"You're trembling, Miss Fullbright."

Valentine's voice was so low it was barely a rumble through her bones. "Shall I give you my coat or are you well enough to return inside?"

Catherine looked at him, and this close she could see his face very well. His gaze was admiring, his focus on her lips, and under the heat of that look, she could not answer. Why on earth was he looking at her that way? Men never looked at her like this.

"I thought I told you to put on a shawl."

"You did, but—"

"Too late." He placed a finger over her lips. "I can't resist you now."

She tried to protest, but instead, to her astonishment, she found herself surrendering, closing her eyes and feeling his hand come around her waist.

One heartbeat, two . . .

Other **AVON ROMANCES**

Be Mine Tonight *by Kathryn Smith*
From London With Love *by Jenna Petersen*
How to Seduce a Bride *by Edith Layton*
Once Upon a Wedding Night *by Sophie Jordan*
The Perfect Seduction *by Margo Maguire*
Sinful Pleasures *by Mary Reed McCall*
Sins of Midnight *by Kimberly Logan*

Coming Soon

Deliciously Wicked *by Robyn DeHart*
Taken By Storm *by Donna Fletcher*

And Don't Miss These
ROMANTIC TREASURES
from Avon Books

The Duke in Disguise *by Gayle Callen*
His Mistress By Morning *by Elizabeth Boyle*
Tempting the Wolf *by Lois Greiman*

SHANA GALEN

No Man's Bride

AVON BOOKS

An Imprint of HarperCollins*Publishers*

This is a work of fiction. Names, characters, places, and incidents are products of the author's imagination or are used fictitiously and are not to be construed as real. Any resemblance to actual events, locales, organizations, or persons, living or dead, is entirely coincidental.

AVON BOOKS
An Imprint of HarperCollins*Publishers*
10 East 53rd Street
New York, New York 10022-5299

Copyright © 2006 by Shane Bolks
ISBN-13: 978-0-7394-7384-9

Printed in the U.S.A.

For my husband.
Your support and love
mean everything to me.

Acknowledgments

Gratitude, love, and thanks to:

Christina Hergenrader and Courtney Burkholder for working with me on this book.

May Chen for your brilliant editing and helpful suggestions.

Evan Fogelman—you're an awesome agent and, more importantly, a good friend.

Chapter 1

London, 1801

"**D**addy, please. Please." Catie pounded her small, aching fist against the walls of her prison under the stairs. She barely rattled the door. She'd been locked in the tiny closet for hours, and all the crying had rendered her weak and pitiful.

She was pitiful.

Just like her daddy said she was.

"Please," she cried again, but no one came. No one ever came when she cried. No one cared.

She pulled her knees to her chest, trying to make herself small, trying to give the mice and rats as much room as possible. She was ten. She shouldn't be scared. Her mamma was always telling her to act like a big girl. But as her tears wet and chilled her knees, she shivered.

Please, God. Please.

Catie heard a creak and opened her eyes. Was it her imagination or was—

"Catie? Are you in there?"

It was her cousin Josephine Hale. Catie would know Josie's voice anywhere. And though it was dark, she could see Josie in her mind. Josie was tall for her eight years and skinny, with a shock of short red hair and freckles. She was probably wearing her eye patch. Josie's sight was perfect, but she was going to be a pirate one day.

"Catie? Where are you?"

"I'm here," she croaked. Behind Josie, their cousin Ashley Brittany held up a lone white candle. The red flame danced in the drafty house. Ashley was also eight and the most beautiful girl Catie knew—and not just because Ashley was here to save her. With her long hair of spun gold, her huge green eyes, and her porcelain skin and Cupid's bow mouth, Ashley was as beautiful as the picture of the goddess Athena in the schoolbook Catie had once seen.

Like Athena, Ashley was a warrior. "We've come to save you," Ashley told her now.

Josie reached out to Catie, and Catie jumped into her arms and hugged her tight. "How did you know how to find me?"

"Your sister was making fun of your crying at

church this morning," Ashley said. "We figured out what happened and came as soon as we could. I'm sorry we couldn't come earlier."

Catie swallowed. It was Sunday evening? She'd been locked under the stairs for almost two days.

"Maddie's waiting outside," Josie told her.

Maddie was Madeleine Fullbright, another of Catie's cousins and the fourth in their circle. Maddie was eight, almost nine. Nearest in age to Catie, Maddie also resembled Catie the most closely. Both had long dark hair and olive skin, though Maddie had huge blue eyes whereas Catie's were plain muddy brown.

"Let's go," Josie said.

Catie paused for only a moment. Her daddy would be very angry if he found her missing. He might even hit her, like he sometimes did when she made him very angry. But Catie could not go back in the closet. Anything but that. "Yes, let's go."

With Josie behind her, Catie followed Ashley and her candle until they turned the knob of the door to the dining room.

"We'll go out the window," Josie whispered. "Maddie will help us down."

They opened the door, stepped inside the dining room, and Lizzy jumped out from behind a chair and into their path. "Where do you think you're going?" She was only seven, but already Catie's sister was a miniature version of their father. Lizzy put her hands on her hips and stood with legs braced apart as he did. It would have been comical, a little blond child with an angel's face standing in the center of the room, making demands of three girls all bigger and older. Instead, Catie felt fear shoot through her like a thousand tiny pins falling onto her body.

"Lizzy, what are you doing in here? Go back to bed," Catie whispered.

"No." She shook her head and pointed at the doorway. "You better get back in that closet Catherine Anne. Go back now, or I'll tell Daddy."

Catie knew she'd do it too. Not only was Lizzy mean and spiteful, she was their daddy's favorite. And she intended to keep that favored status. "No, Lizzy, please," Catie begged.

Lizzy took a step forward. "My name is Elizabeth."

"Yes, I'm sorry, I forgot," Catie said quickly. "Please go back to bed."

The blond angel scowled at her. "Say it. Say *Elizabeth*."

"Elizabeth," Catie whispered. "Don't tell Daddy."

Elizabeth smiled. "Say, please."

"*Please.*"

Lizzy appeared to think about her options for a moment, then shook her head. "No. I'm going to tell. Daddy said I could decide when you could come out. I didn't say you could come out yet."

"Little brat," Josie hissed. "Let me get my hands on you."

Catie jumped in front of Josie. "No! She'll scream and wake my daddy."

"That's right." Lizzy stuck out her lip and crossed her arms. "Get back in that closet, or I'm going to tell."

While Lizzy made her demands and stomped her small feet, Ashley moved stealthily behind Lizzy. Ashley chose that moment to grab Lizzy around the throat, clamping her hand over Lizzy's mouth. Sometimes Catie wished she had older brothers to teach her these things.

"Now, you listen to me, Lizzy," Ashley hissed, holding Lizzy tight. "You aren't going to tell anyone about tonight. You hear me? If your daddy wakes up, you are going to tell him that you let Catherine out."

Lizzy shook her head and struggled to free herself from Ashley's iron hold.

"You'll do what I say," Ashley ordered. "If you don't, you better not ever sleep again because I'll come in the middle of the night and get you!" With a shove, she released Lizzy and pushed her to the floor. Then Ashley bent over her so that her long blond hair tangled with Lizzy's until the two heads were almost indistinguishable. "Now go to bed."

Catie watched as Lizzy jumped up and scampered away. She prayed Ashley's threats had worked. If not, her daddy was going to be very, very mad.

Josie went to the window and helped lower

Ashley. As soon as Ashley was out of sight, Josie turned. "Jump, Catie!" Josephine held the window curtain aside so Catie could slip out of the dining-room window and join her cousins on the walk in front of her parents' house. Catie gave a last glance over her shoulder, into the black house, where her daddy was sleeping.

"Catie, are you coming?" Madeleine called. She was a small shape in the dark beside the golden-haired Ashley.

"Yes!" Catie answered. Her stomach convulsed at the thought of what her father would do to her if he realized she'd escaped, but she would rather die than go back into the rat-and-spider-filled closet. "I'm coming," she said and scrambled out the window.

Ashley and Maddie caught her, and as soon as she was on solid ground beside her cousins, she hugged them as hard as she could.

Ashley hugged her back just as hard. "You're okay now," she said. "We've got you, and we're going on an adventure." Her father called Ashley a little hoyden, and Catie knew her spunky blond cousin was almost certainly the instigator of her rescue.

Madeleine took Catie's hand in hers, her warm grip calm and reassuring. "Is your mommy all right? And Lizzy?" Maddie asked. She was always concerned about others.

"Aunt Cordelia and Uncle Edmund are snoring away in their beds," Josephine answered, climbing out the window behind Catie, then taking her other hand. "And Uncle Edmund made that little brat, Lizzy, Catie's prison guard. When I'm a pirate, I'll make them all walk the plank."

Catie hugged Josie, feeling her cousin's sharp shoulder blades under her hands. As Catie had imagined, Josie had her auburn hair tied under a strip of cloth and had fashioned an eye patch out of an old handkerchief.

With Josephine on one side of Catie and sweet Madeleine on the other, the three girls followed Ashley, their leader. Catie didn't know where they were going, and she didn't care. She was free of rats and spiders and cruel little sisters. She could breathe, and though the night was cold, especially as she was dressed only in her nightgown, the air felt good on her tear-stained face.

A half hour later, the girls climbed into Maddie's room in the Earl of Castleigh's safe, quiet town house on Berkeley Square. Catie looked at her cousins, at their dirty dresses, their eyes sparkling with adventure. She was dizzy with the adventures of the night as well. Either that, or she was weak from hunger.

Maddie convinced everyone to wash their faces, and then she brought out clean nightgowns for all. Finally, they all climbed onto Maddie's bed. Catie saw that it was growing light behind the curtains, and she knew she needed to get home before her father found her missing.

Please, God, let Lizzy keep her mouth shut.

Catie didn't understand why Lizzy was believed when she was not, why Lizzy was coddled when she was turned away. Her father had said she should have been a son. But he didn't hold being a female against Lizzy.

Maybe because Lizzy was so pretty or because she looked like him. All Catie knew for certain was that her father looked for reasons to punish her.

"You know," Catie said, looking at her cousins and friends again, "once we grow up and marry, we won't be able to have adventures like this anymore. Our husbands won't let us."

Madeleine looked at Catie. "Is that why your daddy hurts your mommy?"

Catie sighed. As the eldest, she was expected to know everything. "No, he does it because he can. Because he's a man," she answered. "Men are stronger and meaner, and they have rights. When you get married, your husband will treat you the same."

"No, he won't," Madeleine said. "My daddy is nice to my mommy."

"She got lucky," Catie said. "And he's rich. If your daddy wasn't rich, he wouldn't be as nice."

"When I become a pirate," Josephine told them

confidently, "I won't need a husband. I'll have loads of treasure all for myself."

"And I'm going to have lots of adventures," Ashley said. "I won't have time for a husband, especially a mean one."

"But how will you have money for adventures without a husband?" Josephine asked.

"Well, I don't care how poor I am. I'm not going to marry at all. Ever." As soon as the words were spoken, Catie knew she meant them. How could she marry, when all her life she'd seen clearly what men were and what they could do? And it wasn't only her father who was cruel. She'd seen his friends hit their wives and kick dogs in the street. How could she know which men were like her uncle William, Madeleine's daddy, and which were like her father?

"And I'm not going to marry either," Madeleine chimed in. "Never. I don't need the money. If you want, Catie, you can come stay with me. You, too, Ashley, when you're not on an adventure, and you, Josie, when you're not on your pirate ship." She paused, and then because she was Madeleine and could never be cruel, she added, "Your sister can come, too, Catie, if she really wants."

"I'll tell her, but she thinks she's special." At least that's what their father always told Elizabeth. He always said, "If I have to be cursed with daughters, thank God one is small and pretty.

You'll marry a prince and make us all rich, Elizabeth."

Now Catie told her cousins, "Elizabeth thinks she's going to marry a prince."

"She's a fool," Ashley said. "But I'm not."

"Me, neither," Catie said, then sat up straighter. "I propose that we make a pledge, a promise never to marry. I'm the oldest, so I go first. I, Catherine Anne Fullbright, swear never, ever, ever to marry so long as I live. Now your turn Maddie."

"I, Madeleine Richael Fullbright, swear never, ever to marry so long as I live. Now your turn, Josie," Maddie said.

"I, Josephine Linet Hale, swear never, ever, to marry so long as I live. I promise to be a pirate!"

"Now you, Ashley," Catie directed.

"I, Ashley Gweneira Brittany, swear not to marry for as long as I live. But you know what this means, don't you?" She didn't wait for an answer. "We're going to be spinsters."

For a moment the four cousins were quiet, and then Catie said, "I'd rather be a spinster than beaten and locked in a closet."

"I'd rather be a spinster than a silly girl who thinks she's going to marry a prince," Ashley said.

"It won't be bad to be unmarried if we're all unmarried," Josie said.

"So we'll make it fun. We'll be the Spinsters' Club!" Catie said, impressed that she had thought of it.

"That's right," Josephine agreed. "We'll stick together. No men or mean girls allowed."

Catie was the first to sit up, stick out her hand, and the other girls followed. Soon all four sat in a circle on Maddie's bed, hands joined in a silent yet binding pact.

Chapter 2

Ten years later

On hands and knees, Catherine backed into the doorway, surveying the shining floor of the drawing room. She'd just spent three hours dusting, sweeping, mopping, and polishing, and she was finally done. She sat up, feeling her back twinge in protest. The muscles in her arms and legs were on fire. No matter. She was finished. She was free.

She could spend the rest of the afternoon curled up in her bed, reading a book or even sleeping. Sleep sounded like the best option at present. She was so tired. She'd been up since dawn helping with the laundry, cooking breakfast, and straightening the mess her father had made when he'd come home drunk the night before.

With a sigh, Catherine rose, hefted the heavy pail, and lumbered down the stairs. The house was unusually quiet today. Neither of her parents nor her younger sister was home. Not that she missed them. She preferred days like this, but all the peace and solitude did give her pause. She wasn't used to it, and she knew it wouldn't last.

Going through the kitchen, Catherine went out the back door and poured the dirty water into the yard. The sheets on the clothesline were almost dry, and she checked the sky to make sure the rain would hold off another hour or more. Satisfied, her clean linen wouldn't be drenched in the near future, she set the pail by the door and went wearily back up the steps.

That was when she heard them. Her mother, her sister, and her father. They were talking and laughing, making their way up the stairs to the first floor. For a long moment, Catherine hovered in the kitchen, wondering how long she could hide down here. How long would it be before they missed her? She bit her lip to ward off a rueful smile. Probably as long as it took before they wanted something.

"Catherine Anne!" She heard her father call in his booming voice.

Well, she had known it wouldn't be long.

And she knew better than to tarry. She scampered out of the kitchen and was almost to the drawing room before her father bellowed again. "Yes, Father! I'm here."

She opened the door and was poised to give a quick curtsey, when she saw the mud. There were two sets of boot prints tracking mud across her clean, polished floor. One track led to her father, seated on the couch, one muddy boot dirtying the upholstery. The other boot was smaller, daintier, and it led to the chair her sister occupied.

"Where were you?" her father asked, sitting up. "Where's the tea?"

Catherine gaped at him. Normally, she would have rushed to bring the tea, but she couldn't stop staring at the mud tracked across her clean floor.

"What's wrong?" her father finally asked. "Why are you just standing there like a patient in Bedlam?"

She pointed to the floor. "The mud. I just—"

"Oh, who cares about the floor?" her sister Lizzy said, waving Catherine's concern away. "You can clean it up later. I have news."

But Catherine didn't want to clean it up later. She'd be folding the linen later, then helping the cook with dinner, and probably darning her father's socks if her mother had her way. At this rate, she was never going to get any sleep. "But I spent all afternoon polishing the floor, and now it's dirty again."

"Do you know where we've been all day?" her mother said, ignoring Catherine's complaints, as usual.

Before going on, Mrs. Fullbright glanced carefully at her husband. Catherine doubted she even realized she did it, but she continually checked his moods and sought his approval before speaking or acting.

Catherine sank onto a footstool at the far side of the room. "Where have you been?"

Certainly not here, helping to clean the house.

"We have been at Lord Valentine's."

Catherine nodded blankly. The name was familiar, as familiar as the name of any of her sister's beaux. She had half a dozen, and they changed as often as Lizzy changed her hairstyle. Valentine was supposed to be some sort of political prodigy. At the tender age of thirty, the man was already a leader in Parliament. Catherine did not have time to follow politics, but her cousin Madeleine did, and she called Valentine a true reformer.

Whatever that meant.

And if he really was a prodigy and a revolutionary, why was he interested in her insipid sister, who had not a thought in her head but which hair ribbon would look best?

"Do you know why we were at Lord Valentine's, Catherine?" Lizzy asked.

"No . . ." But she had a bad feeling. Her family had identical looks on their faces: like they'd just robbed the Treasury and gotten away with it. "Why?" she said drawing the word out.

"To sign the betrothal agreement, silly!" Lizzy cried. "I'm betrothed to Lord Valentine!"

Catherine blinked and then ducked as Lizzy jumped up and twirled around the room.

"I am going to be the Countess of Valentine." She rushed toward Catherine and grabbed her by the shoulders. "And one day, dear, poor, ugly sister, I will be the Marchioness of Ravenscroft. It's practically royalty!" She released Catherine and stood with her hands on her hips. "So what do you have to say about that?"

Catherine opened her mouth to speak, but somehow "No, please God, no" didn't seem the right response, so she closed it again. It was a good thing, too, because her father was watching her, his gaze shrewd.

"I'm sure you are pleased for your sister." He dropped his muddy boots on the floor.

Catherine managed to nod. She was pleased. She couldn't think of anything better than having her sister out of the house.

Except that the privilege would come with a price.

"You know what this means, don't you?" Her father's voice was ominous. Or perhaps it just sounded that way because she knew what he was going to say. He'd been saying it since she was a child. Elizabeth was his darling, his pride, his joy, his ticket to wealth that the position of second son had not afforded him. But there was one thing standing in the way of his Elizabeth's success: Catherine. It was an old-fashioned rule, but Edmund Fullbright was an old-fashioned man.

The older daughter must marry before the younger.

"You'll need to marry before your sister's wedding," he told Catherine. "Do you have anyone in mind?"

Catherine shook her head. She wasn't socially adept like her sister. She wasn't pretty like her sister. She didn't flirt like Elizabeth. She knew no men; none except her father, and he was more than enough.

"You'll need to attend the Beaufort ball tonight then," her father instructed.

"But Father, I—"

"No whining, goddamn it!" He stood, and all three women shrank back. "You'll go, and you'll smile, and you'll flirt, and you'll find a husband." He crossed the room, until he towered over Catherine. "Because if you don't, I'll find one for you."

"Maddie! Maddie! Where are you?" Catherine rushed down the gravel walk leading to the Earl of Castleigh's stable. She knew all the noise she was making would probably scare the horses, so she tried to calm herself. A moment later, she was running again. "Maddie!"

A dark head popped out of the stable door. Madeleine Fullbright's blue eyes grew wide with alarm. "Catie, what is it? What's the matter?" She rushed forward, catching Catherine just as she propelled herself into her cousin's arms.

"You have to help me. Lizzy's getting married, and my father is forcing me to go to the Beaufort ball, and if I don't find a husband, he's going to find one for me, and I just know it will be to some horrible brute he finds on the street and pays to take me off his hands."

"Whatever are you talking about?" Maddie said, easing Catherine onto a bench. "Take a deep breath. Calm down."

Normally this was a comforting place for Catherine. She loved horses and loved to ride, though she rarely had the chance. But just now, she wanted to be alone with Maddie, away from the eyes and ears of the stable lads and the grooms, moving in and out of the building. "Maddie, can we go inside? Please? I need to talk to you in private."

"Very well, but only if you promise to calm down. You're scaring me."

Catherine made a show of taking a deep breath and forced a smile. "All better. Can we go now?"

"Fine." Rising, Maddie untied her apron, and Catherine helped her pull it off, then the two linked arms and walked up the path and into the morning room of the Castleigh town house.

Though she'd been in the house a thousand times or more, it never failed to impress Catherine. The gleaming marble staircases; the polished wood floors that clacked under her old, worn boots; the sunlight streaming through the huge windows and dappling the richly painted walls with light. She loved to run her fingertips over the velvet and brocade furnishings. The heavy, sumptuous fabrics cushioned her hands and made her feel like a princess, if only for a little while.

A servant appeared with tea almost as soon as Maddie and Catherine took their places on their favorite window seat, and Catherine took a moment to savor the feeling of being waited on. Maddie, used to the little luxuries around her, folded her legs underneath her and leaned back against the casement. She wore a pale blue morning dress and a sheer fichu tucked inside her bodice with a collar that floated over her dainty shoulders and collarbone. The morning sun glinted off her chestnut hair, highlighting the strands of auburn and gold woven throughout.

Her blue eyes were the color of a robin's egg, her peach skin flawless, and her figure petite but voluptuous. Catherine was well aware that though she and Maddie had been virtual twins as children, they no longer resembled one another. As Maddie had grown, she'd taken their shared features and chiseled and refined them. Catherine had just grown taller and heavier. Her figure was curvy without any trace of daintiness. Her skin was olive, almost tan. Her hair did not curl like Maddie's. It was dark brown, almost black, without any other shades threading through it. Her eyes were still the color of mud.

When Catherine looked in the mirror, which

was but rarely, the only things she liked about herself were her eyebrows and her mouth. Her eyebrows arched nicely, contouring her face and eyes. Her mouth was wide and perpetually rosy. She had a nice smile and all her teeth. It could have been worse.

"Now start over," Maddie said after the tea had been poured. "Lizzy is engaged?"

"Yes, and I've been ordered to find a husband, too. Tonight, if possible."

"Goodness!" Maddie put her arm on Catherine's. "What's the hurry?"

"The old threat. My father swears he won't marry Elizabeth until he's got me out of his house. Those were his exact words, by the way. Maddie, I'm worried that my father might do something rash," Catherine said, lowering her voice.

Maddie leaned closer so that her cup of tea steamed between them. "Like what?"

"Gamble me away the next time he plays faro all night or kidnap some brute off the street and force me to marry him."

"Don't be ridiculous." Maddie laughed and sat back. "He won't do anything of the sort. My father wouldn't put up with it, and if Uncle Edmund so much as tries, you'll be welcome here any day."

Catherine smiled to reassure Maddie. How could her kind cousin, with her idyllic house and her ideal parents, understand what it was to live under Edmund Fullbright's roof? Sweet, naïve Maddie was incapable of understanding that escaping Catherine's father was near impossible. He would be rid of his daughters on his own terms or none at all.

"I hope you're right about my father, Maddie, but just in case he turns out to be a wee bit more nefarious than you believe, I want to stop the marriage between Valentine and Elizabeth. I need your help."

Maddie shook her head. "That would not be very nice. I don't like Lizzy very much, but that doesn't mean I want to ruin her match."

Catherine tried very hard not to roll her eyes. Maddie was too good. "Maddie, I'm not trying to stop it forever. I just need to buy myself time."

"Time for what?"

"To think of a way to escape."

"Escape! Catie, be reasonable."

Catherine put her arm on Maddie's. "Maddie, I just need your advice. That's all. *Please*."

Madeleine gave a resigned sigh.

Catherine decided to push her advantage. "I know you don't approve, but help me this once. You move in Society far more than I do." This was a gross understatement, but Maddie had the grace not to say so. "How can I halt the engagement?"

"It will be difficult."

Catherine clasped her cousin's hand. "Maddie, please!"

"Oh, very well. Perhaps if you could keep them apart . . ."

"That's better." She squeezed Maddie's hand.

"When will they next meet?"

"Tonight at the Beaufort ball."

"You shall have to keep Lizzy from attending."

Catherine raised her brows. "I thought you knew Elizabeth better than that."

"You're right. She is a bit headstrong."

Catherine snorted.

"Very well, then," Maddie said, ignoring the snort. "You must attend as well and—"

"*Me* attend? No, you have to help me avoid that." Just the thought of all those people crammed together made her hands clammy.

"Catie, there's no other way. Besides, you know you need a bit of confidence, and this will be good for you. While you're there you can keep Lizzy away from Valentine."

"How?"

Maddie threw her arms out. "I don't know. Tie her up and hide her in the bushes."

Catherine nodded, impressed. "That might work."

"I was only joking, Catie," Maddie said in a warning voice.

Catherine gave her a placating smile. "I know." But she was inwardly thrilled at the new plan. It might even be worth braving the ball.

She was off to a good start, and she would be able to buy herself some time. But she still needed to talk to Josie. Josie would help her escape. And she needed to talk to her soon, or it would be too late. She suspected her father had already concocted a devious plan, one not even his brother, the Earl of Castleigh, could prevent.

Chapter 3

Quint Childers, the Earl of Valentine, heir to the marquessate of Ravenscroft, strolled from the floor of Parliament flushed with success. He stepped outside, lit a celebratory cheroot and, staring up at the bleak London night, began to smoke. MPs swarmed out behind him, many of his fellow Whigs pausing to slap him on the back and congratulate him on his latest victory, and Valentine congratulated them back.

The reform bill he had slaved over, the bill he had written, revised, and pushed through the House practically on his hands and knees, had finally passed. It was a complicated bill, but the bottom line was that there would now be more aid for the poor of England. Quint felt like a new mother.

"Going to the Beaufort do?" the new Earl of Westman asked, pausing beside him.

"Hmm?" Quint stubbed out the cheroot and watched Westman lift his arm to hail a passing hack. Westman was about the same height as Quint and an imposing figure. The hackney driver swerved to stop at the corner.

"The Beaufort do. Are you going? If so, we can share this coach."

For a moment, Quint had no idea what Westman was talking about, and then it came to him in a rush. Elizabeth. The Beaufort ball. He had told her he would be there at eleven. He pulled out his pocket watch, glanced at it.

"Damn!" It was after midnight.

Westman raised a brow at him. "Is that a yes or a no?"

"It's a yes, but goddamn me. I had no idea it was so late."

The two men started down the steps. "Arguing a bill like the Valentine-Cheswick Reform Act can make a man lose his sense of time. I watched the debate. Your efforts were well worth it, I'd say."

"If only the ladies would take your view of things."

"Women take an interest in politics? What kind of country would this be then? But I see your predicament. You are late for an engagement."

"Very late." It was so late, in fact, that he dared not even return home to change his clothes.

The roads were crowded and blocked with the carriages of the *ton* scurrying to this rout or that soiree, and the journey to the Beaufort ball took the better part of an hour.

The time in the hackney gave Quint plenty of time to think how to apologize to the beatific Miss Elizabeth Fullbright. They hadn't been engaged more than two days, and already he had disappointed her. Damn! He could not afford to lose her as he had so many other suitable ladies.

He was an intelligent man, and it wasn't like him to make the same mistake over again. But here he was, once again, allowing his work to get in the way of his wooing. He should know by now that no lady liked to feel as though she ranked second to public policy. And wasn't Elizabeth Fullbright at the ball, feeling that way right now?

He would not lose her. He needed a wife, and not just any sort would do.

His wife should be an intelligent woman. She had to be able to entertain his political friends. Her conversation, the habits of her mind, her wit and vivacity, would be on display for all.

In addition, his wife should be charming. Society would be her playground and her classroom. She should be at ease with all classes and sets; however, her background must be impeccable.

He did not care about money. He had money. But his wife's family had to be respectable. Quint would brook no scandal.

And, finally, his wife had to be beautiful. Quint had noticed that men with beautiful wives generally went further than those married to less attractive ladies. Quint intended to go far—all the way to the post of prime minister.

Love did not fit into Quint's notion of marriage. His mother and father had not loved each other when they married—the idea was preposterous. But they were quite fond of one another now, and Quint was certain that, given time, he would come to love Elizabeth and she him.

The hack finally stopped, and he and Westman went inside the ball, parting after the butler announced them. Immediately Quint began to search for Elizabeth.

One problem with his list. The women who fit its criteria were usually in high demand by other men as well, and many of those gentlemen had far more time to attend the theater, musicales, and the routs the *ton* hosted than a man such as he—a man concerned with the welfare of his country—had at his disposal.

No wonder he had been eager to secure Elizabeth. Now that they were betrothed, no other man could touch her. She more than met the requirements on his list, and though several rumors concerning her father—his activities, morals, and scruples—gave Quint pause, the fact that Edmund Fullbright was the brother of a wealthy, powerful earl eased Valentine's worries. Most importantly when it came to Elizabeth, she had accepted his marriage proposal.

Still searching for his lovely intended, Quint accepted a glass of champagne from a passing footman and then stopped the servant to ask if he knew where Miss Fullbright might be.

The footman did not, but he promised to inquire and return with the information. Quint nodded and sipped his champagne, at the same time watching the dancers on the floor of the ballroom.

He was surprised Elizabeth was not dancing. Certainly she could not want for partners. Then just as Quint emptied his glass, the footman reappeared. "Are you still looking for Miss Fullbright, my lord?"

"Yes."

"No one has seen her, sir. You might check the terrace. Through those doors."

"Thank you." Valentine slipped the man a shilling and arrowed for the terrace. But when Quint stepped outside, he found the balcony empty. It was early April, and there was a chill in the air. Not many ladies would brave the cold on a night like this. Frowning, Quint surveyed the area more carefully. Had the footman been mistaken or—

The bushes at the far end of the balcony rustled,

and then two hands appeared on the balustrade. There was a grunt and then a head and shoulders appeared, and as Quint stared in amazement, a girl hauled herself up and onto the stone railing. She swung her legs over and then leaned down to brush her skirts off, as though she did this sort of thing every day.

"I can't decide if you're a cat burglar or a guest hoping to make a fabulous entrée."

The girl's head snapped up. "Who are you?" she said, taking a step back.

"Who am *I*?" Quint chuckled. The interloper had courage. He pulled out a cheroot. "I'm a guest with an exceedingly conventional entrance. No match for you. I came in through the front door."

She backed up again until she was flush against the stone banister. "So did I. I was only in the bushes because"—she glanced over the side as though looking for an inspired excuse—"because I lost something."

"Did you find it?" Quint lit the cheroot.

"No." The bushes below her heaved and swayed. "I mean, yes. I don't require any assistance."

"Well, you might if you don't step away from the banister." Quint walked toward her. "It sounds like there's something down there."

She immediately stepped in front of him, blocking his view. "Why do you say that?"

Something grunted, and a branch below cracked. Quint raised a brow. "Because I bloody well hear it, that's why. Now step away before you're hurt."

She shook her head and continued to block him. She was a tall woman, barely a head shorter than he, and he could not see past her. "I'm afraid I cannot do that," she said. "I cannot move un-less—unless you come with me. I couldn't live with myself if you were hurt by that—dog."

The dog made a very human grunting noise. The woman was obviously daft. She was either truly afraid for him or didn't want him to see what was over the railing.

Quint craned his head one last time. What was she hiding? Her lover? All he saw was darkness.

"Very well, I will retreat if you will," he said, giving in. He moved back, and she followed. "I came outside because I was looking for Miss Full-bright."

"Oh!" She paused midstride. "But *I* am Miss Fullbright."

But the woman looking at him was not Eliza-beth at all. In fact, she was a poor substitute for his intended. Whereas his Elizabeth was petite and fair with a fall of blond curls and big blue eyes, this woman was tall and olive-skinned with hair so dark it was black. Pieces of that hair fell haphazardly over her eyes so that he could not determine their color, but he saw no resemblance whatsoever to his betrothed. Perhaps she was so daft she was now impersonating others?

"I must be mistaken. Did you say you were Miss Fullbright?" He could see no harm in giving her the opportunity to rectify her erroneous claim.

"I did. Who are you?" she asked. She swiped a strand of hair from her face and when she did so, Quint caught the resemblance. Her eyes were not the brilliant blue of her sister's, but they were the same shape, and she looked at him with the same mixture of skepticism and curiosity.

"Forgive me," Quint said and bowed. "You must be Miss Elizabeth Fullbright's sister." Damn it, but he could not remember her name. Claudia? Cordelia—no, that was the mother. Calista?

"And you must be Lord Valentine," the girl said. Then, to his amazement, she looked him over. She studied him from head to toe as though he were a piece of meat at the butcher's shop or a bolt of muslin she wanted for a dress or—he flexed his hands as her gaze traveled back up again, pausing for a moment on his groin—as though he were a prostitute in a line of them, and she was choosing her partner for the evening.

The gall of the woman, and he had heard she was shy and insular. How wrong that report had been!

"Congratulations on your impending nuptials," she said when her eyes were back on his face. "Though I feel I should offer you my sympathies instead."

The bushes behind them rattled savagely. "Perhaps we should retire farther away." She indicated the far corner of the terrace. Quint would rather have stayed and observed what other suspicious movements the bushes made, but she was already moving.

When they reached the appointed spot, she perched on the balustrade. Behind her were the dark lawn and the misty lights of the city. The breeze whipped up, trailing loose strands of her hair over her shoulders. He caught the faint scent of peaches on the wind, and then it was gone.

"Well, it was a pleasure to meet you, Lord Valentine." She stuck her hand out, and he shook it almost automatically. "Once again, my condolences on your engagement. Good night."

Quint recognized the dismissal, but he was not ready to go. Not by far.

"Madam," he said, "you offer condolences. I believe the accepted practice is to offer felicitations."

He watched her straighten her shoulders and had the distinct feeling she was bolstering her resolve as well. Good God. Was it that much of a burden to wish her future brother-in-law a happy marriage?

She looked up at him. "I do not wish to overstep my bounds—"

"Oh, no. You must speak now." He waved her onward. "I insist."

"Very well. How well do you know Elizabeth,

sir? What I mean to say is, have you known her long?"

"A month, perhaps a bit less," he answered. "I met her at the start of the Season."

"I see. And have you had an opportunity to talk much with my sister?"

Quint drew his cheroot and watched her through the fragrant smoke. How did one define *much*? He had spoken with Elizabeth enough to know she would make an acceptable wife. That did not require extensive conversation, though. He would have plenty of time to know all her thoughts and opinions over the years of their marriage.

Quint doubted the young upstart before him would appreciate the efficiency of his selection process. He was willing to wager she was the romantic sort. Finally, he said, "You are certainly full of questions tonight. And I had heard you could be timid."

She blushed at that. He saw the color in her cheeks even in the dim light. The woman was a mélange of contradictions—bold one moment, bashful the next.

"I admit, I am not usually so forward, sir, but I cannot help but wonder how well you know my sister. Have you spoken with her much as opposed to"—she waved her hand as though searching for the words—"just looking at her?"

Quint was speechless for a moment, unable to predict the direction of her questions. It was a bit unusual for an orator as great as he to find it difficult to gauge his opponent's intent, but he had no idea at what Elizabeth's sister—Camelia?—was hinting.

Quint stubbed out his cheroot and decided a direct approach might be best. "What are you suggesting, Miss Fullbright? If you are implying there has been anything improper between us—"

"Oh, good Lord, no!" She laughed then as though the statement were the most preposterous thing she had ever heard. "I simply wondered how well you knew Elizabeth. In short, sir, I wondered if you knew what a *wicked shrew* she is." She raised her voice on the last and seemed to say it to the balcony at large. She looked back at him. "I can see by your look that you do not."

Immediately Quint schooled his face into the unreadable expression he used when a political opponent made a point that was technically correct but which Quint had no intention of granting him. "I fear I am at a loss for words, Miss Fullbright. Your sister is a very sweet girl, and I cannot imagine why you would disparage her so."

The girl muttered something that sounded like, "I'm sure you can't," and then she smiled at him. "I'm only trying to save you from a dreadful mistake, Lord Valentine. You seem a nice enough man." At this she looked him over again. "Intelligent, handsome—though your hair is a bit long—and I would not want to see you shackled to such a *horrible witch* as my little sister." Again, she seemed to say this to the terrace behind him, and Quint swore the bushes at the other end rattled at her words.

He made to speak, but she held up a hand to silence him. And then, perhaps sensing this would not be enough to quiet him, she rose from the banister.

Knowing who she was now, he could not help but judge her against her sister. He had been right in thinking her the taller of the two. She must have a good five inches on Elizabeth and was at least thirty pounds heavier. But it might be more, as her dress was too big for her, and she wore a wrap pulled like a shield about her.

When she stood, she was nearer his height, and he was able to look directly into her eyes. They were much darker than her sister's. He guessed them to be brown. And her hair. It was the thickest, darkest coil he had ever seen. There was the scent of peach wafting toward him again, and for one moment, he thought her beautiful—far more beautiful than her sister—and then the moment passed and he wondered how he could ever have compared the two.

"My lord, I will not keep you, but I would be remiss in my duty as a fellow human being if I did not warn you against marrying Elizabeth."

"Your duty as a fellow human being?" Quint said through clenched teeth. "What about your duty as a sister?"

She laughed again, and this time he had difficulty resisting the impulse to throttle her.

"I owe Elizabeth no duty, I assure you. She is a spoiled, demanding little shrew, as you will see for yourself. Do not say I did not tell you so. Now, if you will, please leave me alone."

"Gladly."

She made a gesture that he supposed was meant to dismiss him, and as he was more than eager to oblige her, he started for the doors to the ballroom. At the last minute, he turned back. "It seems to me"—Caroline? Claudette?—"madam, that you, not your poor sister, are the shrew. I pity your family and the man you marry."

She laughed again, and he turned away from her—vexing how often and inappropriately the chit laughed—but he paused when she called, "You are absolutely correct, sir. I am a horrible shrew. Tell all of your friends. Take an advertisement out in the *Times*. I won't relinquish my hand without a fight!"

As soon as Valentine entered the ballroom, Catherine began to shake. To calm her nerves, she began to count. The predictability of the numbers always soothed her.

Twelve, thirteen, fourteen . . .

Even counting wasn't calming her nerves at this point. She had almost been caught. She'd tied Elizabeth up and left her in the bushes, and Valentine had almost caught her.

Fifteen, sixteen, seventeen . . .

She began to shake anew, thinking of the way she had spoken to him. She was not a rude person, but desperate times and all that. The problem was that not only had she been rude, she'd been critical. What had gotten into her? She was usually such a nice girl. Oh, she hoped she never saw Valentine again.

And yet what else could she do? Lord knew she didn't care whether or not he married Elizabeth. He seemed the sort of man who was unlikely to be swayed by someone like her at any rate. But she'd had to at least delay the nuptials. She needed time to plan her escape.

Catherine rushed back over to the shrubs where she'd left Elizabeth and peered over the edge. She could just make out her sister's golden hair and white gown in the thick foliage. Lizzy was staring up at her. Catherine would have liked to give her a three-fingered wave and skip off, but she could not be that cruel.

"I'll come back for you when Valentine is gone," she called. Lizzy shook the bushes and said something, but with the gag in her mouth, Catherine couldn't understand.

"I'll be back," she promised and headed toward the ballroom to keep an eye on Valentine. She stopped just before entering to give herself a moment to rally her courage. The room was full.

No, to say the room was *full* was like saying the old king George was just a little bit off. The room was brimming over, and George III was mad as a loon.

Catherine tried to calm herself by reflecting on the fact that with so many people crushed together inside, there were many other people far more interesting to look at than she. No one would care about her.

Unfortunately, she also detested small, tight spaces, and she could see nowhere in the room that would afford her any space to breathe.

Taking a last deep breath of freedom, she plunged inside and squeezed through as best she could, searching for Valentine. Not that she wanted to speak to him. She just wanted to make sure he didn't decide to return to the balcony to investigate the rustling bushes further.

"Where have you been?" Her father's fetid breath hit her cheek, and his rough hand grasped the tender flesh of her upper arm. "Why aren't you dancing?"

"I—" she began, but he shook her violently, and she could not finish. Catherine could only be thankful they were in public, else he would have done far worse than shake her.

"I told you to find a husband."

She stared at him, at his small black eyes and large red nose with the broken blood vessels. How she hated him sometimes.

"You've sat on your arse and lived off my largesse long enough," he continued. "I'll have you married before my Elizabeth, or you'll know the back of my hand."

"Then I suppose you'd best release me so I can simper and flirt. Or are you going to make a scene? I can imagine how that will influence my chances."

"Little hoyden," he spat. "I'll be glad to be rid of you."

And then the bruising hold was gone, and her father disappeared through the crowd. Catherine's brave façade shattered, and her teeth began to clatter.

One, two, three . . .

The noise and the heat from the crowd in the Beauforts' ballroom seemed to press in on her. She tried to gulp air and could not.

Four, five, six . . .

Her heart began to pound, and her throat closed up. She had to escape. Ever since she'd been a small child, she'd had a fear of loud noises and tight places. The night her cousins had rescued her from the closet under the stairs had not been her last confinement there. And her father, whether sober, drunk, or depressed at having lost at dice, always found her pitiful cries amusing.

But she could not cry here and now. She had to get out. She had to have space and air to breathe. Edmund Fullbright would not be pleased if she escaped back onto the veranda at the first opportunity. Her only hope was that he would be not be sober enough to know anything a half an hour from now. She'd smelled the alcohol on him, and it penetrated his every pore. Soon, he would be too drunk even to remember her name. Catherine was counting on that fact as she squeezed through the room and into the foyer.

By the time she made it through the crush, she was perspiring and pulling in short, panicked breaths. She felt dizzy, and her chest was constricting, and just when she feared she would pass out, she felt a familiar hand on her shoulder.

"Catie, are you well? Oh, no. You're not. Quick. Sit down."

She was led to a chair against the wall and encouraged to take deep breaths. A footman was sent running for a glass of wine, and then that was thrust under her nose as well. She drank a small sip, then looked up to see Josephine standing over her.

Josie bore the closest resemblance to the picture of a pixie that Catherine had ever seen. With her cropped auburn hair, pulled back by combs into a wispy crown about her head, her small pointed nose, and her perpetually mischievous smile, Josie looked like trouble.

And she was.

Her only saving grace was her huge, dark green eyes. They were fringed with long, dark lashes, and tilted upward. When Josie wielded her eyes, no one could stay angry at her long.

"All right now?" Josie asked, those green eyes full of concern.

Catherine, her voice still not recovered, nodded.

Josie shook her head. "Why do you do this to yourself, Catie? You hate these things. Why not just stay home?"

Catherine swallowed another portion of wine.

"Now, take a deep breath. There is nothing to fear here. You just need a bit—"

"Of confidence. Yes, that's what you always say." Her voice was raspy but strong. Catherine took another sip. "I'm in trouble, Josie. I can't go back through there, so you shall have to go outside and untie Elizabeth. I left her in the bushes beneath the veranda."

Josie's eyes widened. "What?"

"I wanted to keep her away from her fiancé, but as it was, I was almost caught. By *him*."

Josie blinked at her, and then erupted into a fit of laughter. "Oh, this is too much. Are you telling me that right now your evil sister is tied up and sitting in the bushes beneath the veranda?"

Catherine nodded.

"And that when you were tying her up, her own fiancé almost caught you?"

"I was climbing back onto the balcony, and Elizabeth was still thrashing around. It's not a long drop, and he heard her. I think I managed to convince him it was a dog, but what if he goes back out?"

"Who cares? I say we leave her there until morning. Maybe the gardener will find her."

"Josie, we can't!"

"The little wretch stole my grandmother's earrings and won't give them back. I hope she gets frostbite."

"Oh, no! It's not that cold outside, is it?"

Josie smiled and plopped down next to Catherine in the chair. "No. I was joking. Maddie told me about Lord Valentine and Lizzy. How did your thief of a sister manage to win him?"

"Her charm, I'm sure."

"What charm?" Josie took the glass from Catherine and swallowed its contents. "It's a tragedy. Lord Valentine is so handsome. I would have thought Lizzy's betrothed would have two heads and three arms."

"No, only one head that I saw." And a very nice head at that, Catherine thought. A very nice everything. He was tall, taller than she by several inches, broad-shouldered but not so broad that his chest reminded her of a tree trunk, and his eyes were the loveliest shade of brown—a polished mahogany color that she could get lost in.

Not that she intended to get lost in the man's eyes—or any man's eyes for that matter. At twenty, she was an avowed spinster. If Elizabeth wanted to marry the man, bear his cuffs and smacks when he drank too much and cry when he stayed out all night with whores, leaving her and her children home alone, then that was Elizabeth's concern. Not hers.

Unless she didn't delay Elizabeth's marriage.

"Josie, I need your help."

Josie laughed. "I thought you'd never ask."

"You'd better wait until you hear me out before you agree. I have to take drastic measures."

Josie's eyes lit. "Oh, now, this will be too much fun. How drastic?"

"I have to escape my father, escape London before Lizzy and Valentine marry. If I don't, I'll be forced to marry as well."

"I see." Josie rolled the empty wineglass in her hands. "It's a wonderful idea, but we don't have any money."

"What about your grandfather's pirate treasure?" Catherine whispered, aware that Josie didn't like to speak in public about the treasure. "What if we found the treasure? You could lend me a tiny bit—just enough to help me escape to America—and then once I got my feet under me, I'd pay you back."

Josie looked surprised at the suggestion but not opposed. "It might work," she said after several long seconds of uncharacteristic contemplation. "But I'll need time to find the map and figure out where to start searching."

"How much time?" Catherine grabbed Josie's arm. "I'm running out."

"Then you'll have to make more. Keep Valentine and Lizzy apart a bit longer, and in the meantime, ward off your father's potential suitors for you."

"Ward them off? How? He's probably paid any suitors he's found, and, as you pointed out, I don't have any money."

Josie rolled her eyes. "Just be unsuitable. Suitors don't like unsuitable girls."

When Catherine still looked blank, Josie added, "Be horrible and nasty—the kind of woman no man would want to marry."

"But how do I do that?"

Josie slung an arm around her neck. "Act like Lizzy. The *real* Lizzy."

Chapter 4

"**G**et out here right now, Catherine Anne," her father shouted from the other side of her bedroom door. Catherine quaked at the sound of anger in his voice. She did not like to anger her father, but she had no choice. Just as she'd anticipated, he'd brought three of his own handpicked suitors home this afternoon, and the men were waiting to meet her in the drawing room. Well, they were going to have to wait. She wasn't going down there.

Her father pounded on the door again, and Catherine jumped.

One, two, three . . .

Oh, he was going to beat her for this. She'd be

black-and-blue for weeks. What had Josie told her
to do?

Play the shrew. That's it. Josie had assured her
that was the only way to run the men off and ensure they would not want to marry her.

"Catherine Anne!" her father bellowed.

Four, five, six . . .

What would a shrew say? "Go away!" she
called, leaning with all her weight against the
door. He banged again, and her whole body
inched forward, but the triangle of wood she'd
wrenched under the door held. Barely.

"Get out here right now, little—dear." His voice
sounded high and false, and Catherine knew he
was trying to impress her suitors with his fa-
therly kindness.

Well, she was trying to unimpress them. To
that end, she screamed, "I'm never coming out!"
That didn't seem like quite enough, so, knowing
it would mean more misery later, she added. "I
don't have to do anything I don't want to!"

"Why you ungrateful—" Her father's voice cut
off, and Catherine pressed one ear to the door to
hear why. Were the suitors running off to court
sweeter, more docile brides?

She couldn't hear the men, but she thought she
heard Elizabeth's voice. Then she heard her father move away, and there was a light tap on the
door.

"Catherine, open the door. It's me, Elizabeth."

Catherine considered. It could be a trick.

"Catherine, open the door. It's my room, too."

Still, Catherine hesitated. She had heard her father move away, and it wasn't as though Elizabeth could make her go down.

"Catherine, if you don't open this door, you'll be sorry later," Lizzy warned. Considering Catherine had had to bribe Lizzy to keep her mouth shut about the events at the Beaufort ball by giving Lizzy the only thing Catherine had of value, the jewelry their grandmother had left her, she could not afford to anger Lizzy again. Especially when her father was in a bad mood with her and inclined to grant Elizabeth any favor she asked. Next thing she knew, Lizzy would have Catherine sleeping in the attic.

Catherine removed the wood brace and moved away. Elizabeth opened the door. She was dressed as though she was the one with three suitors waiting downstairs. In addition, to the sapphire jewelry Catherine had been forced to give her, Elizabeth wore a light blue cambric day dress with a fluted ruff. Despite the fact that the style was from last year, Elizabeth looked fresh and new in it. If only people would look past her pretty face and figure and see the true Elizabeth. Behind those cornflower blue eyes lay only malice and temper.

She put her hands on her hips and frowned at Catherine, who wore an old, stained brown work dress. "Catherine! No wonder you didn't want to open the door. You look a fright—as usual.

Change and come downstairs. Daddy has three men here to see *you*."

She spoke the last word as if she were truly awed that any man would be interested in her sister, even though they all knew her father was offering her up to the highest bidder. As the niece of an earl, she could offer breeding and connections to wealthy merchants who had money but no other means of moving into the upper classes.

"And if you don't come down soon, I might just steal them away from you. And unlike your sorry attempt with Valentine at the Beaufort ball, I will succeed."

"Go ahead," Catherine said, sitting on her bed.

"Why, I think all three are half in love with me already. What will Lord Valentine say?"

"Who cares?"

"You do. You tied me up to keep me away from him. But he sent a note to say he'd come today. Are you jealous that he won't give me up so easily?"

"Not at all, and I'm not going downstairs. You can have them all."

If they wanted Elizabeth, then they wouldn't be interested in her. On the other hand, what had her father promised these men to get them here? If they were after money, they might not be so easily dissuaded.

Catherine glanced at her sister. Well, she would have to dissuade them. Lizzy was looking in the mirror, adjusting her gown and babbling on. "But you haven't even met them. Here. You can borrow my old blue ribbon if you want." She pawed through the litter of items on her dressing table— actually there was only one, and the two girls were supposed to share it, but Elizabeth never allowed Catherine near it—and pulled a long length of blue satin ribbon from under a comb and straw bonnet. "You should do something to get that ugly mop of hair out of your face."

"I don't want the ribbon," Catherine said, holding up a hand. "I want the men to go away."

Elizabeth turned back to the mirror. "No matter. It wouldn't suit you anyway. Perhaps I should try it. Everyone will be complimenting my eyes."

But Catherine had other ideas for the ribbon. While Elizabeth stared at her own reflection and pinched her cheeks, Catherine crept off the bed and started for her. A moment later, she grabbed Elizabeth and pulled the ribbon from her grasp.

But Elizabeth didn't let go. She let out an angry yelp and yanked it back, turning slightly in an effort to use her weight to win the battle. Her elbow thrust out and knocked over a lamp, and it crashed to the floor.

"What the hell was that?" he father called, and Catherine smiled. Already, the plan was working. But the ribbon would not be enough.

She ran to the windows and yanked the cords

off the drapes so that they fell, shading the room. The cords were thick and strong. Perfect restraints.

"What are you doing?" Elizabeth said, backing up now. "You'd better not tie me up again. Daddy will beat you if he finds out about the Beaufort ball."

"He'll beat me anyway."

"I can make it worse."

Catherine was going to have to risk it. "Come here."

Elizabeth tried to run, but she didn't move fast enough. Catherine tackled her to the floor and began binding her sister's arms.

Elizabeth let out another squeal, and their father called, "What in the devil is going on up there?"

"Help!" Elizabeth called when her attempts to fight were rendered futile. "She's got me!"

And to her surprise, Catherine found herself laughing. She pulled the cords tighter, immobilizing Lizzy's hands behind her back. Then she tied a knot so tight it would have to be cut to free her sister. She jumped back, and Elizabeth immediately scrambled to her knees.

Catherine heard her father coming up the stairs, and she locked eyes with the imprisoned Elizabeth. Lizzy stuck out her tongue. "Now you're in for it."

And that was all it took. Catherine ran to the door, jammed the block of wood under it, and then advanced on her sister, hands raised, fingers curled in tickling position. "That's what you think."

Quint heard the screams even before he'd reached the house. They were horrible, bloodcurdling screams that surely meant someone was being murdered.

He jumped off his horse, didn't even bother to tie the gelding to the post, and ran to the Fullbrights' front door. He pounded away, all the while her screams—and he was now convinced they were Elizabeth's—echoed around him.

Someone inside the house must have heard him pounding because a young man opened the door. He was wearing his hat and holding his walking stick, apparently intent on departure, but Quint didn't pause to ask questions. He took the steps two at a time and found two other men in the drawing room. They were standing, holding hats and gloves and looking pale with discomfort.

"Where is she?" Quint asked first one man, then the other.

They shook their heads, but one of the two men, a gent who had to have been at least sixty, said, "They're in her bedroom. Her father's gone—"

Quint turned to race up the next set of steps, but the sound of thundering cattle on the staircase gave him pause. Not that he had ever heard thundering cattle, but he imagined they sounded like the god-awful racket coming toward the drawing room.

"Help! Help! She's killing me!"

Quint and the other two men jumped out of the way just as Elizabeth and her sister Charity—no, that couldn't be right—barreled into the room. Elizabeth's foot caught on the hem of her dress, and both of the girls went sprawling. When they stopped tumbling over one another, Elizabeth began howling again. Was her older sister beating her or—

Wait. She was tickling Elizabeth. Tickling her unmercifully, true, but tickling the girl so that her screams were actually high-pitched giggles.

The girls' parents burst into the room next, the father laying rough hands on the elder and pulling her off her younger sister, who looked about, saw the men and Quint, in particular, and began to bawl. Quint took a step back from the force behind the tears. The girl had a healthy pair of lungs.

Meanwhile, her older sister was flailing about, her black hair flopping in her face, while her father attempted to hold her still. "Settle down, Catherine."

Quint smiled. Ah, that's right. Her name was Catherine.

"Let. Me. Go." And then she sank her teeth into her father's arm.

Quint saw it coming and winced. Her father, in the meantime, barked and threw his rabid daughter off him. She went sprawling, landing on her bottom. But unlike her sobbing sister, now ensconced in her mother's arms, Catherine did not so much as gasp. She picked herself up off the floor, lifted the torn and dusty hem of her brown dress, and strode regally toward the armchair, whereupon she took a seat. She straightened her irreparable dress, shoved a heap of black hair from her face, and blinked at the two men standing beside Quint.

"My father says you want to see me," she said, tone low and dangerous.

"Not I," said the first man, a chap in a black suit, holding a balled apron in one hand. "I must be going."

"I'll join you," the older man said, and the two practically flung themselves down the stairs.

"But wait. She's really a good girl. Very obedient," Edmund Fullbright called, going after them.

Mrs. Fullbright looked at Quint. "Lord Valentine, please do sit down. You mustn't leave. This is all just a"—she glared at her elder daughter—"misunderstanding. If you'll give us just one moment to collect ourselves."

She put an arm about Elizabeth, helped her up, and the two limped, arms wound tightly around each other toward the stairs to the family's private chambers. Catherine made to follow, but her mother saw her and hissed, "Get away, you ungrateful devil. I ought to beat you myself for this."

So the elder sister made her way back to the chair in the drawing room while mother and younger daughter disappeared up the steps. Quint felt a twinge of pity for Catherine, but it didn't last long. The chit had been behaving abominably. She deserved to be scolded, though if he'd had a daughter, he doubted he would ever have used such words on her.

Catherine took her seat again, and the look she gave him dried all words of sympathy from his tongue. She didn't want his pity. And so instead, Quint made her a bow. "Wonderful show, Miss Fullbright. When is the next performance?"

She scowled at him, but he could see she was relieved that he hadn't tried sympathy.

"You think me entertaining, sir?" A lock of hair had fallen forward and she brushed it back again.

"Immensely." He gestured to the chair opposite her. "May I?"

"I don't care what you do," she answered, looking away.

"You were only too full of advice when we met at the Beaufort ball last week," Quint reminded her. He looked about the room, taking in the dilapidated furnishings, the cheap knickknacks, and the general gloomy atmosphere. If he'd wondered why the Fullbrights had put their seventeen-year-old daughter on the marriage mart so quickly or why they'd jumped at his proposal, the answer was patently clear.

The Fullbrights needed money. Obviously, Edmund Fullbright decided what was good for one daughter was equally good for the other.

"I can only assume the three men I encountered here were meant to woo you."

She gave him a narrow-eyed glare, and he almost laughed. The three men he saw earlier couldn't handle a spirited girl like Catherine. Even if much of that spirit was for show, she was no shrinking violet.

"I do not think you'll be receiving any proposals from those three." He motioned to the stairs. "I think you may have even frightened them away."

"Good," she said. "If only I could now frighten you away, my work would be complete."

He grinned. "Unlikely. I spend much of my time in Parliament with Tories screaming their lungs out, promising to incite my constituents to violence against me. I think I can handle a little girl's tirade."

Her jaw dropped at that. She did not like being called a little girl or having her efforts belittled.

He was about to speak again, when he saw the blood trickle onto her lower lip. Without thinking, he rose and bent over her. Immediately, she pulled back, as though she expected a blow.

"I'm not going to hurt you. Come here." He reached for her chin, but she leaned farther back.

"Please. I'd prefer you didn't touch me."

"Yes, well, you're bleeding. At least take my

handkerchief, so you don't stain—" He looked at her old, dirty dress. "Just take it." He pressed the cloth into her hand and watched her dab her lower lip with it.

She touched her lip, drew the cloth away, saw the blood, and replaced the handkerchief. She looked up at him briefly, and said, "Thank you."

Looking directly into her eyes, he was momentarily at a loss. They were the eyes of a lioness— deep, golden brown hazel, wide set, and startlingly clear against her olive complexion. One reason Quint had chosen Elizabeth was because she possessed the prized blond hair, blue eyes, porcelain skin, and petite form that were currently in fashion. But it was no hardship on him to do so.

He had never found brunettes particularly alluring, and he usually disliked the dark look many of his country servants had after working out in the fields, but this girl, with her dark hair and bronze skin, was astonishingly alluring. She was not beautiful, not in the way Elizabeth was. But there was something earthy about her, something raw and exotic and sexual that attracted him.

Involuntarily, his eyes traveled down the length of her throat to the small expanse of flesh revealed at the bodice of her gown. He wondered, if he'd been able to see more of that flesh, if she would be honey gold all over—breasts, stomach, legs.

Immediately, he forced his eyes back to hers.

She was still holding the handkerchief to her lip. She pulled it away again, and he saw that the bleeding had slowed. Retaking his seat, he watched her push the hair from her forehead yet a third time.

The clock on the mantel ticked off the minutes, and that was the only sound in the room until Quint could no longer stand it. "Do you think your sister will be coming back down?"

She shrugged, lifted the handkerchief, and touched her lip. It was slightly swollen now, a splotch of red radiating out from her lower lip to tinge her cheek.

"Could you be persuaded to go up and fetch her?"

The girl gave him an incredulous look. "No, I could not."

"You don't like your sister very much, do you?"

She gave him a long look. "Whatever gave you that idea, Lord Valentine?"

"You have nothing to be jealous of, you know," he said, sitting back and making himself comfortable. "You're attractive—in your own way."

"What a compliment," she said, tone wry.

"And I am certain you could find a suitable husband if you only applied yourself more."

She stared at him. "I shall remember that the next time my father brings home three apes who are bent on trying to lure me into their lairs."

"Apes sleep in trees."

"That's not my point."

"I am beginning to see that." He remembered her parting words at the ball. "You do not wish to marry, do you, Miss Fullbright?"

"A young lady who does not want to marry? Ridiculous idea, Lord Valentine." She slanted those hazel eyes at him, and he had to cover his smile.

"It is ridiculous, especially your method of avoiding the institution. Climbing about on verandas and throwing tirades, Miss Fullbright?"

"You have another suggestion?"

"No, merely a question: Why don't you want to marry?"

"I have a better question," she said, finally allowing the handkerchief to drop from her mouth. She sat forward as though intensely interested in her subject now. "Why do you *want* to marry?"

"A variety of reasons," he answered, uncertain why his cravat felt as though it had shrunk. "Many reasons," he finished weakly.

"Name three." She pounced, and he was back on the defensive.

"I approve of the institution of marriage, for one," he began. "It's good for the moral code of the country, and—"

She waved a hand. "That's meaningless rhetoric. Give me a good reason. A personal reason."

He felt like telling her his personal reasons were none of her business, but he was trying to make a point here. It was probably his duty as a man and a member of Parliament to convince her to marry. What would England come to with hordes of unmarried women running about, all with *ideas* and such about why they should not marry?

He had read *Lysistrata,* by God, and he wouldn't have his country run by a gaggle of clucking, misguided women.

"I suppose I also want to marry because I need an heir. One day I will become a marquess, and I need a son to follow after me."

She seemed to consider, then nodded. "Yes, I suppose children are a good reason to marry. I will miss children. What is your third reason?"

Quint thought for a moment. What the devil was his third reason? He'd never considered *why* he would marry; he only knew that he must. And then it came to him.

"For my career. The right wife can be an asset for a man like me."

Immediately, he knew he'd given her the wrong answer. He'd forgotten she was the romantic sort. Her face clouded, and she shook her head. She began to speak, then shut her mouth and stood. "Men. You are all the same. It disgusts me."

She made to leave the drawing room, but he called after her, "Then I have not caused you to reconsider?"

"Reconsider?" She rounded on him. "Reconsider what? Reconsider joining an institution devised by men to benefit men at the detriment of women? An institution that has nothing whatsoever to do with love or esteem or even affection but relies wholly upon political stratagems formulated by men? Now you tell me, Lord Valentine, why should I marry?"

She stood and stared at him, waiting for an answer that he seemed unable to give. Surely he should be able to think of something. The *Times* had called him one of the greatest orators of his time, by God.

And yet the girl, this unkempt and uncivilized girl, had left him speechless. It was not to be borne. She stared at him a moment later, and then without the least trace of victory in her eyes, said, "That's what I thought."

And she strode from the room, her ugly brown skirts swirling as though she were the queen.

"Have you gone completely mad?" Ashley said when Catherine opened the door to the attic. She'd been banished there for a week.

Their maidservant slept there as well, but at present Catherine was alone in the attic and the house. Elizabeth and her mother had gone to stroll in Hyde Park, as it was the fashionable hour. It would have been more fashionable to ride, but the family had neither a horse nor carriage.

"Come in." Catherine opened the door wider, but Ashley just stood in the doorway and stared at her.

Ashley had changed little in the eighteen years Catherine had known her. She'd grown up to be precisely the beauty everyone had said she would. Her hair was the shade of ripe wheat, her skin so white and flawless that it shamed milk and honey, and her eyes were the most startling shade of pale sea green. She was of medium height with a perfect figure, and she had an amazing flair for fashion.

Not that she concerned herself with matters of fashion very often. Ashley was neither vain nor conceited. She would have made a better man than woman, for she was courageous, willful, and never dissembled, even when one wanted her to.

"That's what you have to say for yourself?" Ashley remarked. " 'Come in'?"

"Sit down?"

"Have you gone absolutely daft? You are sleeping in the servants' quarters now?"

Catherine sighed. "As you see."

"Oh, never mind that." Ashley stomped inside and bent under the low ceiling. "More importantly, Devlin told me he heard that you took a shot at a gentleman caller this morning, tried to set the house on fire, and tackled Lizzy."

Catherine smiled. If Ashley's brother had heard of her actions, the plan was working. "The last part is true. Where on earth did Devlin hear the rest?"

"I think he was at the butcher's. The man

claims the two of you were practically engaged."

"What?"

"Yes, that's just what I said." Ashley flounced inside and flopped down on Lizzy's new bed, careless of her riding dress or the intricate style of her blond hair. "I made Devlin take me right back over there, and then the butcher admitted you weren't quite engaged. But what about the rest of it, and why are butchers courting you? I thought we promised to be adventurers, not wives." She said the last as though it were a curse.

Hoping her cousin's tirade was over, Catherine sat next to her. "I am going to be an adventurer. Josie and I are planning an exciting adventure right now. But until we're ready to leave, I have to keep my father from marrying me off. I thought if I caused a bit of commotion, it would put off some of the suitors my father has been bringing home. Men like that butcher."

Ashley sat forward. "Really? That's actually a very good idea."

"Thank you."

"But don't you think starting fires is taking the scheme a bit too far?"

"I didn't start a fire or shoot at anyone. I did tackle Lizzy, but—"

"She deserved it," they said in unison and then laughed.

"Good for you," Ashley said. "Let me know if there's anything I can do to help."

"I was hoping you would ask that." Catherine had been sitting in the attic for several hours contemplating her next plan of attack as well as praying her father would not break down the door and beat her senseless for her earlier behavior. He had gone out after the incidents of the afternoon and hadn't yet returned. Thank God. As much as she'd like to run and hide at Maddie's home, Catherine knew that would only make her father angrier and guarantee her own punishment was that much worse in the end.

"I've been thinking, and I feel that continuing my efforts to dissuade my father's suitors are not wise. I can't keep acting like this," Catherine said. "You know how my father is."

Ashley nodded, uncharacteristically silent. She was not the kind of girl to be afraid of anything, but she was cautious around her uncle Edmund.

"I have to work even harder to delay Lord Valentine's wedding to Elizabeth. I made one attempt at the Beaufort ball, but I must do more. I need more time."

Ashley nodded. "Yes, I see your point, but the announcement appeared in the *Times*. Valentine will be in a hurry to get Lizzy to the altar now. He's a proud man."

"Arrogant you mean. The only reason he wants to marry Elizabeth is because he needs an heir, and he thinks it will help his career. He doesn't care one fig for her."

"Nor she for him, I imagine," Ashley said.

"So what do we do? How do we keep them from the church?"

"I don't know, but I promise to think about it. I'll talk to Madeleine and Josephine, too. Between the four of us, we'll come up with a plan. Until then, don't do anything rash."

"Me? Rash?"

Ashley laughed. "Very well. *I* won't do anything rash. Just sit tight, Catie. We'll halt that engagement if it's the last thing we do."

Catherine sighed. Leave it to Ashley to put it in the most dramatic terms possible.

sold the girl had he offered her for a pound and an eel pie.

He poured another glass of gin. Not only was it unprofitable, it wasn't right to marry Elizabeth before Catherine. The elder should marry first, or the family looked desperate. Edmund had been the younger son of an earl, and though Edmund cared for little else the man he'd called father had taught him, some rules and social rituals stuck with him. He *needed* to marry Catherine before he could allow Elizabeth to wed. And he needed to marry the girl soon. Already Valentine was chomping at the bit, asking when he could call the banns, pressing for a wedding date.

Valentine would be a good son-in-law. Edmund smiled and took another swallow of gin. Then he frowned when he saw the glass was empty. He filled it a third time, taking note that the bottle was almost dry. Stupid cow. His wife had been stealing his liquor again. Later he'd show the strumpet what happened when she stole what was his.

But now for Valentine. Edmund had looked into Quint Childers. The man was wealthy—not a Croesus by any means—but he would do. Still, Edmund hated to waste his one good daughter on a marquess. He knew with Elizabeth's pretty face and tight little figure he could score a duke at least. When she'd been a child, he'd promised her a prince, and he still thought the plan entirely feasible. But the little chit was happy with Valentine, couldn't stop cooing over how handsome he was and how well-mannered. Stupid cow. He had other plans for her.

But what to do with Valentine then? One did not just toss away a good future marquess. Edmund took another sip of gin and another, and then through the haze an idea came as clear as the song of an angel. The idea was so good, he sat up straight and rigid, and said, "Oh!" And then he dissolved into fits of laughter.

He laughed and laughed. He laughed so long and so hard that after a while his wife knocked on the door and asked if he was well. He cuffed her, sent her away, and then he laughed some more.

Yes, he would have his marquess and both daughters married too. Pulling on his coat, he stumbled through his house and then out the door. He'd tell his little Valentine to call the banns now—this Sunday. Edmund Fullbright was ready for his daughter to wed.

All he needed to do was make one little stop at the chemist, and everything would go as planned.

Chapter 6

Catherine checked her appearance in the mirror one last time before she followed her cousins down to Lord Castleigh's ballroom. Tonight was her last chance to warn Valentine away from Elizabeth.

It had been over two weeks since the earl had come to the house, and in that time she had not seen him. She had heard plenty of him from Elizabeth and her mother. The banns had been called, and the wedding preparations were under way. In fact, the family was so busy, Catherine was virtually left alone.

She was actually left alone when her father, mother, and sister had traveled to Valentine's ancestral estate in Derbyshire to meet the Marquess and Marchioness of Ravenscroft. Catherine had been given leave to stay with Maddie, and she'd been able to ride every day.

It had been a wonderful respite, but then the family had returned. Her father seemed to have given up marrying her off, and that was the most worrisome turn of events.

Her father never gave up that easily. He had to have an ulterior plan.

Pinching her cheeks to add color, she glided down the staircase in her new white silk gown. It wasn't actually hers. She wore one of Maddie's dresses from last Season. The two cousins had cut and pinned and sewed for days to alter it for Catherine's proportions. Now Catherine felt almost like she belonged here. She had rarely worn silk before, and the fabric was light and airy against her skin.

The gown had been Madeleine's contribution to the plan. Josephine and Ashley had helped Catherine with the rest, and now she saw them smiling at her as she descended the stairs. At the bottom, Josephine clasped her hands, and said, "Perfect! You look treacherously beautiful. Lizzy will bite her tongue all night!"

Catherine nodded and took a deep breath. The ball was not terribly crowded yet, but the guest list was extensive. She would have to act quickly, before too many people arrived, or she would be shaking too badly to implement the plan. Her hands were already clammy, and her heart was beating faster than usual. Oh, why couldn't she just hide?

Despite Josephine's encouraging words, Catherine did not feel beautiful. She felt like everyone was looking at her. How was she ever going to attract Valentine's attention? What if he ignored her and made her look a fool?

More guests were arriving, and Catherine knew she should join the receiving line. Ashley gave her a last reassuring squeeze. "You know what you have to do?"

Catherine nodded. "I must make Elizabeth show Valentine her true colors."

Ashley nodded. "Right. Then he'll call off the wedding, and you can remain a founding member of our club."

Josie and Maddie patted Catherine's hands. "Keep your chin up. Think confidence!"

Catherine nodded and forced her feet toward the entry hall, where her father, mother, sister, and Lord and Lady Castleigh stood greeting their guests. They made room for her to join them, and her father leaned over, and hissed, "Now you choose to look presentable? What are you up to?"

Catherine just smiled and bowed to a baron and his wife.

Next Elizabeth leaned over. "You look like a fool, you know. Trying to outshine me?"

Catherine smiled at her. "Well, no one will be

looking at me." She greeted Sir Gareth and her aunt Imogen, Ashley's parents, and accepted their compliments.

"No one ever looks at you, except when you act like a fool. Is it not time for you to begin gulping for air and shaking?" Elizabeth hissed.

Catherine turned back to the line in time to see that Lord Valentine had finally arrived.

Thank God he's here was her first thought. *Oh, Lord he's handsome* was her second. Catherine never noticed men except to avoid them. Some were taller or fatter or louder than others, but these were characteristics of the species, not points that held her interest.

Valentine held her interest. It was difficult to look at him and not be absorbed. His face, with its high smooth cheekbones and the contrasts between the hard planes of his chin and forehead and the softness of mouth and lips, intrigued her. And then there was his hair, which she had called too long, but which she now decided was perfect. The straight, brown edges scraped his collar and flowed back from his forehead like a bird's wing.

Like his, her hair was dark, a black her sister compared to mud. But Valentine's hair was the brown of topaz, the golden brown of rich, aged whiskey, the brown of virgin earth when it's freshly plowed and gleaming in the early-morning dew.

Catherine blinked. Lord, she couldn't keep

staring at him this way, thinking of him in these terms. If she weren't careful, she'd start believing herself in love with him. Even though she didn't intend Lizzy to marry him until after she and Josie had escaped, she knew the wedding would happen eventually. What would not happen— what was not possible or even within the realm of possibility—was that she herself would ever have him. A man like Valentine would never look at a woman like her.

And then he was before her, executing a formal bow. Catherine forced her legs to bend into a curtsey. She opened her mouth and said something, which she hoped was a polite greeting, but Valentine gave no indication he had heard. He stopped in front of her and stared. He stood so long, his gaze so hot and intense, Catherine began to tremble from nerves. Her cousins' plan was not going to work. He obviously thought she looked hideous. Finally, he barked, "What are you wearing?"

Catherine glanced down at Maddie's gown, then back into Valentine's lovely eyes. "A-a gown?"

"Put a shawl over it. It's practically indecent." And then he moved on. Catherine watched as he bowed to Elizabeth. While Lizzy's gown was just as low-cut as her own, Catherine noted that Valentine had no criticism for her. He smiled at Lizzy, his own face turning beautiful when he did. He drew Elizabeth close, into his warmth, and watching them, Catherine felt a painful stab through her heart.

She had never felt a stab of this magnitude before. She knew what it was. She'd experienced it as a child when Elizabeth had been given the cake Catherine had wanted or the doll or had received a kiss from her mother when Catherine had none.

Jealousy.

Catherine wanted to rip out her own heart. Anything but this feeling of covetousness for something that belonged to her sister, especially something as worthless as a man.

Valentine and Elizabeth moved away, but not before Elizabeth turned her head and smirked at Catherine. She always knew when she had something others wanted. The rest of her family moved away as well, and the receiving line dissolved until only Catherine remained.

She knew Valentine and Elizabeth would begin the dancing soon, and she also knew she would have to lure Valentine into dancing with her, but it was going to take every ounce of courage.

"Are you well?" Josie asked, coming to stand beside her. "Are all the people making you ill?"

Catherine shook her head. "No, but I-I don't want to go through with this."

"You can do it, Catie," Josie said immediately. "I know you're scared, but—"

"That's not it. Well, that's part of it. I am scared, but I'm also"—she grasped Josie by the elbow and dragged her into a corner—"I'm jealous!" she whispered.

"Jealous of what?" Josie asked. "Of Elizabeth's dress? Madeleine's gowns are the highest quality. I swear you are as pretty as Elizabeth. In fact, she pales beside you."

"No, Josie, I'm not jealous of Elizabeth's looks. I'm-I'm jealous of . . ." She lowered her voice even further. "I think . . . I mean, I might feel something for . . . oh, it's Valentine. *I* want him."

Josephine threw back her head and laughed. For a moment Catherine thought she truly resembled the popular image of pirates from books and papers. Of course, Josie laughed. The idea of Catherine and a man like Valentine . . .

"Who *doesn't* want him, Catie?" Josie said. "He's terribly handsome." So Josie wanted him too?

"But, Josie! We're never going to marry."

"What? Because I'm never going to marry means I can't even look at a man? I never will marry, but when I'm rich as a pirate, I plan to have lots of lovers."

"Oh, Lord."

"Catie, stop standing here. You and I are going to escape as soon as I find that treasure map. But I need more time. My assignment is to find the map. Yours is to remain unmarried until I do. Now get to it."

Catherine felt like saluting, but Josie gave her a little push.

Catherine entered the ballroom to the sight of

Elizabeth and Valentine dancing. She felt another pang of jealousy and a sharper stab of uncertainty. They looked so good together—Valentine's dark hair and eyes beside Elizabeth's pale blond beauty. Who was she to part them?

One, two, three . . .

Then she caught Elizabeth's eye. Her younger sister sneered at her, and then Catherine knew it was up to her to save Valentine and herself. Valentine was not the true target.

Catherine waited until Elizabeth was dancing with another man before approaching Lord Valentine. She did so overtly, making sure that Elizabeth saw her. As she moved toward him, crossing the ballroom, she received encouraging waves from her three cousins. He was standing by himself for the first time that evening, and Catherine knew this might be her only opportunity. But when she approached him, he barely glanced at her before looking away again. Still, there was something in his look that made her remember she hadn't yet donned a shawl. She felt almost naked.

"My lord," she said, standing beside him, refusing to allow him to make her more nervous than she already was.

"Miss Fullbright." His voice was cold, and he obviously had no interest in speaking to her.

She followed his gaze and saw that he was watching Elizabeth dancing. He did not look jealous. The closer she looked, the more he appeared simply satisfied by what he saw. She narrowed her eyes. Lord, the look on the man's face was nothing short of proprietary. He looked quite pleased with his newest acquisition.

Catherine straightened her shoulders. *Caveat emptor.* "You are still intent on marrying my sister, I see."

He gave her a sideways glance. "And you are still intent on persuading me otherwise."

She shrugged. "I did try. But now that we are to be brother and sister by marriage, perhaps we should begin anew."

Without taking his eyes from Elizabeth, he answered, "If that is your wish."

And then they stood in silence.

Four, five, six, seven . . .

Catherine sent an appealing look to Josephine across the room. What was she to do now? Valentine had not asked her to dance; and he did not seem at all interested in continuing their conversation. This sort of behavior would only please Lizzy, not tempt her into throwing a tantrum.

Josephine bit her lip and consulted with Ashley, who was beside her. The two whispered while Catherine shifted from foot to foot, hoping no one came between her and Valentine.

Eight, nine . . .

The ballroom was growing more crowded as

the theaters let out, and the late arrivals made their appearance. Catherine watched the crowds and was forced to take a shaky breath. She could not panic now. Breathe, breathe.

Nine, ten, ten, ten . . .

"Are you well, Miss Fullbright?" Valentine said suddenly. She turned, and he was staring at her, concern in those lovely mahogany eyes.

Her first instinct was to assure him she was quite all right. Her family mocked her fears of crowds and tight places, and the weakness embarrassed her. But now that his eyes were on her, she wanted to keep them there. What would Elizabeth have done in this situation? Catherine had watched her flirt and charm men for years. Elizabeth would have wrapped Valentine around her fingers. She already had.

Catherine took another shaky breath—quite authentic—and said, "I'm sorry, sir, but I do not feel well at all. I think a bit of air—"

That was all she need say, and his hand was on the small of her back, and he was assisting her toward the French doors of her uncle William's ballroom. The doors opened directly onto the lawn, and Catherine had entered through similar doors into other areas of the house often. As soon as she stepped outside, she recognized where she was and remembered the stone bench just a few feet away.

"If I might sit down for a moment," she said

before Valentine could leave her to fetch one of her cousins or aunts to help her, "I believe it would help."

"Of course," Valentine said, taking her arm and leading her to the bench. He walked stiffly beside her, and Catherine was well aware he did not wish to be there.

He seated her on the bench, then moved an appropriate distance away, and Catherine had to think quickly to keep him close by. It was imperative her sister find them talking together. The very sight would so anger Elizabeth that she would finally show her true self. Then Valentine wouldn't possibly wish to marry her, and Catherine would be free of the marriage threat hanging over her head long enough to escape with Josie.

"Thank you so much for your kindness," she said softly, so that he was forced to move a step closer to hear her. "I am feeling better already."

"Yes, your color is back," he said, though his eyes were on the house and the activities of the ballroom. No matter. She did not need him to pay attention to her, merely to be by her side rather than Elizabeth's. But there was something rather exciting about having him all to herself like this. In the semidarkness and shadows, his expressions were a mystery to her. And yet she could feel his presence and smell the scent he wore. She shivered, afraid and intrigued all at once.

She had not forgotten what men were capable

of. She had not forgotten her father's vicious words and roughness, and so she could not understand why she, who knew what men were, wanted a man to touch her, caress her in that moment. She closed her eyes, remembering the feel of Valentine's strong hand on the small of her back. The hand had guided and reassured her, and yet she knew that same hand could hurt.

She opened her eyes and looked at him, and to her surprise, he was staring at her. He did not look away when their gazes locked. He shifted and then he was closer, his knee brushing hers as he stood over her.

One, two, three . . .

"Are you still intent upon not marrying, Miss Fullbright?" His voice was lower than it had been. It resonated through her.

"Quite so, sir."

He was looking down at her, and she finally had to look away. She was afraid what would happen if one of them did not.

He reached out and placed a finger on her cheek, turning her face back to his. His finger was warm against her skin, a tantalizing contrast to the cool evening. She shivered.

"May I ask why?" He did not remove his finger. In fact, he seemed to be moving it closer to her mouth.

"I-I am not inclined to marry," she said, though she hardly knew how to speak anymore. "I do-do not wish to be under a man's thumb." She had not meant to give so much away, but when the words were out, she glanced quickly up at him.

He took his hand away. "Ah, so that is the reason for this streak of independence. Surely you realize that by not marrying, you merely remain under your father's thumb."

"The devil you know . . ." she whispered, but she did not think he heard. And if Valentine would only play his part, she wouldn't be in her father's house much longer.

Valentine took the place beside her and stared out over the lawns. He did not speak, but his knee touched hers. Catherine's breathing hitched. The feel of him beside her made her shake. She wanted to lean into his solid warmth, feel him put his arms around her. Equally strong was the impulse to run, to escape this man and all men.

"You're trembling, Miss Fullbright," Valentine said, voice so low it was barely a rumble through her bones. "Shall I give you my coat, or are you well enough to return inside?"

Catherine looked at him, and this close she could see his face very well. His gaze was admiring, his focus on her lips, and under the heat of that look, she could not answer. Why on earth was he looking at her that way? Men never looked at her like this.

"I thought I told you to put on a shawl."

"You did, but—"

"Too late." He placed a finger over her lips. "I can't resist you now."

She tried to protest, but instead, to her astonishment, she found herself surrendering, closing
her eyes and feeling his hand come around her
waist.

One heartbeat, two . . .

"Quint, there you are!" a shrill voice called
across the lawns. "I've been looking all over for
you."

Catherine opened her eyes and turned to see
Elizabeth rushing toward them. As recognition
dawned, Elizabeth's movements changed from
graceful to jerky. Catherine stiffened, ready for
the full force of her sister's wrath, knowing it was
inevitable and also that it was necessary.

Valentine stood and stepped away from the
bench. "Elizabeth, dear, I'm sorry to have left you.
Your sister felt unwell."

Catherine saw the angry retort on Elizabeth's
lips and willed her to say it, willed her sister to
show Valentine what she truly was. Elizabeth
glanced at her, and Catherine knew her sister saw
the expectation on her face, and quite suddenly,
as though Elizabeth had seen through the entire
ploy, her face relaxed and then transformed into
a mask of concern.

"Oh, my! Catie, are you well? Would you like
me to fetch Mother?"

Catherine glared at her. Where were the accu-
sations, the tantrums? Had she not seen Catherine sitting with Valentine? Had she not seen that
his arm had been wound about her? One more

heartbeat and she would have been kissing him!

But Elizabeth was all worry and distress. She took Valentine's place beside Catherine and put her hand on her arm. "Oh, dear, not again. Poor, Catie."

Catherine almost laughed. Poor Catie? When had those words ever escaped her sister's lips?

"It's silly, really," she said, looking at her fiancé. "Catie is terribly afraid of crowds. She can barely attend a ball without dissolving into a fit of hysterics."

Catherine jerked at the exaggeration, and Elizabeth dug her nails into Catherine's arm.

"We usually have to take her home and put her to bed. Quint, would you be a dear and fetch my mother? I don't want to leave Catie in this state."

He bowed. "Of course. I shall send her right out." He started for the house, and Elizabeth's face transformed, the full force of her fury focused on Catherine.

Just as quickly it dissolved when Valentine slowed, looked back, and said, "Good night, Miss Fullbright. I do hope you recover quickly."

"Thank you," Catherine managed before the pain from Elizabeth's nails digging into her arm made her gasp. She tugged her arm away and stared at the half-moons of blood welling up. "Lizzy, that hurt!"

She glanced up in time to see Lizzy's hand coming toward her, but not in enough time to avoid the slap. Her sister's hand cracked across her cheek with enough force to snap Catherine's head back. She cried out and leaned forward in an attempt to keep her balance on the bench, but Elizabeth merely used the opportunity to try and backhand her. Catherine caught her wrist and pushed back, but she was off-balance and went sprawling.

She did not fall far or hard, but the indignity of it hurt quite enough. "That was for what you did to me at the Beaufort ball." Slowly, Elizabeth rose and stood over her, treading on the hem of Maddie's gown. "You stupid bitch. What were you trying to do out here? Lure him away from me?"

Catherine didn't answer. Instead, she stared at the dark smudge Lizzy's dainty ball slipper had left on Maddie's silk gown.

"As though a man like Quint Childers would be interested in an old hag like you. Stick with what you are good at, spinster, and stay out of my way. If I catch you near him again, I'll kill you."

"Elizabeth!" Both girls jumped and swiveled to see their father striding toward them. "Get inside now before you make a scene and ruin everything."

"But, Daddy, she—"

"Get inside," he growled. "The Duke of Chawton has just arrived, and when I return, you had better be dancing with him."

Elizabeth spared one last glance at Catie and then rushed toward the house. From the ground, Catherine looked up at her father, wondering if there was any point in attempting to defend herself when he would side with Lizzy anyway.

But she would not sit still and wait for him to strike. She stared at her father's shoes and knew if he tried to hit her, she would throw everything she had back at him. Even if she had to scrub chamber pots for a week, he would be the one sorry tonight.

And then suddenly his shoes were gone. She looked up, almost afraid it was a trick, but all she saw was his back. He was walking away, returning to the house and the ball.

Catherine tried to rise and then saw the drops of blood near the mark from Elizabeth's slipper. Maddie's dress was ruined. If she returned to the ball now, Elizabeth would tell everyone she'd tripped or had a nosebleed. Valentine would pity her. Elizabeth was on her guard now. Catherine knew she'd never get close to him again.

She was doomed to whatever her father had in store.

Chapter 7

Quint paced his bedroom, listening to the clock chime four. It was the day of his wedding, early morning, and he could not sleep. Back and forth he paced, his bare feet sinking into the thick burgundy-and-blue Turkish rugs covering the hardwood floors. His bedroom was his sanctuary in an otherwise unimpressive town house in Mayfair. He'd bought the house because he did not want to live in his parents' residence in Grosvenor Square. He'd wanted his own space. His house boasted a small dining room and study on the ground floor; a large drawing room and smaller ladies' parlor on the first floor; and two adjoining bedrooms on the second floor, along with several smaller bedchambers.

Quint supposed those were intended for the residents' children. But he did not plan to live here long with his wife. As soon as he and Elizabeth married, they would begin to search for a new house that would suit them both.

With that intention in mind from the start, Quint had not taken much time or effort to furnish the house in style. His wife could have charge of that duty. The one exception was his own bedroom. He'd commissioned a large full tester bed with Chinese silk hangings in dark blue and matching bedclothes. The furnishings in the room were tulipwood of the best quality. His favorite piece was his large mahogany desk with lion's paws for feet. He had an identical piece in the small study downstairs and another in his office in Westminster. Quint liked consistency, and he arranged each of the desks in the same manner, with matching pens and inkwells. In this manner, wherever he chose to work, he was at home.

He paced to his desk now and opened a folder on a new investment proposal he was researching for the prime minister. The government and Mr. Perceval would thank him if he recommended the proposal and England prospered. Likewise, if he recommended the proposal, and it turned out to be a swindle, his name would be vilified. He could not afford to make a mistake, in this or any area of his life.

He stared at the pages before him until the

words blurred. Standing, he began pacing again. He was restless and impatient, and he didn't understand why. He wanted to marry, and he knew the woman he had selected would make an excellent wife. She was a bit young at seventeen, but he was no old man at thirty, and a young bride meant a malleable bride.

Still, he felt a niggling prickle of unease on the back of his neck, just at the hairline. It was not an unfamiliar sensation. He'd felt it often before a vote on a bill in the House. Usually when things would not go his way.

Why the ominous prickle should appear right before his wedding was a mystery, but he'd felt it the last week or more—ever since the betrothal ball his fiancée's family had given.

Quint crossed his bedroom and opened his dressing-room door. It was a small closet, and on the other side was another door, now open, which led to his bride's room. Though they would not live here more than a few months, he'd had it refurbished specifically for Elizabeth. It was his wedding gift to her. Last week he'd had the room painted, papered, and upholstered in pale blues and lavenders. But now, as he stared at it, he could not picture Elizabeth there. When he looked at the bed he saw—

But it was not true that he couldn't see Elizabeth in the room. He could picture her standing by the window, an impatient look on her face, and he could see her primping in the mirror of the tulipwood dressing table. He could even imagine her at the large kingwood-and-tulipwood armoire, sorting through clothing, attempting to pick the perfect gown for an evening out.

But he could not see her in the bed, could not see himself sharing it with her. When he looked at the bed, he saw—

He turned and strode back to his own chamber. Standing before his own bed, draped in dark blue, he willed himself to imagine Elizabeth there.

The image of a hazel-eyed, olive-skinned girl appeared before his eyes. Her silky black hair fell in soft waves to her waist, caressing generous curves. She was naked—her golden breasts covered by long, lustrous tresses—but the slight swell of her stomach and the curve of her hips drew his gaze. He wanted to reach out and touch those jutting hips, wrap his hand around her waist, and pull her lush, warm body against his own. He could smell her now, her fragrance rich and heavy like ripe peaches. Closing his eyes, he imagined taking her mouth with his and running his hands down along her body until he cupped that sweet derrière and pressed her hard against—

Quint opened his eyes and, hands on the coverlet before him, took a shuddering breath. The little witch had enchanted him. That was the only explanation.

He hadn't cared one whit for the chit before the

betrothal ball, but from the moment he'd seen her in the low-cut white satin gown, he could not take his eyes from her. Damn fool girl. Why hadn't she worn a shawl with that gown? Better yet, why hadn't she stuck to dressing in the poorly fitted gowns he was used to seeing her wear? He did not want to know that underneath those ugly shapeless things, she was so ripe and lush a man's hands ached to caress her.

Unlike so many of the pale, cool beauties of the *ton*—hell, unlike his own betrothed—Catherine was alive. Her skin, her hair, her complexion glowed with luxuriousness he needed to taste, to touch. Beside her, Elizabeth looked pale and wan. A slip of a girl beside a goddess.

Quint had tried to avoid Catherine at the betrothal ball, but she had sought him out. Even then he attempted to ignore her. He tried to be cold, but she thawed his reserve until he found himself alone with her, arms about her, mouth so painfully close to touching hers that he felt he would go mad for wanting her.

And he still wanted her. There was no doubt in his mind that the ache in his groin and his agitated state were due in part to Catherine Anne Fullbright.

Quint was not a rake. Nor was he a saint, by any stretch of the imagination. He was a disciplined man. He did not want or need a woman in his bed every night. And he did not seek to bed every woman he met. There were women available to him, and he occasionally partook of their charms. He was a vital man of thirty, and he had needs. His needs were not pressing. There were often weeks when he did not even think of women, especially when he was consumed with important political affairs. More than anything else Quint sought a mate with the same goals as he. He fully intended to be faithful to Elizabeth, and he hoped one day he would come to love her, as his own parents had learned to love and cherish one another.

Quint knew what he wanted, and that was why he could not understand how he—an honorable man, a disciplined man, a rational man—could not cease fantasizing about his fiancée's sister.

Was he so depraved that he imagined betraying his wife before they'd even exchanged vows?

Was he so degenerate that he could not stop images of Catherine—Catie, her sister had called her—lying under him, her legs wrapped around him and her breathing hard and rapid?

"Damn!" He turned and swiped his hand over his desktop, toppling several books and sending papers dancing all over the room. There went all his careful notes for the prime minister.

Shaking his head, Quint knelt to restore the desk to order and his temper to its usual evenness.

There was a quiet knock at his door, and his valet, Dorsey, said, "Are you well, my lord?"

"Fine," Quint called. "Come back in an hour. I'll be ready to dress for the wedding."

"Yes, my lord."

Quint listened for the receding footsteps and then returned to his task. With each paper he ordered, each book he set to rights, each pen he set in its usual place beside the blotter, he wiped Elizabeth's sister from his mind. He ordered his bedroom as he ordered his thoughts, and there was no place for Catherine Fullbright in either.

The bedroom door slammed open, and Catherine sat up with a scream lodged in her throat.

"Elizabeth, go to your mother's room. Now." Her father stood in the doorway, the light behind him, his shadow falling over Catherine's bed like a shroud.

Catherine watched as her younger sister scrambled out of her bed, passed her father, and hurried out the door. It was Elizabeth's wedding day, and Catherine had only moved back in the room from the attic two days ago. Perhaps her father had forgotten he'd allowed her to move back?

"Father," she stuttered. "Remember, you said I could sleep in here now."

But he remained blocking the doorway, and Catherine shrank back when he raised the lantern he carried and stepped into her bedroom.

He was not alone. Beside him was a large man, almost as wide as the door and almost as tall. He had his ham-sized fists outstretched, and he leered at Catherine with obvious intent.

"F-f-father, what do you want?" Catherine pulled her knees up against her chest and tried to make herself small. With the two men in her bedroom, the room already seemed unbearably tiny and cramped. She struggled for breath as her heart pounded incessantly in her temples.

One, two, three . . .

"Well, what do you think?" her father said to the beefy man, holding the lantern closer to Catherine so that she was visible. She lowered her head, and her father grasped her chin and yanked her face back up. "Stand up girl. Show him what you got."

She screamed as he hauled her from the bed. Her nightshirt ripped on the bedpost so that it fell open over her shoulder. She caught it before it could expose more skin. Head ringing, she clutched her father and looked up in time to see the beefy man grinning down at her. God help her, she could see the bulge in his pants.

"I like her. Ten pounds, you say?"

Catherine blinked. Ten pounds? Was she being sold? Here and now, thrust out of her warm bed and bartered away like a piece of meat?

"Ten pounds," her father agreed, and stuck out his hand. The beefy man handed him a wad of blunt and then reached for Catherine.

She screamed. She screamed like she had never

screamed before, so loud that it would wake not only the house but the neighbors and the whole city of London.

"Stop that infernal wailing," her father bellowed. "I gave you a chance. I brought you suitors and took you to balls. But you wouldn't listen." He bent low and his rank, brandy-soaked breath wafted over her. "You and that little hoyden cousin of yours had to make *plans*." There was dried spittle on his lips, and she could see he hadn't shaved for several days. Stray, gray hairs grew in at all angles on his chin and cheeks. "Now, you see that I keep my promises."

He hauled her up and all but threw her at the beefy man, but Catherine reached out at the last moment and grabbed her father's hand. Her thoughts were wild now, desperate and jumbled, and all she could think was *no, no, no!*

She held fast to her father's hand, even when he tried to pry her fingers loose.

"Get off me," he said, but she held on. And somehow she leashed her terror, gathered it into a ball, and used it to fuel her courage. She looked up and into her father's face. He was staring down at her, his expression uncertain. She did not think he had expected this from her.

"Daddy," she cried, using the endearment she hadn't spoken since she was a little girl. "Please, don't do this to me. Please. Anything but this."

"I won't have this insubordination," he roared. But she held on. "You're no longer my daughter."

"Daddy, please, no. Please. I'll marry. Whomever you choose. Anything. Please don't give me to him." She glanced ay the brute again. "Please, please."

"You'll do whatever I ask?" he said. "Marry whomever I say?" When she looked into his face again, she saw the slightest hint of a smile. Her blood turned to ice, and she felt her stomach heave.

"Anyone?" her father pressed. "Even your sister's betrothed?"

Catherine swallowed the acid in her throat. She wanted to scream *no*. What her father suggested was wrong. Immoral. She glanced back at the beefy man, then back at her father.

Catherine swallowed the acid in her throat and nodded.

"Good." Her father strode to the door and clapped his hands and Meg, their much-abused housemaid, came in carrying a tray of tea.

Catherine looked from Meg to her father. "What is that?"

Her father poured the steaming brew into a large cup and thrust it into her hands. "Drink it, or I keep his money." He nodded at the beefy man.

Catherine swallowed. "But, Father, this will never work. Valentine is no fool. He'll know I'm not Elizabeth. Even if I'm veiled, he'll know."

Edmund Fullbright smiled. "Don't you worry about Valentine. I bribed one of his footmen to give him the same brew you'll take. Now drink."

The brute shifted, his gaze never leaving Catherine's breasts.

Catherine gulped the foul-tasting brew, not caring that it scalded her tongue.

Three hours later, she stood in the chapel. It was cool and quiet inside, but to her everything appeared hazy and blurred. She swayed, but her father's hand on her elbow steadied her. She was glad that she could not see clearly, glad that her groom's face was obscured, and that the tea her father had given her before the ceremony numbed her. She did not want to think what she was doing.

She did not want to think of Elizabeth at home, crying, as Catherine took her place. She did not want to think what Valentine would do when he lifted the heavy veil and saw his bride.

But perhaps he would not notice. She'd seen him sway and stumble and knew he, too, was drugged.

The parish priest was speaking, saying her name, and behind her, she heard her father cough. He'd done so each time her name was required. He'd hacked and coughed, concealing the sound of her name, so that she did not even know whether her name or Elizabeth's was spoken.

And then she was being shaken from her lovely quiet place. She was urged to speak, and she obeyed. It seemed so much easier to obey now that she had drunk the tea.

She spoke the words required of her, listening to the voice coming from her lips in wonder. It did not sound like her, and yet she liked listening to the voice. She did not want the voice to stop.

But she was hushed, and the voice went dead, and Catherine wished she herself were dead because then her heavy veil was lifted, and she looked into mahogany brown eyes. The shock and disgust on Valentine's face was a physical blow. And then all went black.

Catherine stretched and tried to open her eyes. They were so heavy, though, that she almost rolled over and went back to sleep. Her whole body was terribly burdensome. She could not seem to move it. Every time she did, her head ached. But she could not sleep all day. She had to go to Elizabeth's wedding.

With an immense burst of will, she opened her eyes and tried to focus. The room was dark, the bed's blue silk drapes drawn. She blinked. Her bed did not have drapes. Reaching out, she parted the luxurious material and peered into an unfamiliar room. The curtains, also blue, were pulled shut, so she had no idea of the time, but she felt as though she'd slept for a week.

She closed her eyes again and tried to think where she was. She'd been asleep in her bed and then—

Catherine shot awake. Everything flooded back to her so quickly that her head throbbed with the effort to contain it all. Bits and snippets of images poured over her.

Her father bursting into her room.

The beefy man's ham-sized fists.

The cool church.

Valentine lifting her veil.

No!

She had to find Valentine. Lifting her head from her pillow, she forced herself to ignore the pain and sit. As she did so, the sheet she wore fell back. Catherine gasped, noting she wore nothing underneath. She was naked in a strange bed.

There was a groan and beside her something moved, and then a man's arm emerged from the silk bedcovers beside her.

Catherine screamed and clutched the sheet, pulling it to her chin. She kicked at the man and scooted as far toward the edge of the bed as possible.

"What the hell?" he said. She was pulling all the sheets to cover herself and revealing him in the process, and her eyes widened as she realized he, too, was naked.

One, two, three, four . . .

Good Lord! She was in bed with a naked man. She pinched her arm, hoping it was a dream.

Her arm hurt, and she did not wake. Then the man rolled over, turning so that she could see his bare chest all the way to where the last vestiges of sheets barely covered him at the hips.

Catherine stared, unable to take her eyes off

him. And then she jumped up, tripped over the sheets, and stumbled to her feet. She screamed again, backing away from the now-naked man and wrapping the sheets tightly around her. She had to escape, to get away from this man. But she could not go home. She could never, never, never go home. Anything but that.

"Who the devil—" Valentine was looking at her now, frowning, seeming confused. He did not appear to recognize her yet or understand what was going on, but Catherine knew. Oh, God, she knew all too well what had happened.

Her father's plan had succeeded. He'd forced her agreement, drugged her, then drugged Valentine, too. And now Quint Childers, the Earl of Valentine, was staring at her, naked and aroused, and lying in the bed they'd shared.

Chapter 8

"Stop screaming," Quint said, when he found his voice. "I can't think with you screaming."

The woman closed her mouth, her hazel eyes wide and frightened. He ran a hand through his hair and tried to understand what was going on. One minute he'd been sleeping, dreaming that a soft, warm woman was beside him. The next moment, he'd been shoved, thrust into coldness, and had his senses assaulted by a high-pitched keening. His head throbbed with a dull ache that numbed his usually quick wits.

What the hell was going on? And what was he doing in his bed? He thought back, mentally retraced his steps, but the path was not easy. It was dark and winding, and at first all he could remember was a church. Talking to Edmund Fullbright in a church. And he'd been angry—they'd both been angry because—

Quint bolted upright and swore. Catherine yelped and jumped back, taking all of his bedclothes with her, and then he swore again. He was naked, with a morning erection he could not hope to hide.

At least now he knew why she was screaming. "Damn, damn, damn! That goddamn bastard. I'm going to have his head."

Quickly, he rose and pulled on his dressing robe. In two strides he was at his desk, pen in hand, fumbling for paper. And then he paused. How the hell was he going to fix this with a pen? He needed a pistol. He needed to find Edmund Fullbright, shove the pistol into his mouth, and pull the trigger.

Quint gripped the desk. No, he had to be rational. He had to think.

He looked at his pen again. He would write a letter and decry the wrong that had been done to him. He'd tell how his father-in-law had drugged him. He didn't know how, but he knew that the deed had been done. He'd been drugged and only half-lucid when he and his bride had exchanged vows, and he'd lifted his bride's veil and found not Elizabeth but Catherine.

And then her father had taken him aside and showed him the marriage license. There, swimming before his blurry vision, was Catherine's name, not Elizabeth's. Fullbright had warned Quint not to make a scene. One sister or the other, what was the difference? He was married to a Fullbright now, a niece of the Earl of Castleigh, what else did he want?

Quint had told Fullbright in no uncertain terms that he wanted Elizabeth. And then Mrs. Fullbright had come in with Catherine and tea. More tea.

Quint thought of the tea he'd drunk yesterday morning. That was how Fullbright had done it then. And he'd never thought, not until he had that second cup.

Now he pulled paper after paper off his desk, tossing the used sheets on the floor, but he could not find a clean one. Quint dropped his aching head in his hands. It was no use. He'd seen the marriage license. And he had signed it. He was married to Catherine. He'd said the vows to her, and he didn't even remember whether the priest had said her name or Elizabeth's. And now, to seal the deal, he had slept with her. He didn't think he had taken her, made love to her, but he could not be sure, and what did it matter anyway? She would be ruined. Even if he arranged an annulment, she was already ruined.

He was ruined—all his hopes and dreams, his plans for the future disappeared into dust when he'd lifted that veil. He allowed his head to fall into his hands. He allowed himself a moment of mourning for what might have been, and then he steeled himself. This wasn't over, not by far.

Slowly, he turned back to the room and faced Catherine. His wife.

She had pushed herself into a corner, her face pale and wary, as though she feared he would pounce on her at any moment. She looked afraid and confused, and with her hair down about her shoulders, very much like he'd pictured her in his fantasies. Quint pushed the image away and tried to keep his thoughts honorable.

"We need to talk," he said.

She nodded.

"Your father—"

"I won't go back," she said, her voice shaky but strong. "I'm sorry. I didn't want this to happen, but I will *not* go back."

Quint frowned. "Then you knew?" he said. "You willingly took part in his plan." He tamped down the burst of anger that threatened to flare up again. Now he knew the kind of woman he was dealing with.

"No!" She stepped out of her corner, the words spoken so vehemently that he almost found her believable. "I had no choice. He-he—if I hadn't gone along he would have . . ." She trailed off, and he watched her glance about his bedroom, then turn her gaze on him. Her hands tightened on the pile of silk bedclothes at her throat. He wondered if she realized they gaped at her side, showing him the curve of one honey-colored breast.

He looked away. He didn't want to feel lust for her right now. He was angry, so angry, and lust would only complicate the matter. He wanted to strangle her. How dare she deceive him like this? How dare she and that bastard father of hers do this to him and Elizabeth?

She was speaking again, and he glanced at her, fury making her words hard to understand at first.

"I don't understand how this happened," she was saying. Catherine gestured to the bed. "How did we end up here? I don't remember—"

"You were drugged," Quint said without preamble. "Opium, as I'm sure you well know."

She closed her eyes. "The tea. He made me drink it before we left for the church."

He leaned forward in his chair and pounced. "So you were drugged, but that doesn't change the fact that your name was on our marriage license. You stood with me in the church and said the vows."

"I didn't want this," she said, her voice a mere breath.

"I don't believe you." He could see the shock on her face, but he didn't care. "Tell me, why should I believe you? You all but seduced me the night of the betrothal ball."

She curled her lip, mirroring his own disgust. "You wanted to be seduced."

"Well, I didn't want this marriage. I didn't want *you*."

She flinched, then took a breath.

"You've made your feelings for me plain. What are you going to do?" Her voice still shook when she spoke, but he wasn't sure exactly what she was afraid of—the fact that she was naked in a room with a man or the threat of having to spend the rest of her life with said gentleman.

"There's nothing I can do." He ran a hand through his hair again. Bloody hell, he wanted to kill that bastard Fullbright. But his anger was already smoldering, being replaced by something like despair. "I know of no escape."

"But we could get an annul—"

He shook his head. "Annulment, divorce. Either choice leaves you a ruined woman. Where will you go? Your father will not take you back, and your family will be disgraced."

"I told you that I won't go back." The color had returned to her face now, and her hazel eyes were bright with anger. Even doomed as they were, he could appreciate her strong will. She took a step forward. "And I won't accept this marriage."

Quint gave a bark of laughter. "Is that so? And just what do you propose we do, Miss Fullbright? There is no way out of this without causing a scandal. And not just a scandal that people will whisper about for a Season and then forget. If we even hint to the public that we were duped into this marriage, you and I will never recover."

He knew the words he spoke were true, knew the rational part of his mind was beginning to emerge, and yet the facts, logical as they were, were no easier to accept. With bile in his throat, he forced himself to go on.

"We must use all of our skills to persuade the public that I changed my mind and intended to marry you all along."

"And who will believe that? What about the banns, the betrothal ball?"

Valentine looked at her as though she were a simpleton. "People will believe what I tell them. I've built my reputation on honesty and integrity." And made the mistake of believing others were the same. What a fool he'd been.

Bedclothes still clenched tightly to her chin, she advanced on him. "So that's what this is about. You are worried about your wretched career. Well, I couldn't care less about your political advancement. I won't be your wife. I'll-I'll run away."

"Oh, no you will not." The little deceiver might have helped trick him into marriage, but she would not ruin his career, too. Quint stood and stared down at her, though she was not much shorter than he. "Do you think I want to be married to you? A woman who stands here and tells me she cares nothing for my entire life's work? A woman who isn't half as pretty or remotely as charming as her sister, and I am stuck with you for life? *Life*. Do you think that's what I want?"

She took a step back, but he caught her wrist.

"Do not dare think I don't know what you did, you little liar. But my hands—our hands—are tied. There is no way out. And I will not have you do anything rash that might jeopardize both our reputations. I need a partner, not a liability."

Catherine wrenched her wrist free of his hold and took two steps back. "You want a partner? Ha! You want a lapdog to follow you about and nod at your every pronouncement. I'm sorry I'm not the sweet, biddable wife you'd hoped to get, but I assure you Elizabeth would not have been so either."

"I suppose now I will never know. Damn it!" He slammed his hand down on the desk, angry at the situation, his own foolishness, and his loss of control. "Damn it all to hell. I don't even know what to do with you." He made a dismissive gesture. "I should just send you home. Let your father deal with you." It was an idle threat, but her body tensed in immediate fear.

"I won't go. And if you even try—"

"Don't presume to tell me what you will or will not do. You'll do what I say." Quint couldn't stop the words from spilling out of his mouth. He did not intend to speak them. He didn't even mean them, but something about her defiance and the reckless look in her eyes set him spinning.

"You pompous, self-centered bastard," she spat. "You don't have to worry about me. I won't be your problem much longer."

She swept the train of the bedclothes over one arm, marched to the door, opened it, and stomped into the hallway.

"Where the devil are you going now?" Quint said, following her. "You can't walk about London dressed in a sheet."

"It's not your concern," she called over her shoulder, now descending the staircase that would lead to the entry hall. "Go back to your room and feel sorry for yourself."

Her voice began to fade, and he had to start down the first flight of stairs. He passed a maid who was staring after the woman dressed only in a bedsheet and who then goggled at him in his dressing robe.

"I'm not going back to my room," he said when he'd caught sight of her again. "And you are not leaving. Get back into that bedroom."

She'd reached the last three steps and descended them without even pausing. As she marched toward the front door, Quint's butler rushed forward to open it for her.

"Webster! Do not open that door!" Quint roared. Webster paused, but she breezed past the man.

"Thank you anyway, Webster," she said as

though she'd known the man for years. "I can open it on my own."

Webster bowed, "Yes, madam."

Quint ran a hand through his hair and rushed down the last steps. "I order you to stop. Now! *Elizabeth!*"

His new wife's back went ramrod straight, like a stag who has been shot with a mortal arrow. She paused, hand on the doorknob. Quint held his breath, praying to God she'd reconsidered.

She looked back. "My name is Catherine." And she opened the door and walked into the London morning.

Quint looked at his butler and then back at the line of servants peering down the hall and over the staircase. As one, they looked down and proceeded to work diligently at their tasks.

Quint grabbed the door and slammed it shut. Idiot woman! Let her go out there and make a fool of herself. This was exactly what he'd meant when he'd said he didn't want her doing anything rash.

From outside he heard a man yell, and then there was a crash, and Quint shut his eyes. Dear God, the woman was already stopping traffic. Quint pulled the door open again, saw his wife strolling, head high, shoulders bare, sheets pulled up to her ears down the walk in front of his house. He whipped back to his servants. "Fetch my boots and my horse." They gawked at him. "Now!"

* * *

Quint went after her. It had taken more time than he liked to fetch the horse from the mews and to saddle the beast, but Quint had used the minutes to tug on the pants he'd worn the day before. Unfortunately, the quick search of his room had not uncovered Catherine's clothing.

Quint spurred his horse forward, following the trail of surprised and whispering people Catherine had left in her wake. He saw her a moment later, and he thanked God it was early enough that most Londoners were still abed. She could have been hurt or accosted by now.

"Catherine!" he yelled, galloping up beside her.

She barely glanced at him. "I see you remember my name."

He tightened his grip on the reins to stop himself from snatching her right then. "It was a small mistake. And an understandable one."

"I see." She marched on.

He decided to try reasoning with her. "Catherine, I know you're upset right now, but you have to come home."

"I have no home," she said, and he could have sworn she increased her pace.

"I meant come to my home. Just for now. Temporarily. Until we sort all of this out." Quint looked ahead, trying to determine where she might be headed. As he did so, he saw the Secretary of the Navy's coach approaching. He ducked his head as the secretary peered out the window at him.

Catherine did not even notice. "I don't think so."

Quint was becoming desperate. Another block, and they would reach the heart of Mayfair. Not to mention, it was later than he'd first thought. The streets were already beginning to crowd. He tried one last attempt at reason. "Catherine, I'm going to ask one more time." He spurred his horse forward so that it blocked her path. "I'm begging you," he said, choking on the words as though they were poison. "Please turn back."

She barely glanced up at him, stepped to the right, and walked straight by the horse, dragging the bedsheets in the dirt after her.

That was it. Quint was a reasonable man, but he had his limits. The moment she was on his opposite side, he leaned down, caught her by the arm, and swept her over the horse on her belly in front of him.

As he expected, she did not go willingly, she fought him, losing a good portion of the bedclothes in the process, but he was able to throw one sheet over her. Then it was just a matter of holding her down and starting for home.

The horse he rode was a gentle mare, and Quint thanked God for that blessing. He could not have controlled a nervous horse and held on to Catherine. He had one arm clamped firmly on her bottom, which stuck up on one side. Her head hung down on the other, her long black hair trailing on the ground.

"Let go of me!" She squirmed and swiped at him before grabbing on to his leg again for fear of falling.

"Hold on, you silly chit. We're almost there."

That statement only elicited another round of squirming and fighting until he finally grabbed her around the waist and yelled, "Unless you want me to lift this sheet, and swat your bare bottom right here, sit still!"

Fortunately, that did the trick. She stopped fighting and lay stiffly on the horse's back. Unfortunately, he'd yelled the threat at the top of his voice, and people on the street were now staring at him. Not that they hadn't been before, but somehow he'd attracted a crowd following him, and as soon as he turned up to his town house, the whole city would have his name on its lips.

Quint decided there were two ways to deal with the situation. One, he could cringe, run, and hide inside the house.

Two, he could make the best of it. People would talk no matter what, but his actions might influence what they said.

At his front walk, he slowed his horse and tossed the reins to one of his footmen. Then, with a wave to the crowd, he gathered Catherine and her sheet up. He pulled her off the horse, tossed her over his shoulder, and, smiling, marched into the house.

Chapter 9

Catherine closed her eyes. All the blood was rushing to her head, and she felt so dizzy she could not have protested had she wanted to. The horrible *politician* bounced her into the house and up the stairs. Catherine was almost glad she had not eaten anything in two days. If she had, she would surely have lost it.

Finally, he ceased jouncing her up flights of stairs, and she opened one eye to see the red carpets of the second-floor hallway. He was taking her back to the bedroom. This was it. Now, he would beat her and rape her. After the way she'd acted, she knew she had it coming.

But instead of opening the last door of the hallway, the one she knew led to his room, he stopped short and walked into another room. This one was done in pastels, all muted blues and lavenders. At least she thought it was before her world spun violently, and she was dropped unceremoniously on a bed.

Immediately, she curled into a protective ball, covering her face and head. But she also fisted her hands. He might get in the first blow, but he wouldn't have the chance at another.

Nothing happened. Catherine cracked one eye open.

Valentine was standing over her, hands on his knees, trying to catch his breath. "Sorry I had to do that."

Catherine frowned and opened both eyes. He was *apologizing*?

"I warned you not to act rash—"

"Bastard!" she spat the word, hoping it would goad him to action. Why did he not just hit her and get it over with? She was ready to fight now.

"Ah, good. You're feeling better already. Splendid."

Catherine uncoiled and sat up. What was wrong with this man? She insulted him, and his retort was "splendid"?

He was backing toward the door now. "I'm going to have to lock the door, but I promise to send a tray of food."

Catherine's indignation shot her to her knees. "Don't you dare lock me in, Valentine. I'm not staying here."

He was already at the door. She scrambled off the bed, barely managing to preserve her modesty with the sheet.

"It's only until you calm down, and we can talk rationally."

"I don't want to talk rationally!" she said. "I want out of this marriage."

"So do I!" And he closed the door, locking it, just as she reached it and began pounding. But it was no use. The door was locked, and she was imprisoned. She went back to the bed and tried to comprehend what had just happened. She had awakened beside him, naked. They had obviously been sleeping together for some time, and yet, he had not raped her. She would have known if he had forced himself on her. Perhaps the opium had incapacitated him so much that he had not been able to take her? More likely, he found her so repulsive that he did not want her.

And then she had argued with him, fought with him, and stormed out of his house. He must have been furious. He'd gone after her, and yet, when he had her back, he didn't beat her. Not even when she insulted him further.

She didn't understand this man. He was not acting at all like her father would have.

Suddenly, her door was hastily opened, a covered tray shoved inside, then it was closed and locked again.

Perfect beginning. Now the servants were afraid of her.

She wandered over to the tray, lifted the linen napkin, and stared. Wonder of wonders, Valentine had kept his word and sent the food. What was wrong with this man? Why was he being so nice? Did he not realize that she didn't deserve the food? She had been defiant and rude. Shouldn't she be punished?

She peered at the food again. Perhaps there was some punishment in it. Perhaps it was poisoned and would make her violently ill.

She ate a piece of cheese and some bread, drank a half glass of wine, waited, but nothing happened. Catherine sat back on the bed and slowly the thought occurred to her that Valentine was not punishing her at all. In fact, he was not going to punish her.

Was it possible Valentine was a man like her uncle William, kind and even-tempered?

No, she would not let her guard down yet. It might be a trick, a ploy to lull her into complacency.

Catherine finished her meal and lay back on the bed, surveying her surroundings. If she had to be imprisoned, this was a nice enough jail. The room was small but the space well used. There were two windows, both draped with a lightweight lilac material. They seemed to overlook a small badly tended garden in the rear of the house.

The furniture was heavy but not overbearing. She allowed her gaze to rove over the tall kingwood-and-tulipwood armoire in one corner. It was a beautiful piece, decorated with parquetry and ormolu mounts. Across from the brass bed where she lay, sat a beautiful combination writing desk and dressing table, also in tulipwood and also with extensive ormolu. The last piece was a washstand with a tile-paneled splashback. She stood and went to washstand, pleased to find the pitcher was full of cool water. She poured about half into the washbowl and rinsed her face, then crossed to the lovely armoire, hoping inside there might be some article of clothing she could wear.

But the three inner shelves were empty except for extra linens and a stack of lace handkerchiefs. They were embroidered, and Catherine lifted one and stared at it. In the corner, the initials EV were embroidered in script.

Catherine dropped the handkerchief. Elizabeth Valentine. This room, these handkerchiefs, were meant to be Elizabeth's. Catherine put her face in her hands.

She was doomed. She knew that now. She was married, and no matter how much she wanted Valentine to find a way out of the union, she knew in her heart it was nigh impossible. He'd talked of scandal, and he was right. The scandal would ruin her reputation and his career.

She cared little for herself, but she knew he would protect his career above all else.

So what now? He didn't like her; he didn't even

trust her. He thought she'd planned this bride swap. He certainly didn't love her. It seemed to her that a marriage without love was the worst sort of prison, especially when one partner loved another. Valentine had called her Elizabeth. He obviously loved her sister. And Lord knew Catherine was nothing like her sister.

How fitting that Catherine should be forced into marriage with a man who would spend all his days pining for her horrible, spoiled sister. Elizabeth didn't begin to deserve this man. Not that Catherine did. If he was really as kind as he seemed—and that was just preposterous; it had to be a ruse—then Catherine knew she could never deserve him.

If she ever got out of here, she would find a way to make her father pay for this. How could anyone treat others' lives so carelessly? How could he trick a man into marriage and condemn his own daughter to a lifetime of misery?

And what of her sister? Catherine was under no illusion that Elizabeth loved Valentine. The girl loved no one but herself. But to have the man you were betrothed to taken away, capriciously given to another, and be made a fool of before all Society.

Did her father realize what he'd done? Did he even care?

And how could he possibly get away with this? Valentine had said her name was on the license and she'd said the vows, but what of the banns, the engagement announcement, and the betrothal ball? Surely Society would notice that one sister had been substituted for the other. Valentine was so worried about sullying his reputation, but Catherine could not but believe they were already the favorite topic of the *ton*.

Not that she cared one jot for the *ton*. She had more important concerns. Her face flamed when she thought of her behavior this morning. What had she been thinking, marching through the streets in nothing but a sheet?

She could never have imagined doing anything so reckless in all her life, but something inside her had snapped when Valentine had threatened to send her home. Terror had overridden reason, and she had indeed behaved rashly, as Valentine suggested. But what did he know of rationality? Valentine had not been pulled out of a sound sleep and sold to a leering thug for less than the cost of employing a housekeeper.

She would not go home, and the more she thought about it, the more she realized that she could not allow Valentine to end the marriage. If he did so, she would have no choice but to live on the street. That, or run to her uncle William's. She wiped a trickle of wetness from her cheek. Oh, what did it matter? She'd run before, and her father always found her. He always got her back. If she left Valentine, her father would get to her. He would sell her again or worse . . .

Valentine, with his excessive worry about

scandal and his reputation, was nothing compared to her father. Why, the earl had not even struck her after her behavior this morning. She'd been impudent and insulting, and the man had done nothing but apologize. He hadn't laid a hand on her. Yet.

She did not want to be married. She did not want to be some man's wife—subject to his whims and his fists and his anger. But what if her marriage had actually relieved her of that life? What if this marriage to Valentine had saved her from the whims of another man, even worse than the man she called husband?

She stared at the shadows on the ceiling and considered. She might be wrong about Valentine. After all, hadn't she always said that the devil you knew was better than the devil you didn't? But what if Valentine was her one escape from her father?

But even this revelation did not relieve the trapped feeling in her chest. What would Valentine do with her now that she was his? What if she had misjudged him and, given time, he was no better than her father?

One thing was clear to her. She might be his wife in name, but she would not be his wife in truth. She would not share his bed or his life. As long as she was here in London, she still had her cousins, her only friends. She could run to them for protection, if only temporarily.

Sometime later there was a knock on the bedroom door. Catherine had fashioned a sort of toga from the sheets, and now she checked that it was secure.

"Miss Fullbright?"

It was Valentine. She pulled the knot at one shoulder tighter. "What do you want?" Now, he would beat her.

"May I come in?"

He was asking permission? What kind of trickery was this? She tried to forestall him. "Do you have my clothes?"

"I'm not going to stand in the hallway and yell through the door. I'm coming in."

She heard the sound of the lock turning, and Valentine poked his head in. He peered about the room, obviously worried she'd gone on a rampage and destroyed it, then he peered at her. Catherine crossed her arms over her chest and felt her cheeks explode with heat. Now that she saw him again, her earlier escape seemed even more childish. Had she actually thought that stomping into the street wearing nothing but this sheet would solve anything?

And then he stepped into the room, and she had the impulse to run away again. Not just because she was afraid he would hurt her. The sight of him, even now that he was fully clothed, reminded her of his nakedness this morning. She hadn't meant to reveal anything when she'd pulled the bedclothes off him. She had not meant to see the expanse of his chest, lightly furred with dark hair. She had not meant to see his bronze arms, hard and muscular. She had not meant to see those long, lean legs or to look when he'd risen to catch a glimpse of his small, tight bottom. And she had especially not meant to see that part of him that made him unquestionably male. Had he been sleeping beside her all night with it hard and ready for battle?

She shrank back from him. Was it hard now? Was he ready to use it on her?

"I've come with gifts," he said.

Catherine paused and blinked. Gifts? Had she heard him correctly? Why was he bringing her gifts?

He held out a piece of cloth to her, and when she did not take it, he shook the robe open. "I can have clothes ordered, but perhaps this will do until that's been accomplished."

Catherine stared at the robe. She didn't understand this man. She understood his words, but not the reasons behind them. Why was he being so kind? Where was the trap in this?

"This is very kind of you," she said finally, taking the robe. She would have to wait until he left to put it on, and without stays or a shift, she would still be far from proper, but it was better than the thin sheet. She wondered how far his kindness extended. "Am I still a prisoner?"

"That depends on you." Valentine eyed her directly, his gaze assessing. "Have you given up your rash ideas and begun to see logic?"

Catherine crossed her arms. Why did men always think they were the only sex capable of rational thought? "If you mean am I going to attempt to escape in only my sheet again, the answer is no. But I will not go home. I know you wish to be rid of me, but I would go to the Americas before I return to my family."

"I understand."

She raised her brows. She did not think he could possibly understand all her father was capable of, nor did she think he understood what she was telling him. She was now, for better or worse, his wife.

"Would you feel better if I said that I have written several letters, discreet inquiries to my friends, asking their advice on the situation?"

That did not make her feel better, not at all. What could other men know of her situation? Mightn't they all simply tell Valentine to send her home? If that were to happen, she would need to prepare to escape first, so she said cautiously, "And you will share their replies when they arrive?"

She could tell by his scowl that he didn't like that request. How like a man to use knowledge to make himself feel powerful. But to her surprise, Valentine nodded. "I will share them. For now, will you do me the honor of dining with me for dinner?"

"Do you the honor—? A few hours ago, you called me a liar and looked as though you could have cheerfully strangled me. Now you want to dine with me?"

He cleared his throat. "I am not happy with our circumstances. I am not happy about what you did—"

"I told you, it was my—"

He held up a hand. "Nevertheless, I am trying to be reasonable. There are several matters I wish to discuss with you—matters I think better dealt with now than later."

Suspicion tickled her spine and spread warm fingers over her shoulders. Now what did the man have in mind? If he so much as hinted at sharing a bed—

There was a bang and a shout, and then the sound of voices outside. Catherine whirled toward the window and saw Ashley's face and her fist pounding the pane.

"What the devil?" Valentine swore, while Catherine ran to the window and unlatched it.

"Ashley! What are you doing? Get in before you fall." Torn between joy at seeing her cousin and fear that Ashley would fall, Catherine clasped Ashley's hands and made to pull her inside. Ashley was heavier than she looked, and Catherine grunted, but then Valentine was beside her, lifting Ashley effortlessly inside. Catherine sighed with relief. Ashley was safe. And now Catherine had an ally.

As soon as Ashley's feet were on the ground, Catherine tackled her, hugging her hard, but

Valentine went straight back to the window. He swore under his breath. Catherine stared her cousin. "You didn't."

Ashley gave a sheepish smile. She wore black trousers and a loose-fitting shirt. Her glorious hair was caught under a workingman's cap. "How could I leave them behind?"

"Hold on," Valentine was calling out the window. "I'm coming to get you. And you"—he pointed at the ground—"do not even *think* about climbing up." Then he leaned from the window so far Catherine was afraid he would tumble out. She and Ashley ran to the window on the other side of the bed and peered out.

Josephine was hanging on to the rusty trellis. She too wore men's clothing, and with her thin figure and cropped hair, she resembled a young boy. The trellis she clutched looked stable enough, but it ended a few feet before Catherine's second-floor window. Josie was reaching up, her fingers mere inches from Valentine's. And then she seemed to sway, lose her balance on the trellis, and Catherine and Ashley screamed in unison. The moment they were certain their cousin would fall, Valentine clasped her hands in his and lifted her off the trellis and into the room.

Before she ran to Josie, Catherine saw that Maddie was still on the ground below. She was the only one of the three dressed in a gown, so she obviously did not intend to scale any buildings. Thank God one of her cousins had some sense. Catherine ran to Josie. Valentine had just released her, and Catherine gave her a hard hug. "You almost got yourself killed! What were you thinking?"

And then she looked at Valentine. "My cousin, Lady Madeleine, Lord Castleigh's daughter. Would you bring her up before she decides to climb up, too?"

Valentine went to the door, and she heard him call directions to his butler.

Catherine turned back to her cousins, her heart still pounding from fear, but by now the girls were laughing. "We made it!" Josie said.

"Of course we did," Ashley said, slapping her on the back. "Third time is the charm."

Catherine gaped. "Are you both mad? You might have fallen and died. And what if this had been the wrong window?"

"We knew it had to be right," Ashley said. "We'd tried two others already."

Catherine's legs felt weak, and she had to back up and take a seat on the bed. She could just imagine her cousins scaling the house, falling, and ending up a broken pile of bones on the lawn below. And that was just the worst-case scenario. All the girls but Maddie were wearing men's trousers and shirts. Had they been traipsing about London in broad daylight like that? It was one thing for them to dress as boys and run about London in the middle of the night when they were eight. But now they were grown women of the *ton*. It didn't help that Catherine had made her own scene this morning. Lord, the papers would be in news ecstasy after reporting on the four of them.

"Oh, stop worrying," Josie said. "We did it for you. We had to rescue you."

"And just in time, too," Ashley said, her gaze falling to Catherine's sheet. "What was he doing to you?"

Catherine flushed, but before she could answer, Josie reached into her coat and extracted a large cutlass. Valentine, who was coming back into the room, paused.

"Don't come any closer," Josie warned. "If you touch her, I'll cut off your nose. And that's just the start."

Valentine touched a finger to his nose and then glanced at Catherine. His expression was one of amusement and disbelief. But Catie knew anger couldn't be far away.

"You can put it away, Josie," she said. "He hasn't hurt me or tried to touch me."

They heard footsteps racing down the hall, and a heartbeat later, Madeleine burst into the door. "You found her."

Valentine stepped back and then Catherine was surrounded by her three favorite people in the world. Ashley, Madeleine, and Josephine were crowding around her, hugging her, and talking all at once. Ashley was the first to make herself heard above the din.

"If he hasn't touched you, Catie, where are your clothes? Why are you dressed in only a sheet?"

Catherine shook her head. "I woke up this morning and my clothes were gone. I had to use Lord Valentine's sheets to cover myself."

The three cousins turned back to Valentine, now standing with one shoulder braced on the doorjamb. Josephine lifted her grandfather's cutlass again. "What did you do to her clothes? Was that part of your plan? To force her into your bed and have your way with her?"

Valentine held up his hands. "I assure you I was just as surprised as Miss Fullbright to awaken thus. I have no idea where her clothes are. She seems to have been left here with nothing."

Maddie clutched Catherine's hand. "So then you didn't want to marry him?" She looked at the other girls. "I told you. I knew my father was lying."

"We all knew," Ashley said. "But we didn't know what to do when they said your name during the wedding, and then *he*"—she pointed to Valentine—"lifted the veil, and there you were. And you looked so happy that we thought maybe we had misunderstood."

Catherine shook her head. "No, no misunderstanding. My father drugged me. He has finally had his way."

"And sacrificed you to the wolves," Ashley added.

"I would hardly call myself a wolf," Valentine muttered.

"We can't let Uncle Edmund get away with this," Ashley said.

Catherine saw Valentine start. "Now, don't do anything rash."

"But we have to do something," Josie said. "Catie is trapped in this marriage, and we've lost her forever."

"Oh, for God's sake, Miss Hale. I live only three blocks from Lord Castleigh's house," Valentine said. "And the three of you are welcome to visit, providing you use the front door."

"But it's not the same," Maddie cried, turning away from him. "You have to come with me. I know my father will make this right."

Catherine knew her kind uncle would do all in his power—even to his own family's detriment. But Uncle William could not help without causing scandal, and even if she were safe under his protection, her father would find a way to get to her. "I am certain Uncle William would help if I asked," she said, "but I don't need his help."

"Yes, you do!" Maddie cried.

"Don't be a fool," Ashley said.

Catherine looked at Valentine, still standing in the doorway. She knew he was watching her, waiting for her response. Was she with him or against him? Would she accept this marriage—at least temporarily—or fight it and force them all to face the consequences?

Catherine turned resolutely back to her cousins. "Listen, girls," she said, "Lord Valentine and I have discussed this. There's no way out."

Ashley's jaw dropped. "You're giving up? You're just going to accept this and marry that-that *man!*" She pointed an accusatory finger at Valentine.

"I'm not giving up, but I don't see another way right now."

"Well, I do," Maddie said, taking her hand, and Catherine was surprised by how firm her grip was and how determined the set of her jaw. "You're coming home with me. Daddy will take you in."

Catherine snatched her hand back. "No, Maddie. I won't do that to you. Any of you. It wouldn't help anyway. You know my father would find me and then . . ."

"Then let's all run away," Josie said. "We were going to anyway."

"Don't talk nonsense," Valentine said, coming into the room. "Don't ruin your own chances for a good match."

Maddie shook her head. "But we don't want to make good matches. We don't want to marry."

"You're eighteen and don't know what you want," Valentine broke in before Catherine held up a hand. "You, you are Lord Castleigh's daughter." He inclined his head at Maddie. "You will be expected to make a good match and continue the family tradition. You"—he nodded at Ashley—"Sir Gareth is a friend of mine. You're expected to marry a baron at the least. And you"—he glared at Josephine—"put the sword away. If your father knew you were going about acting like the black sheep of the family, your grandfather, he would drink himself to oblivion."

Ashley put her hands on her hips. "Well, you seem to know so much about everything, Lord Valentine, why don't you think of a way to get Catie out of this? Or perhaps you wanted this all along? It seems you want to get all of us married off."

He shook his head. "I assure you, Miss Brittany, my interest is all for my bride. Remain a spinster if you wish, but don't put ideas in Catherine's head."

Now it was Catherine's turn to glare at him. The presence of her cousins made her brave. "Put ideas into my head? What? Am I an imbecile who cannot think for herself?"

He waved her protests away. "Of course you can, but we've already decided this."

Catherine turned her back on him. Oh, she wished he would just go. She pulled her friends close. She needed the security their circle gave her, and she wanted to reassure them. "Valentine has promised me he will try to find an escape from this mess. In the meantime, you three are still the Spinsters' Club," she said. They giggled at the childhood name. "There will just be one less of you temporarily."

"And that's all you have to say?" Josie cried. "But what will you do? You are married to a man you do not even know!"

The devil you know, Catherine thought, but again, she needed to calm her younger cousins. "I know you are worried, but right now this seems the best choice. If I'm selfish and ruin myself, Valentine, and our families, then how does that make me any different from my father?"

"You could never be like your father," Madeleine whispered. "And you know we don't care about Society's rules. We'd rather live in disgrace than sacrifice you to him."

Maddie was crying now, and Catherine took her hand. "You won't lose me. And I'm hardly sacrificing. Look at him."

The girls turned as one and studied Valentine, who was once again slouched against the door. "You said yourselves he was handsome and kind. There are worse fates."

"But what if he beats you?" Josephine said.

"Then I'll run away, and I'll come to one of you."

"Come to me," Maddie said. "Promise."

"I promise."

Ashley was the first to turn back to Valentine. "And don't think we'll let you get away with anything," she snapped at him, then motioned for Josie to come forward with her sword.

"If I hear that you hurt her, you'll be sorry."

Maddie didn't say anything to Valentine. She only hugged Catherine and promised to send enough clothes for a few days.

"We'll be back tomorrow." Ashley said the words to Catherine, but she suspected they were meant for Valentine's ears. "We won't abandon you."

Maddie and Josephine nodded, and then, with a sinking feeling in her belly and a heavy heart, Catherine watched them file out of the room. She and Valentine were left alone.

He crossed his arms over his chest and jammed his shoulder into the door again. "Are your cousins always so wild?"

Catherine went to the window and peered out, hoping to catch a last glimpse of the three of them leaving. "How do you mean?" She craned her neck.

She heard Valentine chuckle. "No matter. You've just answered my question. How exactly are you all related? I'm sure I should know, but the information has escaped me at present. Your father and Lady Madeleine's father are brothers, I believe."

"Yes, and Josephine's mother, my aunt Mavis, is their sister."

"What about the adventuress? Miss Brittany?"

"I suppose that technically Ashley is not really Maddie and Josie's cousin. Her mother and mine are sisters. But Ashley is the sort of girl everyone wants to know. Truly, we are all more like sisters than cousins."

"What is this talk about the Spinsters' Club? I have not heard of it. Where does it meet?"

Catherine looked back at him and tried not to smile. "It's a private club. No men allowed. I'm afraid I cannot tell you more than that. Against the rules."

He frowned. "I see. You realize I have my own methods of obtaining information."

She smiled. "I shall see you at dinner."

She turned back to the window, and when she heard him leave, she picked up the robe and slipped it on. Hopefully, Maddie would send clothes before the dinner hour. And what then? She looked back out the window. Obviously, it could be scaled. She could leave anytime she chose. She would remember this, and if Valentine tried to touch her, if he drank too much and hit her or threatened her, she would know how to run away.

Maddie's clothes arrived an hour later. She'd sent two dresses and underclothes, but none of them were Catherine's. Catherine wondered if she would ever see her own things again. Perhaps her father had already sold them or given them away. It was growing late, and she'd received no letter or note from him, no call from her mother or sister. She felt as though she'd never existed in their lives.

She had not expected to hear from her father—

had not wanted to hear from him, in any case. But what of her mother? Did she not care about her own daughter?

Catherine unfolded the dresses, shaking out the wrinkles, and as she did so, a pair of trousers fell out of the folds of one. Catherine picked them up, then shook out the other dress. It hid a shirt and an old jacket. She sent a silent thank-you to Maddie. These would be a start if she ever needed to escape. She took an extra pillowcase from the armoire and folded the men's clothing into it, then hid it under her mattress.

Perhaps tomorrow she would be the one scaling the wall.

Chapter 10

When Quint strode into his dining room that evening, he did not expect to see his bride. In his experience, women were almost always late, either because they were so vain that they could not leave their mirrors or because they desired to make grand entrances.

He almost wished he wouldn't see her. Then he could pretend this whole swindle of a marriage had never happened.

But Catherine Fullbright was waiting for him. She stood at one end of the dining room, staring idly at a painting of horses grazing in a field. After the events of the long day, Quint did not feel like talking. But this was his wife, little as he liked to remember that. He supposed he had better say something. "Do you like art, madam?"

She turned, and he noticed at once that she was finally dressed. She wore a blue-and-white polka-dotted calico gown that was more suited for a day dress and which was also too short and too tight. The sheet she had worn all morning revealed less of her figure. He took a deep breath and tried not to stare. She had gone to some trouble to look presentable by pulling her hair up and away from her face. In the candlelight flickering from the chandelier, her golden hazel eyes shone.

Catherine looked at the picture one last time before replying, "Actually, I care little for art. But I do like horses."

"Do you ride?" As soon as he spoke, he regretted the words. The image produced in his mind had nothing to do with horses. But the damn dress she wore was too tight at the bosom and strained a bit at the hips. How could he help thinking of unleashing her straining body, removing her gown so she could ride him? He took a step closer, wanting to see her more clearly, to be closer to her.

"I do ride, actually." She took a step back, and he moved forward again. "My cousin Madeleine and I often ride together." Her voice wavered. She backed up again, bumping her shoulder on the corner. "Sir, please stand back."

Quint stopped and shook his head to clear it of lascivious thoughts. He'd allowed his carnal impulses to guide his actions, and though he might be attracted to her, she made it abundantly clear that she felt nothing for him. This marriage was looking worse and worse.

Not that it had ever looked good. He'd been drugged and deceived. How was he ever supposed to feel affection for a woman who was part of that? And yet, there was no denying he wanted her.

Quint retreated. With a slight bow, he pulled out a chair from one side of the table and inclined his head. He saw her release a pent-up breath. So she was relieved not to be subject to his advances. The long years of their doomed union loomed before him. He had to find an escape.

She took the proffered seat, and he considered his own place carefully. He could sit opposite her and give her the space she needed. Over time, she might not find him so repulsive. On the other hand, he found the idea of yelling at her across the room as they sat at opposite ends of his enormous dining table distasteful. He pulled out the seat beside her. She would have to get used to him sooner rather than later.

He took his place, and his butler entered and began directing the footmen to pour the wine and serve the soup. Valentine inquired after her health and whether the food was to her liking. Catherine smiled and seemed pleased with the food. He waited until she had finished her soup to reveal the train of his thoughts.

"Miss Fullbright—or, rather, I should say Lady Valentine."

She glanced up at him, eyes narrowed. "Miss Fullbright is fine."

He frowned. He would have rather she was still Miss Fullbright as well, but she was his wife now, and as such, she'd become Lady Valentine. One day she would be Lady Ravenscroft. He tried to let that thought sink in. "Perhaps we might compromise. As we are married, why not use given names? I will call you Catherine, and you may call me Quint."

"Quint is your name?" she said with raised brows. "I had no idea."

"I shall be the fifth Marquess of Ravenscroft. My parents thought it appropriate."

"I see, and I accept your compromise."

"Good." He lifted his wineglass and sipped. That had been easy. He did not think his next proposal would be accepted so warmly. "I have yet another suggestion, and this may be less to your liking."

She tensed, looking as though she'd been expecting this. "Go ahead."

"I think that in light of the scandal news of our marriage will certainly cause, it might be best if we were to retire to the countryside. London will have too many distractions." The image of her cousins climbing through the window flashed in his mind.

Catherine blanched, and Quint bolstered his

defenses, preparing for a fight. Her eyes had turned from honey to amber, and he now recognized that as a sign of her anger. Or was it fear?

"Absolutely not," she said, just as the footmen came in to clear away the soup bowls.

Quint waved the men away.

"Do you expect me to leave for the country with a man I do not even know, much less trust? In the country, I'll be alone. I'll have nowhere to run." She looked almost wild as she spoke, her eyes bright and the color high in her cheeks. Quint knew that if he made the slightest movement, she would bolt. Quite suddenly, her behavior toward him all morning began to make sense. She'd challenge him, then retreat, challenge him, then cringe back again. Could it be that she feared him?

"Why would you need to run?" he asked carefully.

"How do I know what you plan?" She scraped back from the table and looked prepared to flee. Quint allowed it. He did not move, made no attempt to make her stay.

"I assure you I have no plans, but I suppose you will have to learn to trust me, whether that is in the city or in the country, it makes no difference."

She shook her head. "It makes a difference to me. My friends are here. And you need to be here in case you receive a letter from one of your friends with a solution to ending this marriage."

He leaned back in his chair. "A letter from my friends can reach me just as easily in Hertfordshire as in Town. But if we remain in Town, we will attract attention. People will come to call, and I will be expected in Westminster."

"That is not so very bad."

Quint went on as though she hadn't spoken. "People will want to know about our marriage, and they will ask us to dinners and balls because we will be of interest."

Now her face went pale.

"I'd like to put the social events off for a bit, if possible."

"As would I."

Quint noticed that she was clutching her hands together. She took two deep breaths. So her behavior at his betrothal ball had not been a ploy. She was truly uneasy in crowds. Another reason for retiring to the country. He would build her courage and her trust in him. And perhaps he would begin to reveal the nature of her soul as well.

"Good, then I'll make arrangements for us to leave in the morning." He began to stand, and she stood too.

"No! I did not mean that you should make arrangements to leave, just that we should avoid the public. Perhaps we could go into seclusion here. Only my cousins and your friends would be allowed inside."

"I won't be a prisoner in my own house." He

began walking toward the door, and each step he took, she matched, backing toward the door.

"And I am already a prisoner. Please, don't come any closer!"

Quint stopped, leaned on the table, and closed his eyes. She was terrified of him. What the hell had he done to make her afraid? It galled him. He wanted to shake her and tell her that there was no reason to fear. Somehow he doubted that tactic would work.

He opened his eyes. "Catherine, I'm not going to hurt you. You needn't look like you think I'll attack."

"I'm sorry." She put her hands over her face. "I just-I wish I could go home. And yet I don't want to go home. I can't go home ever again." Her voice was small and frightened, and he wished she trusted him enough to allow him to hold her.

The poor girl's life had been changed irreparably, and she was fighting that fact as hard as she could. She was holding on to her past, her old way of life, and he could hardly blame her. He'd held on to his own illusions as long as possible. But now he had to face the situation. They were not going to dissolve this marriage—not without more disgrace and shame than he was willing to bring to his name or his family. She was alone in the world now. Except for him.

"Catherine, I know this isn't what you wanted, but please tell me you understand that part of your life is over. You must accept this marriage."

"But you said you would write to friends—"

"And I have, but it is something I do to ease my conscience, to know I have explored every avenue. I have very little hope that any of them will find another solution for us. You are my wife, and I do not expect that to change."

"But why does anything have to change? Why can we not stay here and—"

"No. Everything has changed. Your life as you knew it is over."

Her lip trembled then, and Quint could not stop himself from closing the distance between them. He couldn't stand seeing her—any woman—in so much pain. He placed his hand on the door before she could turn the handle and open it. He knew trust was a gift to be given, never taken. But in this case, perhaps the giver needed a bit of encouragement. He put his arm around her shoulders and pulled her to him.

She stiffened at first, her body rigid with fear, then she melted against him. She was crying silently, and he patted her back and shushed her.

After a few moments, her tears subsided. Quint knew he should pull away, but he did not. He liked the feel of her in his arms. She was taller than most women he knew, and he liked that her height was close to his own. She fit him.

And with his mouth close to her ear, whispering words of comfort, he smelled the skin of her neck and felt the softness of her hair. No wonder he thought of peaches when he was near her. She wore that scent, and her body was giving and supple like that fruit.

And so he did not move. He held her in his arms, basking in her warm body and her sweet smell. Finally, she began to move away, and it took all his willpower, but he let her go. She looked into his face with those indefinable hazel eyes, and a last tear rolled down one cheek. He brushed it away, his hand lingering on the softness of her cheek, then caressing her full lips, and trailing to her chin. He knew he shouldn't, but he could not resist. He leaned down and brushed her lips with his.

The kiss was sweet, her lips as soft and warm as a summer peach. He wanted to open the fruit, taste its sweetness, explore its flavors and textures, but her hand came up. With a gasp, she pushed him away.

"Catherine, I'm sorry—"

Her eyes were full of fear, and she pushed past him, opening the door and scrambling into the foyer and up the stairs. Quint stepped back into the room and shut the door behind him. No point going after her. He'd scared her now, and it would probably be some time before she allowed him to get close again.

He leaned his head back, and he could still feel her in his arms and smell her on him. God, he wanted her. For the first time, he allowed the traitorous thought that had niggled in the back of his mind all day free. He was glad he had married her. The sight of her in his bed, wrapped in his sheets—hell, even seeing her standing in his dining room—excited him. God, help him, but he needed to possess her.

More than ever, the necessity of taking her to the country became clear. He did not want a wife who was afraid of him. His country home was small and cozy. There he would have ample opportunity to get close to her, show her how to trust him.

He was still standing in the dining room when he heard Webster speaking to someone in the hall. Quint opened the door and saw his assistant, Harold Meeps. The small, slight man was laden with sheaves of paper, and his glasses were perched on the edge of his nose.

"Oh, good evening, my lord," Meeps said with a bow that almost tumbled his load. "I hope I haven't interrupted dinner."

"No," Quint strode forward and took a stack of papers. "We've just finished." Glancing at the documents in hand, he noted they were communiqués of various matters before Parliament as well as answers to inquiries he'd made concerning forthcoming bills. "I presume this is not a social call."

"No, sir," Meeps said. "You said you would be away from work for a few days, so I thought I would bring some of it to you. As you can see, my lord, we are already behind."

"Yes, well, that may be a continuing problem,"

Quint answered, waving Meeps toward his study. "I'm afraid I may be away a bit longer than anticipated." He opened the study's door and held it until Meeps had passed through. Quint took a seat at his desk and motioned for his assistant to take the seat opposite. As his study was set up very much like his office in Westminster, the arrangement was familiar to the men.

"Are you still feeling ill, sir?"

Quint paused in the midst of organizing his sheaf of papers and raised a brow at his assistant. "An illness? Is that what they're calling marriage these days? Or is it just my marriage?"

Meeps pushed his glasses back on his nose and wrinkled his forehead. The assistant had red hair and a wealth of freckles, and his freckles stood out more when he was agitated. "You've married, my lord?"

Quint shook his head. Meeps had difficulty remembering anything that did not have to do with politics or affairs of state. The man could recite legislation and political speeches verbatim, but he did not recall the name of Quint's estate or that of his betrothed. "Yes, Mr. Meeps." Quint began sorting again. "I married yesterday morning. Surely there was something about it in the paper. I confess I have not had a moment to look at it. Have you?"

"No, my lord. Too much happening in your offices right now. But I have the *Times* right here." He extracted the newspaper from the bottom third of his stack. "Would you like me to look for a relevant article?"

"By all means." While Meeps clucked over the news, Quint read and signed and replied to the various correspondence before him. He'd just finished his pile and started on the mountain before his assistant, when Meeps let out a small cry.

Quint looked up, pen in hand. "You've found something?"

"Yes, my lord. It's not on the first page, but it's prevalent enough. Here, my lord." He handed the paper over, and Quint read silently.

The piece was not good, but it might have been worse. Much of it was devoted to relating the antics of Catherine and her three cousins, though the article referred to the most recent events as rumor. What was not rumor was the marriage between Catherine and Valentine, and the paper made much of the betrothal ball for the younger Miss Fullbright and speculated as to how Miss Catherine Fullbright had stolen her sister's fiancé away.

Quint threw it down in disgust. There was no longer any question in his mind that he and Catherine would have to leave for the country tomorrow. He might have been willing to give her a day or so to become accustomed to the idea, but no more. If they stayed in Town, they would only create more talk. They could return in a few weeks, when interest in their marriage had waned.

"Meeps," Quint said, rising and ringing for his

butler. "I am afraid you will have to do without me for a bit longer. I find I am required at my estate in Hertfordshire."

Webster entered, and Quint handed him the newspaper with the offending article faceup. Then he scrawled a note to Catherine, instructing her to be ready to leave at first light. "Take this to my . . . wife. Thank you, Webster."

"Yes, my lord."

Meeps was shaking his head. "Sir, you will do what you must, but I cannot support a trip to the country at this time. You need to be in the city, now more than ever."

Quint gathered up a new pile of documents and began flipping through them. "I will keep abreast of things in the country. If anything truly pressing arises, I am not so far from London."

"Yes, but you do not know the latest news." Meeps lowered his voice, and Quint looked up. "We had discussed the possibility of an undersecretary position."

Quint nodded. "What of it?" After his last victory in the House, he was expecting the appointment. Leaving Town should not affect it one way or the other.

"I have heard rumors, sir." Meeps's voice became even softer. "That the prime minister was so impressed with the work you did on the Valentine-Cheswick Reform Act that he is now talking of offering you a position in the Cabinet."

Quint stared at his assistant for the space of

five heartbeats. The news was too overwhelming for him to accept all at once. It took those five heartbeats to allow it all to sink in. "Bloody hell!" He jumped to his feet and slapped Meeps on the back. "Bloody hell! We did it!" With another whoop, he descended on the decanter of his best brandy and poured two overflowing snifters.

After the first few sips, Quint lit a cheroot and savored it. "And what about Fairfax?" Quint asked, referring to his rival.

Meeps raised his glass again. "No mention of the man. Not yet at any rate."

With a smile, Quint filled their glasses again and watched Meeps drain his. Quint did not remember ever having seen Meeps drink before, but the man was keeping pace with him.

"And I propose another toats—er, toast!" Meeps said. "All hail the—"

Quint looked up and saw Catherine standing in the doorway, his letter in hand.

"Catherine!" He slammed the snifter down, feeling like a naughty child. "I mean, Miss-Lady Valentine. Meet my assistant, Harold Meeps."

She nodded at him. "Mr. Meeps."

Meeps held his glass aloft, toasting her. "To you, madam. Many haspy—I mean, *happy*—years together."

"Thank you. Do you think you might give me a moment alone with my"—she swallowed and cleared her throat—"my husband?"

"Certainly."

When Meeps was gone, Quint's wife turned her golden hazel stare on full force. "Do you often smoke, sir?"

Quint stared at his cheroot, taken by surprise. Had she come all the way downstairs to complain about his smoking? He put the cheroot out. "I have had good news. But if my smoking bothers you, I—"

"May I ask the meaning of this note?" She held up the paper he had scrawled a message on and sent with the *Times*. He noted that her hands were shaking, but if she was afraid of confronting him, that was her only tell.

"It means we will be leaving for the country posthaste. You did read the article?" He sipped from his glass again.

She straightened her shoulders, and he saw that amber cast in her eyes again. Bloody hell. The woman had been thinking, most likely preparing her arguments. Quint was tired of arguing. Could he not have even a small measure of peace in his own home? "And don't argue," he added before she could speak. "You're going."

"Am I? Lord Valentine, I am no child of seventeen. I am a woman of twenty."

"I am well aware of that fact."

"And I have been thinking."

Quint clenched his hands. It was just as he'd thought.

"I've been bul—ordered about all my life, and I

have had enough. I will no longer tolerate overbearing men telling me what to do."

Quint set his glass down very slowly. He liked to do things slowly when he was angry; that way he kept his emotions controlled. "I am not overbearing. You are irrational."

She blinked and said through clenched teeth, "I do not want to argue with you. Go to the country, if you will, but I stay here."

Quint took three deep breaths, trying hard as hell not to be overbearing. It was damned hard when the chit was so frustrating. "You will *not* stay here. We leave for the country at first light."

Her eyes narrowed, and she balled up the note he had written.

"Is that your idea of a rebellion?"

"Is this your idea of marriage?" She threw the paper at him, and it hit him in the chest. "I won't be dictated to or ordered about."

"Then be reasonable." He picked up the paper from the floor where it had landed and placed it carefully on the desk. Then he moved slowly around the desk until he stood before her. She took a shaky breath and moved to put distance between them. "Do not make me force you to go."

"That's all you men know, isn't it? Force and brutality."

"Good God. If you knew me better, you'd know how ridiculous these statements are."

"If you knew me better—"

"I intend to get to know you better. *In the country.*"

She flinched back from his raised voice, and he paused, allowing her nerves to settle again before he spoke.

"Catherine," he said quietly, "until such time as you understand the political workings of this country as well as I, you will have to trust me to do what's right for us both."

"For us both?"

He could see now that her anger had overridden her fear. Her eyes blazed with golden fury.

"This has nothing to do with me, and everything to do with your all-consuming career. You think I didn't hear you toasting when I came down?" As she spoke, she backed away from him, holding one hand out defensively. But she was obviously intent on saying her piece. "You're so worried your petty career will be hurt by your marriage to me, you can't wait to hide me away rather than be seen with me."

Quint stared at her. "Where the devil did you get that idea? But while we're on the subject, you must admit you are not exactly the ideal political hostess at present. Stay in Town, and you will be forced to attend social events as well as to host them."

"And you don't think I can?" She halted, crossing her arms over her chest.

"No, I don't. Putting aside for a moment the

fact that you have no clothing, have you forgotten the episode at the betrothal ball? You were terrified of the crowds and the noise. I had to escort you outside so you did not faint."

"I-I only wanted to get you outside to warn you about marrying Elizabeth."

Quint arched a brow. "I saw your color, Miss Fullbright, and you're either a very good actress, or you were very scared. All you have done now is verify to me that not only are you afraid of social settings, but you can be manipulative as well. Which is all the more reason for me to take you to the country."

"And do what with me? I won't be locked up. I'd-I'd rather die. You can't lock me up!" And with that she swung toward the door and pulled on the knob. But she was shaking so badly she could not open it, and the more she pulled, the more she shook. Quint came up behind her, hands hovering over her arms, but he did not know what to do. He was afraid if he touched her, she would only become more upset.

Finally, he reached out and covered her hand with his. She jumped and froze, but he only helped her turn the knob. As soon as the door had opened, she shot out, like a cat from a bath of water. He heard her feet on the stairs, and her bedroom door slam closed.

Quint went back to his desk, lifted his glass, and poured a somewhat less-celebratory brandy.

He had to do something, or this disaster would turn into an all-out catastrophe. He had several points to consider, and he did so, glass of brandy firmly in hand.

Point one: He did not trust his new wife, but the closer he got to her, the better he would know her true character.

Point two: If he was stuck in this marriage—and he didn't see a way out without admitting to the country at large that England's political star had been duped into marriage—so if he was stuck, he wanted a wife he could mold into the perfect political hostess.

He needed her trust for that, and he knew few women were able to distinguish the physical from the emotional. When he had her physically, he would have her emotionally as well.

He might not ever trust her, he might not ever come to terms with that she'd done, but he would know her. He would know what to expect from her and of what she was capable. What if he was wrong—unlikely but possible—and she was blameless in this farce of a marriage? Could Edmund Fullbright have done it all on his own?

Quint didn't know, but he wanted to get close to Catherine and find out.

With that objective in mind, Quint pulled out a clean sheet of a paper and wrote an express post that would seal his fate. And this marriage.

Chapter 11

Catherine knew she had lost the battle. Overbearing politician! She was going to have to go to the country with him, and she'd rather go by choice than by force. But that did not mean she would let her guard down, not even for a second. She did not trust or understand this man. She could not predict his actions. Was all of his kind behavior merely a ploy? What would happen when he had her in the country? There she would be at his mercy. He could have his way with her and lock her up if she did not please him.

Then again, perhaps he was right. Was she overreacting? He had been nothing but kind . . . albeit, a bit domineering. But he had not raised a hand to her and—

She heard a sound from his room and held her breath, listening. Though she'd placed a chair under the knob of the main door and pulled the dressing table in front of the dressing-room door, she was still terrified he would break in. She listened for a long time and when all was silent, she breathed again.

Lord, what was she going to do? Of all the men she might have married, only royalty would have been worse. She knew the role of a politician's wife. They hosted parties, they attended parties, they went everywhere and knew everyone. Catherine's chest tightened just thinking about it.

She was so stupid, so inept. How could she ever hope to fit in among those women? And she knew nothing about politics. Her father had made fun of her whenever he caught her reading, and politics were never discussed at home. She'd been told to shut up and mind her own business when she'd asked about political items she'd read from the papers at Maddie's house.

The little she did know was from listening to Maddie's father talk, but those discussions were infrequent and usually brief.

Now Valentine expected her to impress all of London and further his career with her social finesse. Surely she would fail, and then he'd want to be rid of her. He'd lock her in a small, dark attic, and she'd never be free. She could not allow that to happen.

And yet, how could she prevent it? She would

have to go along, travel to the country with him, tolerate him for now.

Until she found an escape.

Catherine was in a boat, rocking from side to side, the waves pushing the vessel this way, then back again. It was cool and dark on the boat, and it smelled clean and fresh, like oak trees and pipe smoke. She wondered vaguely if she were on Josie's ship. Had Josie finally found her family's lost pirate treasure and bought her own vessel? She'd always said she'd take Catherine away with her when she became a pirate.

Catherine burrowed in more deeply, wondering at the softness of her bed on the ship. And it smelled so good here.

Slowly, she opened her eyes and peered into the darkness. She blinked. It was not the unfamiliar darkness of a ship, but the inside of a carriage with its curtains drawn. The rocking was not waves, but the carriage making its way over the roads.

With a start, she tried to sit, but just as quickly had her arms clasped and her shoulder pressed back down. "It's all right," a male voice said. "Everything will be all right."

Catherine looked up, her eyes adjusting to the gloom, and saw Valentine. She frowned, wondering at his position, then realized she must have been lying on his lap!

She struggled to rise again, and this time he

allowed it. As soon as she was up, she squashed herself into the corner of the carriage, as far away from him as possible. "How did I get here?" she stammered.

Valentine adjusted his coat, and she saw that she'd creased it when she'd been lying on him. Dear Lord, how long had she been draped over him like that?

Valentine looked up at her and, seeming to read her mind, said, "You've been asleep these last two hours. I tried to wake you this morning, but you were obviously exhausted."

Catherine cursed silently. This was exactly the reason she had vowed to stay awake. She could stay up practically all night, but no matter how early she went to bed, she found mornings difficult to tolerate and preferred to stay abed as long as possible. When she'd been young and a yell from her father had not wakened her, he'd thrown cold water over her.

"But how did you get into my room?" Catherine asked. "I had the doors blocked."

Valentine smiled, and she hadn't seen the expression in so long that she'd forgotten what a nice smile he had.

"You apparently did not realize that the dressing-room door opens from the inside. I merely opened it and pushed the dressing table aside."

"I see." She looked down in embarrassment.

"Catherine," he said, "I know you do not want

to be here. I understand you can't trust me right now, but I swear by all that's sacred to me—on my mother's family ring"—at that he pulled a small box from his jacket and held it out to her— "I will not harm you or lock you up."

Catherine stared at the box. It was wooden and intricately carved. Another gift? She'd rarely received gifts in her life, and when she did they usually came with a price. She looked into Valentine's eyes. "What's inside?"

"Open it and see." He held the box out to her again.

Still, she did not move to touch it. "And then what? What happens when I open this?"

"I hope you'll put it on. It's your wedding ring."

"But I don't want—"

"I know. If you don't want to think of it as a wedding ring, look at it as a symbol of my promise to you." He reached over with his free hand and opened the box. Inside, the gold ring shimmered with rubies, garnets, and sapphires. "This ring is your assurance of my good faith."

Catherine stared at him, then back at the ring. Was she supposed to believe the promise he gave her? If she took this ring, did that mean she agreed to trust him?

Tentatively, she reached out and touched it, then withdrew her hand once again. She could not wear this ring! It was too much. She'd never had something so beautiful and so expensive.

But she wanted it. She wanted to see the beautiful ring on her hand, to know someone had given it to her. Someone had thought her worthy of it.

She reached out once more, and the ring glinted in the light like something enchanted. Catherine drew back again. "I can't," she said. "I-I cannot wear something like this. It's too valuable."

"So are you," Valentine said, taking the ring from the box. He held out his hand for hers. "If you wear this, it does not mean you accept this marriage. I realize now that I've moved too fast with you. I think if we're given some time alone, get to know each other, you will learn to trust me."

Catherine listened, and she stared at his open palm, but she did not move. She liked his words, and she wanted to trust him, but she couldn't help but feel that this was some sort of trick.

And if it were a trick, what then? How was that any different than what she faced now? He would do with her as he pleased, ring or no ring.

"Catherine," he said, and his voice was soft. She'd rarely heard gentleness in a man's voice, and it perplexed her. "Give me a chance. Please."

It was the gentle *please* that undid her. She knew all too well what it cost a man to say that word. Taking a shaky breath, she slipped her hand into his and allowed him to slide the ring over her finger. It fit perfectly, shining brilliantly, even in the dim coach.

"It suits you," he said, twining his fingers with hers.

She looked down at her hand in his, surprised that his fingers seemed so much larger than her own. She was not a small woman like her sister or Josie. She'd always felt too big, ungraceful, and clumsy, but Valentine seemed to have the ability to make her forget all of those feelings. Beside him, she did not worry that she was too tall and awkward. Good Lord, the ring alone made her a dozen times more graceful.

"There are things we need to discuss," Valentine was saying when she looked away from the ring again. "Expectations I have from my wife."

She watched him warily. "Attending and hosting parties and such?"

"Correct, but we must address more personal issues as well."

Catherine stiffened. "I'm not your wife."

"Legally you are. As I've told you, the likelihood of escape from this union is slim. And I can tell you now, after seeing that article in the *Times,* I am even more determined not to end this marriage in any way that might result in scandal. I think you will find it near impossible to achieve a divorce or annulment without my support."

She knew he was right, but her chest tightened anyway. "Then I am trapped," she said, fear rising in her belly. She began to fumble with the ring, wanting to tear it off. He'd said she could trust him, and in the next minute, talked of locking her in this marriage. If the space of a heartbeat was the length of time she could trust him, she wanted none of it.

"No," he said, putting a hand over her ring finger before she could pull the band off. "You are not trapped. I am a broad-minded man, and if you wish no part of my bed, I respect your wishes."

Catherine stared at him, feeling the heat of his hand on hers.

"I can look elsewhere to satisfy those desires, and I will be discreet. You will never find yourself the topic of gossip on that subject."

Her voice had all but left her, but she managed to croak, "And am I free to do the same?"

His look turned dark, and his hand tightened on hers. "I am broad-minded, but I am still a man, and I have my pride. If I am not to be your lover, you'll have no man. I need your word on that."

Relief swelled through her. If he spoke the truth, she would be free and safe. She might have to take on the appearance of his wife, but not the actuality. She would never have to be subjected to his advances, to the same indignities that her mother had borne for so many years. "Very well, I give you my pledge—"

He lifted his hand. "I see you are quick to make decisions, but if you will humor me, I'd like you to give this more thought. There is another option. We could share the marriage bed."

Catherine shook her head. She had a quick

image of her mother one morning after Catherine had heard her screaming. Her lip had been bloody, and she'd walked gingerly, as though in pain. She shuddered. "I-I can't." At his puzzled look, she added, "I don't even know you."

"Your family is among the aristocracy. Among our set, men and women marry all the time without really knowing one another. We shall be in the country at least a week, perhaps more. You have time to get to know me."

He paused, she supposed to give her time to consider.

"Will you hold your decision?"

She wanted to say that there really was no decision to be made. He might claim that he would not touch her, but how realistic was such a promise, especially from a man? Husbands had expectations of their wives, and if she wanted to avoid divorce—to avoid being forced to return to her father—she would need to keep Valentine happy. That might mean spending time in his bed.

She shuddered, but she would do what she had to. At least she could put him off for a little while. "When shall I tell you my decision?"

"Before we return to London. But before we leave the subject, I have one more request."

"You seem quite full of them," she said, and then blinked in horror at her impudence. Her father would have slapped her.

Valentine grinned. "I'm a politician. We rarely run out of words or ideas."

Catherine nodded carefully. Could it be that he was not at all offended by her brashness?

"All I ask," Valentine continued, "is that you do not close your heart to me this next week. Allow me to woo you—"

"Woo me? I am not my sister, sir. I think you shall grow tired of the game."

"Then I will grow tired, but I ask you to allow me to try."

"Why?" She gave him a narrow look. His face went through a myriad of emotions—annoyance, resignation, and finally what looked to her like sincerity.

"I don't trust you any more than you do me, Catherine. You tricked me into a marriage—"

"It was my father!"

He shook his head. "Allow me to continue. But we are here now. We are married." He said the word as though he loathed it more than she did. "I want to try and make this work."

She didn't believe him. Oh, he told the truth when he said he didn't trust her, but he was not wooing her out of any heartfelt feeling. Catherine would have wagered all she had—little more than the clothes on her back and the ring he'd given her—everything he did, he did with his career in mind.

He didn't love her. He loved Elizabeth.

"Fine, then try to woo me," she said. She shrugged. If the man thought pretty words and baubles would work on her, let him make a fool of himself then.

She put her hand over her new ring, feeling its solid, timeless stones against the skin of her hand. She had no gloves, and thankfully she had worn her gown to bed, or she would probably be back in her sheet.

"Then I will start my wooing by saying that you do yourself a disservice, Catie."

She gave him a sharp look, and he grinned again. Lord, when the man smiled at her, her stomach did quick, jerky tumbles.

"May I call you, Catie? Only when we're alone, of course."

"Of course," she stammered. "You work quickly, I see."

Suddenly the carriage seemed far too small, and Catherine looked longingly at the seat across from them. Would he comment if she moved? Would it be a sign of fear? She did not want to show more fear.

He reached out and took her hand again, and it took a vast amount of her remaining courage not to draw it back. "I see you eyeing the other seat," Valentine said, squeezing her hand. "You want to move away."

"I think it would be more comfortable."

He laughed. "I fear it will be a long time before you are comfortable again, Catie." And then he parted the curtains and peered out into the dawn. They were out of London, and the horses were moving at a good clip. Catherine wondered how long she would be forced to sit next to him. Already her shoulders and neck ached from tension.

And her whole arm tingled. He had not released her hand, and the heat of his fingers infused all the surrounding skin. He sat, holding her hand, and peering out the window for a long time. Catherine finally parted her own curtains and looked outside. She watched the low green hills roll by, the fat milk cows, and the cozy, little cottages. She smiled at the laborers in the cornfields, who raised their heads when the carriage passed.

And just as she began to relax, Valentine moved his fingers.

It was a very small movement, and she might not have noticed it at all except that his hand in hers had been absolutely still up until that point. Now she felt one finger move, tracing a small circle on the inside of her palm. She shivered and tried to ignore the sensation. But he repeated the movement, this time the circle grew bigger, his finger tracing the underside of one of hers when the circle was complete.

She looked at him, but he was still staring out his coach window, his face impassive. Perhaps he moved his fingers without thinking. She tried to loosen her hand, to free it unobtrusively, but he did not release her.

With a sigh, she went back to looking out her window, and then a few moments later, he began caressing her palm once again.

Catherine tried to ignore it, but it was difficult when each new touch made her feel hot and cold all at once. Her arm tingled, and she noticed that each new caress was different from the last. One caress was soft, that next more firm. He drew a small circle on her palm, and the next circle was so large, his touch extended over her wrist, making her pulse throb deliciously.

Catherine continued to stare out the window, but she could not believe Valentine's caresses were unintentional. He was the devious one, not she. She had to remember he did all of this for his career. He didn't care for her; he wanted to control her.

But what to do? Should she say something? Ask him to cease? Even as she contemplated her options, he grew bolder, his fingers actually traveling up her arm, tickling the sensitive under skin and tapping over her delicate inner elbow.

At that Catherine could no longer sit still. She was already squirming in her seat, and when his fingers glided over her inner elbow, she turned to him, eyes burning.

"Sir, I must ask you to cease at once."

He turned from his window to regard her, brow raised. "Cease what?"

She glowered at him. "You know what. Cease touching me."

"Am I not allowed to touch my own wife?"

"I'm not truly your—"

"And I am merely holding your hand."

She let out a frustrated breath. "No, you're not. You're *caressing* me."

He gave her a look of mock-horror. "Good God. Can you ever forgive me?"

She pinched her lips at him and glared. "Stop making fun of me. You promised to respect me, and I want you to cease."

"Very well." He turned so that he faced her more fully. "I will cease if you tell me why."

"It makes me uncomfortable," she said, and felt a blush creep up her cheeks. Lord, she hated when she blushed.

"How?"

She frowned. "What do you mean? I just feel unsettled. I don't like it."

"Are you certain?"

She shook her head in disbelief. "Of course I am certain. I know when I am uncomfortable."

"I don't doubt it. But you said you felt unsettled. That feeling is not always unwanted. Sometimes it can even be pleasurable."

Catherine felt her cheeks burst into flame.

"Did my touch give you pleasure?" Valentine asked.

Catherine had to avert her eyes. It was a scandalous question, not fit for a discussion even between husband and wife. Certainly not appropriate for two people who were united by the merest thread. She looked down at the hand he still held and, with his words swirling in her ears, couldn't help but imagine those fingers sliding over her shoulder, her collarbone, flitting across the swell of her breast.

She shivered and tried to free her hand, but Valentine held tighter. "What were you thinking just now?"

"Nothing. I-I—"

He placed a finger over her lips. "There is no shame in feeling pleasure or imagining pleasurable activities. Do you know what I was thinking?"

She shook her head, desperate to know while at the same time wishing he would simply leave her alone. She didn't like the way she felt—the oversensitivity of her skin, the way her nipples hardened against the material of her stays, the dampness between her legs. She felt restless as a filly on a new spring day, and she longed for the cozy, comfortable days of winter.

But now that Valentine had awakened her, he seemed loath to allow a return to sleep.

He slipped his fingers between hers again and leaned closer. "I was thinking about you in my bedroom. I was imagining standing in the doorway, watching you slide that gown off your shoulders, down your arms—"

"Stop, sir! This is not proper." But she could feel the heat and pulse between her legs growing.

"—baring your back," he continued. "I can see

all that honey gold skin until the dress drops to your hips, revealing the dip at the small of your back. And I want to kiss that place. Flick my tongue over it and lave it until you writhe beneath me."

His fingers were sliding over hers once again, back and forth, up and down. And Catherine wanted to silence him, but she did not have the strength. Lord help her, but she wanted him to do all the things he described. She wanted to feel his hands on her.

And then, just when she felt she could be silent no longer, when she felt she must demean herself and beg him to touch her, he released her hand and sat back. Once again, he parted the carriage curtains and peered out into the landscape, his face impassive, his warm, strong hands immobile at his sides.

Catherine stared at him, trying to comprehend the transformation. This man, her new husband, was obviously a man of much control. And he was also a man of much passion. As she stared at his unreadable face, she wondered which side of him she liked more.

Chapter 12

The sun was low in the sky by the time Quint turned to his new bride, and said, "This is it."

She sat forward and parted the curtain, letting a spill of violet-tinged twilight into the carriage.

"Look down at the top of the next rise," Quint said, pointing into the distance. "That's Ravensland." As the coach topped the bank, Quint gave his bride a sidelong look. He watched her face, waiting for any telltale sign of disappointment. His family had large estates, of course. His mother and father lived in Ravenscroft Hall in Derbyshire, but this property was his own—small and simple and unassuming.

If Catherine had usurped her sister and married him for money, he'd know it in a moment.

And he did. As soon as Catherine saw the house, her eyes widened, and the first smile he had seen all day teased her lips. Without looking away from the house, she said, "Oh, it's lovely. I was afraid it would be some monstrous thing that rambled on and on and where I'd get lost." She turned and smiled at him, and Quint was caught staring at the full, ripe peach that was her mouth.

"But it's not," she said, shifting uncomfortably under the weight of his stare.

Quint blinked. What was she talking about? He hadn't heard a word since—"Oh, monstrous. Right, you are. It's a good house, but I don't have the room for a full complement of servants. I hope you don't mind, but I can always hire from the village."

"Oh, no. I don't mind. In fact, I can help out."

"I don't think that will be necessary."

With an abashed smile, she turned back to the window.

Quint was relieved that those piercing brown-gold eyes had left his face. It gave him a moment to collect himself. Whenever he was close to his bride, she seemed to distract him with some new quality he hadn't noticed before. All day in the carriage, it had been her scent. The comparison of her mouth to a peach had not been capricious. He'd smelled peaches, and the closer he leaned to his bride, the more intoxicated he became. When she had been sleeping on top of him, the scent was so strong and so tantalizing that he had been unable to resist stroking her long, black hair.

But his attempts at seduction had been quite deliberate and quite personal. He'd planned most of this last night. He would win her affections while remaining coolly detached. But it would not be easy. Everything about her tempted him, and he knew the signs of a drowning man. Allowing himself to care for this woman was a dangerous proposition. She had tricked him into marriage.

Beside him, Catherine tensed, and he peered past her. They were nearing the house now, and his servants had come out to greet him. There were perhaps nine in all—good people, most of whom had worked for his family for years—but Catherine eyed them as though they were a revolutionary mob after her head.

"Catie, you needn't be afraid." He put his hand on her arm and she jumped.

"I'm sorry," she said, putting her hand to her heart. "I become nervous around new people."

Quint stared at her and forced himself to take a deep breath. What was his job but meeting new people—diplomats, up-and-coming stars of Parliament, even political opponents? The world of politics was constantly shifting and changing. What was he to do with a wife who ran and hid every time she saw someone new?

The coach slowed and pulled around the circular drive, and one of Quint's footmen opened the door and lowered the stairs. Before he exited, Quint gave Catherine's hand a reassuring squeeze. "I'll be right by your side. Just smile, and you'll get through it."

She nodded somewhat stiffly, her face pale and her hands trembling in his. Quint prayed she wouldn't faint or make a scene.

Quint exited first, then with great ceremony, he held out his hand and assisted Catherine from the carriage. When she stepped down, he whispered, "Smile."

She gave a tight grimace.

Quint could see that for their part, his staff was ecstatic to meet their new mistress. The servants clapped and cheered at the sight of Catherine, but this only seemed to make her more nervous.

Quint held up a hand to quiet them. "Your new mistress, Lady Valentine."

The servants cheered again, and Quint felt Catherine go limp beside him. He put an arm about her waist and assisted her up the stairs to the door, but he couldn't stop himself from wondering if this was an act or real fear.

His housekeeper came forward, eager to be first to welcome the new mistress, but Quint whispered to her, "Mrs. Crumb, might we do introductions another time? I fear my wife is overly tired from the long trip."

"Of course, milord. I'll have her things brought to your chambers."

"Then you received my letter?" Quint asked.

"Yes, milord. And this morning the workers began the improvements that you specified."

Quint felt like a scoundrel. He'd sent that letter by express post last night, indicating he wanted the room that would have been Catherine's completely redone. While the room was in need of remodeling, the work was not necessary, especially considering that the other rooms in the house were occupied or untenable. In effect, Quint had ensured he and Catherine would share a bedroom. It was devious and low, not something that Quint would have normally done, but how else was he supposed to get close to her?

And after all she had done, did she deserve any better?

"Thank you, Mrs. Crumb." As the housekeeper led Catherine away, Quint tried to give her a reassuring smile. She looked terrified, not a bit like the devious little liar he imagined her.

At length, when Quint had settled back into his chambers, gone over accounts with his estate manager, and attended to various other tasks associated with being a property owner, he looked at the clock and saw that it was after eleven.

He took a deep breath and ran a hand through his hair. No point in putting it off any longer. It was time he joined his wife in bed.

And he wasn't going to feel any qualms about doing so. She had wanted this marriage enough to have him drugged. She had duped him. Hadn't she?

The rest of the house was dark and silent as he walked up the stairs, lamp in hand, and opened the door to his room. Catherine was sitting in bed, book propped on her knee. She looked up at him, and he paused for a moment to catch his breath. Her long, silky hair flowed over the pretty pink nightgown she wore. Her cheeks were rosy, her eyelids heavy. He had the crazy impulse to go to her, take her into his arms, and just hold her. The impulse was shaken when she saw him. She clutched the covers, and shrieked, "What do you want?"

Quint closed the door behind him slowly and set the lamp on a small side table. "I want to go to bed."

He sat in a silk-striped armchair and began taking off his boots. Dorsey, his valet, had not accompanied him on this trip, and that had not been an accident. Quint wanted no servants interrupting his time with his wife.

"But why do you not go to your own room?" Catherine asked, scooting away from him.

Quint noted her behavior. Could this fear really be an act?

He set one boot on the floor and began on the other. "This is my room."

She blinked at him. "Then where is mine?"

"Yours is under construction. Unfortunately, I have not been as diligent in the upkeep of this house as I should have. I intend to remedy that now. I am afraid we will have to share a room." He finished with his boots and stood to remove his tailcoat.

"Then I will sleep in one of the other rooms."

Quint shrugged off his tailcoat and laid it over the arm of the chair. "All are occupied." That was not strictly true, but she did not know that.

He began unbuttoning his shirt, and Catherine jumped up, grabbing the robe at the end of the bed. "Sir, you promised you would not"—she swallowed and clutched a hand to her throat, closing the robe over her neck—"you promised you would not force yourself on me."

He paused and looked up at her. Bloody hell. She was pale and trembling. Obviously terrified. Keeping his voice low, he said, "Nor do I intend to. I assure you that I will not touch you." He pulled his shirt over his head, and she took another step back.

"I-I do not believe you. How do I know—"

"Catherine, I am tired," he said, "I want to go to bed. Nothing more." And at this point, that was true. Her behavior, as usual, gave him more questions than answers, and he needed time to consider them. He began to unfasten his trousers, and Catherine let out a small yelp.

"Very well, if we are to share a room, then I will sleep on the couch." She pointed to the velvet chaise longue across from the bed, then scurried over to it and lay down.

Quint sighed. He should have foreseen this and had the damn thing removed before they arrived. "You're not going to sleep on the couch. If you won't share a bed with me, then I will sleep on the couch."

"But I don't want—"

"Catie, get in the bed. I'm going to blow out this lamp and lie down on the couch. Unless you intend to lie on top of me, you'd better be in bed."

She scrambled to the bed again and had climbed in when he blew out the lamp. He lifted his coat from the arm of the chair, and, feeling his way across the room, lay on the couch, with the coat over him.

In the darkness, the room was silent. Quint did not even think Catherine dared breathe. He turned on his back, his feet hanging over the edge of the chaise. Shifting onto his side, his shoulder dropped off the couch. He sighed, wishing for his large, comfortable bed.

But there would be many days to come. The better he knew her, the better he understood her, the easier it would be to win his way into his wife's bed. Then he could mold her into the wife he needed. She was like a skittish horse who had to be calmed and soothed, and who, with a bit of attention would become a confident, prancing beauty. That was his Catherine.

Quint rose early the next morning, dressed, and

left his wife sleeping. She had curled into a ball and had one hand fisted under her chin. He restrained the urge to go to her and brush the hair from her face. Instead, he went down to the stable and found his groom. An hour later, he knocked on their bedroom door. It opened a sliver, and honey hazel eyes blinked at him.

"Get dressed," he said. "I have something to show you."

"But I don't—"

"If I have to break down this door and pull you out," he hissed, mindful of a maid dusting nearby, "I will do it. Now meet me on the front lawn in a quarter hour. You'll like what I have to show you."

And he marched down to the lawn and paced away the minutes. He'd stopped pacing and was watching the sun burn off the clouds and glint off the dew at his feet, when he heard behind him, "Is this what I'm meant to see?"

He turned to see his wife in a thin summer dress, standing on the lawn behind him, shivering.

Immediately, he swept off his greatcoat and draped it about her shoulders. He looked into her face and noticed it was pale and tired. "Didn't you sleep well?"

"I might have slept better if I'd been *alone*," she grumbled. "Why did you drag me out of bed so early?"

He grinned. Very well. She wasn't a morning

person. He'd be certain to schedule only after-noon social events.

Without asking permission, he took her hand and led her down the path. They walked in si-lence for the first few minutes. Catherine yawned and blinked at the rising sun, and generally looked about herself as though she could not quite believe what she saw was real. Quint was fascinated by the play of emotions on her face, though it hurt his opinion of her devious nature. As he watched her, it seemed her every thought was revealed. He saw the surprised and mulish look on her face when he'd taken her hand and refused to let go. He saw her face light when she glimpsed a deer standing in the distance, still as an icy pond, watching them. And now he watched her face again as they rounded the next corner and the stables came into view.

He needn't have bothered to pay such close at-tention. When she saw the horses in the paddock beside them, she let out a gasp of pleasure so loud that Quint's stableboy looked up.

"You have horses," she breathed, and he no-ticed that her pace was no longer sluggish. Now she was all but pulling him forward.

"I thought you might like a morning ride," Quint said.

"Oh, yes! Yes!" By then she was almost run-ning, and her smile of joy practically split her face. But when she reached the horses, she slowed and looked back at him. "Which one shall I ride?" she asked.

Quint glanced at the chestnut mare he had been about to suggest she take, and then decided against speaking up. There was a gelding so pale he appeared white that Quint preferred when he was home, and he saw Catherine's face break into a rapturous smile at the sight of the horse.

"You choose," he said.

She glanced away from the white gelding. "Really?"

"Please. Take your choice."

"I—" She glanced at the white horse again and then at the others. With a last longing look at the gelding, she said, "I'll ride the chestnut, I think."

Quint laughed, and she spun round.

"Why do you laugh, sir?"

"Because that was very noble of you, but I didn't bring you out here this morning so you could be noble. You want to ride Thor, don't you?"

Her eyes strayed to the white horse again. "Is that his name?"

"Yes, and you're staring at him like a starving child stares at a mince pie. Ride him, Catherine. He's yours whenever you want."

She blinked at him, and he could see the uncertainty in her eyes. "But what will you ride, then? I am sure Thor must be your favorite horse. He is such a beauty."

"I'll ride Hazard over there." He pointed to a dappled tan-and-brown horse. "Come on, let's go. The morning is getting away from us."

They rode away from the stable, Quint leading the way. Initially, they gave the horses their heads and galloped into the brisk spring morning. When the horses tired, Quint took her on a meandering tour of Ravensland's extensive grounds.

"You have a good seat," Quint said. "And you handle Thor very well."

"Thank you," she said, but he saw the telltale blush.

"Now what have I said to embarrass you?" he asked.

"I'm not used to compliments," she said, looking away. "And I couldn't tell if that one had a double meaning." The last was said so quietly, Quint missed several of the words and it took him a minute to piece the statement together. When he did, he laughed.

"Yes, that seat is nice, too."

"Sir!" she said with a shake of her head, and then she spurred Thor faster. The horses galloped over the green countryside, up small hills and past rambling brooks. Flowers were beginning to bloom in the wild places, and birds sang with abandon from the trees.

A while later they rode beside one another again, and Catherine said, "This is beautiful country. Did you grow up here?"

"No. My family estate is in Derbyshire, but I

spent the occasional week or two here when I was a boy. My grandfather acquired the land and built the house. He intended it for my father, a house of his own until he inherited the marquessate."

"And did your father ever live here?"

Quint shook his head. "My grandfather died just after the house was finished. My father became the marquess at age fifteen. The house was given to me when I became of age, and I hope to live here many years."

Catherine nodded. "I am sure your mother and father are very nice people. What do they think of all that has happened between us?"

Quint gave her a sideways glance. She didn't ask the easy questions. "Naturally, I wrote to my father as soon as I realized what had happened. I asked his advice, but as yet have received no reply."

"Too soon, I imagine," she said.

"Yes."

"Was that one of the 'friends' you told me about?"

He nodded and turned his horse back toward the house. He was growing hungry, and morning was fading fast into a blue-skied April noon.

"What do you think he will say?" she asked, turning Thor and spurring him to catch up.

"I think he will say what he always says in these situations."

"And what is that?"

"To do my duty."

She laughed, and the reaction surprised him. She must have seen the look on his face because she added, "That sounds like something a father would say."

"Yes, yes it does," he agreed. "My father is nothing if not conventional."

"And you are not?"

"Not at all. My father is a member of the old guard. Sometimes I think the man should have been on the boat with William the Conqueror. He has that conquering mentality."

"And you do not."

He saw the doubt in her eyes.

"I want reform. There are people starving in London and throughout the countryside. The poverty is wretched, while so many of us live in luxury." He gestured to their horses and the beautiful rolling landscape surrounding them. "How can I have all this and begrudge a poor man, woman, or child a full belly?"

"You don't have to convince me," she said. "My cousin Maddie runs an orphanage, and she preaches reform all the time."

"Yes, the orphanages are only the beginning. There's so much to do, so many reforms to pass, and they are increasingly more difficult to shoulder through Parliament." He spoke with real feeling, warming to the conversation, until he remembered that he was supposed to be learning more about her. And somehow she had tricked him into opening up.

"And what does your father think of all your efforts at reform?" Catherine asked, and Quint took the opportunity to direct the topic back at her.

"He thinks I am young and idealistic. He thinks poverty has always existed and will always exist. He thinks I waste my time." The stables were coming into view, and Quint raised a hand to the boy waiting for them.

"I see." She was looking into the distance when she said it, and Quint wondered what she was seeing there. Her own father, belittling her efforts? Finding her interests and diversions a waste of time? Or had she and Edmund Fullbright been of the same mind? Annoyed, Quint continued to teeter between believing her the victim of a barbaric father or a deceitful little vixen. Which was she?

Finally, he said, "And my father thinks I am the greatest son a man could have."

She turned then, her eyes wide with surprise. "But you said—"

"A man can be proud of his son without approving all he does. My father thinks I walk on water. Perhaps it's a good thing we have our political differences. If I were any more perfect, he'd petition to have me canonized."

She smiled, and he slowed his horse to give them a few more minutes alone. "I do not expect perfection, Catie. My parents love me in spite of my flaws, and I will treat my children the same."

"Your children?"

He nodded and took another chance to prod her. "I know you have not agreed to that aspect of our marriage, but I want you to know, before you make up your mind, that I will treat our children well, and I will love them no matter what." He watched her closely and saw the flash of disbelief in her eyes.

"The sons, you mean," she said.

The stableboy was approaching now, and he took Quint's reins. With practiced ease, Quint dismounted and was beside her, his hand on her waist as he set her down. He looked into her eyes. "The sons *and* the daughters. If they are our children, Catie, I will love them with all my heart."

Again, he saw the play of emotions on her face—disbelief, scorn, skepticism. "You don't look as though you believe me, Catie," he said, still holding her, hands wrapped around her warm waist. "Why not? Didn't your father love you?"

The veil fell over her face, hiding her emotions for the first time that day. "Let me go," she finally said, pulling out of his arms. "You're hurting me."

He held his hands up, palms out. "I'm not even touching you."

"You don't have to." She turned and fled. He watched her go, and then bent to lift his greatcoat from his feet.

Chapter 13

Catherine didn't know where she was running or why. She simply knew that she had to get away. She couldn't breathe when Valentine was close to her. She couldn't think or reason. For the past two days, it seemed all she did when she was in his presence was to obsess about the way she felt when he touched her. Lord, she did not even believe he had truly begun to woo her yet, and he was already too much in her thoughts.

Not that he could be otherwise, considering she was now in his house and under his protection. Catching her breath, she slowed to a walk, angling away from the house and toward a sparse copse of trees. She needed a moment to be alone. In the past two days, Valentine had spoken first of her sharing his bed and now of their shared children. She'd never considered that she would have either opportunity. She'd vowed to be a spinster, and suddenly she was in the position to be a wife and a mother.

She took a seat on an enormous root poking out of the ground. She wanted children, but she also feared motherhood. Her own mother was little more than a slave to her father. She was at his every whim, his beck and call. She suffered first and most severely when he was not pleased.

As a result, Cordelia Fullbright was a hard, cruel woman. Catherine did not know if she had always been thus, but she remembered her father berating her in front of Catherine and Lizzy. Catherine had learned to see her mother as an object of disgust. What if Catherine was forced to stand helplessly by as Valentine turned their children against her? Or worse, he might mistreat their children.

No, she would never allow that. She would not be like her mother.

Catherine sighed. More and more, she was torn between yielding to Valentine and resisting him. If she yielded, she risked so much. If she resisted . . .

But she was in far too deep to think of resisting now.

Yesterday he had said the decision to share the marriage bed was left to her, but a man who would one day be a marquess would need an heir. And surely he would need a legitimate heir. She was his wife. That was her duty. She could refuse him, and the result?

No heir.

Catherine stood and paced in front of the tree. So the truth of the matter was that Valentine was playing with her. In reality she had no choice. She would bear his children whether she wanted it or not. That was, unless he found a way to be rid of her. And why should he want her to stay? He'd never wanted her to begin with. It was Elizabeth he'd courted, and Elizabeth he obviously still loved. Catherine knew she was a pale second.

She managed to avoid him the rest of the day. She even escaped dining with him as he'd been overseeing a business matter with his steward. But that still left the entire night to be shared, alone with him in their room. She tried to wait up for him, not wanting to be asleep and vulnerable when he came in, but as the hour grew late, her eyelids drooped. There was a creak and she jerked awake. Somewhere a dog barked, and Catherine shook her head to clear it.

She picked up a book. The clock ticked away the hours, the monotonous tock-tock-tock lulling her to sleep. Finally, the words of her book blurred, and the novel grew heavy in her arms.

Her father's house was full of laughing people. Catie could not see their faces, only their huge red lips and gaping mouths. She ran and ran, but everywhere she turned faces popped before her, laughing at her.

The hard floor was cold and damp under her bare feet, the way littered with sharp odds and ends that she could not identify in the dark. She stretched her hands out in the blackness, knowing what she would feel but powerless to stop herself.

Her hand closed on the sticky cobweb, and she felt the spider move over her hand. She jumped back, but her foot skidded over a soft, squishy rat. The rat sank its sharp teeth into her flesh.

Catie cried out and shook her foot, trying to dislodge the rat, and it was then that the spider made its way up her arm, past her shoulder, and onto her face. It crawled into her mouth.

Catie screamed.

"Catherine. Catherine!"

With a wrench of air, she sat, arms up and ready for battle. It was dark, and it took her a long, terrifying moment to realize where she was. Moonlight pooled through the curtains, emitting enough illumination for her to see the man at the edge of her bed.

She pushed backward, scrambling away, feeling another scream in her throat, but Valentine caught her, pulled her close and . . .

Held her?

Suddenly she was on his lap, and he was

rocking her, his hand caressing her hair. "Shh, baby," he whispered. "I won't let anything happen to you."

They were the words Catherine needed to hear, and she relaxed, burying her face in his shoulder. He was not wearing a shirt, and his bare skin was cool against her hot cheeks. He felt so good, so strong, so safe. She wanted to curl up in his arms and never leave.

It was a small thing, an easy thing to turn her head so that her lips were against his shoulder. It was equally simple to press her mouth against his neck, feel the quick pulse beating against her mouth. He did not bend his head to hers. She looked up at him, shy and intrepid all at once. He was staring straight ahead, his jaw clenched.

She wrapped her arms around his neck and pulled his mouth to hers. She'd never kissed a man, and her heart was racing so fast she feared it would jump out of her chest. She did not know what to expect, but his lips were exactly what she craved. They were cool against her heated skin, and he tasted of mint. She pressed her mouth against his, and the shock of the connection buzzed through her.

Her heart galloped on, and her breath was short. And then his arms tightened on her, pulling her closer so that her breasts pushed against his chest. His prickly hair tickled her through the thin nightgown she wore. His hands held her securely, but somehow he also managed to touch her. She felt him move over her waist and her hips. He cupped her bottom and she felt the bulge of his erection against her. Quint groaned, and his hold became almost painful.

She was afraid of him and thrilled by the new feelings, too. His mouth descended on hers again, and her head began to swim. The first tendrils of fear and uncertainty cascaded over her skin. She realized that he was easing her back on the bed, and she was torn. His kisses were consuming. She wanted them to go on and on. She wanted his lips and his hands on her all the time.

But then his hand slipped beneath the hem of her gown, and she felt his tentative fingers on her knee. It was too fast, too foreign a feeling, and she bucked and pushed him away. But her struggle was unnecessary. As soon as she'd tensed, she was free. She opened her eyes, his sudden absence making all that came before seem like a dream.

A match flared, and the lamp on the other side of the bed came to life. Catherine squinted at her husband. His hair was disheveled, his color high, and he was running his hands through his thick hair.

"I'm sorry," he gasped. "I did not mean—" He paused and looked at her. "You were having a nightmare. I only wanted to wake you."

She nodded. In the lamplight, everything seemed different. She was no longer anonymous.

She was ashamed of her actions. What would have happened if she had not stopped him?

Lord, she still wanted him. That was the most humiliating part. She looked at his bare chest and his rumpled hair, and she wanted to press herself wantonly against him. She wanted to touch him and kiss him and lick him.

Oh, Lord. What was wrong with her?

"Are you well now?" he asked.

She stared at him. No, she wasn't well. She was thinking about licking him. That was not normal. But then she realized he was speaking of her nightmare. The faces, the closet, the rat bite and the spider. She shuddered violently.

He started for her, but she held up a hand. "I'm well. I just—" She was startled to find tears on the back of her hand when she wiped her eyes, and this time a wave of her hand did not stop Valentine from sitting beside her.

"It's a dream I have sometimes. A nightmare," she mumbled, trying to keep him from seeing her face.

"Perhaps talking about it will help," he murmured. He took her hand in his and kissed her knuckles. "The room is alight. No shadows. Tell me."

Catherine did not want to tell him. It was silly and humiliating that something from so long ago should still terrify her. She was too old to be afraid of spiders and rats.

And yet she needed to tell him. It was so hard

to keep it all inside. And the dream was so real, so horrifying.

"I'm a little girl," she heard herself say. She stared down at the bedclothes, not his face, but she was glad he did not release her hand. "I'm in a closet under the stairs. Alone. I'm there because I've been bad, and I'm scared because it's cold and dark, and I can't see. I cry to be freed, but no one comes."

Valentine took a deep breath, and she glanced up at him. His eyes were dark. Angry?

"I'm hungry and so frightened, and I'm pounding on the door until my hands are sore. But no one comes."

The tears were streaming down her cheeks now, and she let them fall. And she let Valentine pull her into his lap again. She'd wanted him to. She'd needed him close to say this last part.

"And then I feel something slither over me. A-a rat, I think, and I jump up and my hand is tangled in a cobweb, and I feel the spider, its furry legs all over me. And I scream and scream. But no one ever comes."

"Shh," Valentine said. "You don't have to say anymore. I'm here now. You can sleep, and you'll never have to dream that again. I'll be right here to keep the nightmares away."

He was lowering her on the bed again, but this time his touch was only one of comfort. She closed her eyes as he pulled the sheets up around her.

"Catherine," he whispered just as she began to drift off, "how old were you when he locked you in the closet?"

"Ten," she said. He began to pull away, and she reached out and caught his wrist. "But it was only a dream. You understand that?"

He leaned over her and caressed her cheek. "I understand. Now I understand."

The next morning Catherine received three letters: one from Ashley, one from Madeleine, and one from Josephine. All three were angered that she had been forced to leave Town, for they assumed she would never leave of her own volition. Ashley seemed to take her absence as a personal affront and threatened to come out to Hertfordshire and make sure she was well. Maddie talked more of events in Town, particularly the difficulty her father was giving her about going to the orphanage every day. He worried for her safety.

Catherine wished Josie's father would worry more for her safety. Josie's letter was filled with tales of a Lord Westman and pirate's treasure. As usual, it sounded like Josie was getting into plenty of trouble.

Catherine spent the morning writing letters to reassure her cousins and to give them her opinions on their various dilemmas. Maddie got sympathy and Josie a stern lecture. Ashley was instructed to stay in London for the time being.

Catherine stayed in her room as long as possible, avoiding Valentine. The events of the night before had not been far from her mind. She was ashamed of her forwardness, angry that she had told Valentine about her "dream," mortified that when he saw her again he would pretend nothing happened and mortified that he would not.

There were so many times in the short days of their acquaintance that he had seemed to want her. He'd touched her and looked at her with desire in his eyes. Last night he could have had her. Catherine had no illusions on that score. She would have willingly done whatever he'd asked.

And yet, Valentine had not taken her. He had pulled away, preferring to lull her to sleep than into his arms. She woke in the bed alone this morning. And no wonder. He had no feelings for her. It was Elizabeth he loved.

Catherine finished addressing her letters and put away the writing materials she'd requested. She could hardly avoid Valentine for the rest of the day, or even the rest of her life, as she'd like to. She always waited for things to happen to her. Today, she was going to face the world.

She found her husband in his library. She knocked twice and opened the door. Valentine looked up when she entered. He was sitting at a large mahogany desk that matched his eyes. No wonder his eyes reminded her of that wood. He looked at home behind the desk.

Before him were a stack of papers, a pen, an inkpot, and a pot of tea. She could see the steam still rising from the pot, and could almost feel the warmth of the fire in the hearth.

"Catie," he said, putting down his pen. "Come in."

Chapter 14

Valentine began to rise, but Catherine waved him back down. "No need to rise, sir. I only came to ask if you would make sure these letters are delivered for me." She handed them to him, and he took them, glanced at the names.

"Of course. How are you feeling this morning? I hope you are not too tired."

Catherine looked down at the floor. She stood at the edge of a brown-and-gold rug. Beneath her slipper, a sliver of hardwood floors winked.

"Sir." She finally looked into his eyes. "I must apologize for last night. I do not know what came over me." She looked down again, unable to hold his gaze and speak of such things. "I did not mean to be so forward." She peeked at Valentine. He was staring at her.

"I see." He cleared his throat and stood, coming around the desk. "I assure you, I was not offended."

"It won't happen again." Catherine forced herself not to back away when he came close to her.

"I sincerely hope that's not true."

She took a deep breath. "I have been thinking about our conversation."

He furrowed his brow. "Is there one in particular?"

"The one in the carriage." She shot him a glare. "You know, *the* one. About the—ah, marriage bed."

"Ah, that one."

"I have unraveled your plan."

One eyebrow angled upward as he leaned a slim hip on the desk. Funny how she hadn't noticed how slim his hips were until now. He was lean all over—that much she remembered from last night—but she had not appreciated what a long, lithe shape he had and how attractive that could be in a man.

"I gave myself away, did I?" he said, and his tone was wry.

She blinked and tried to refocus. She looked into his face. "Yes, you did. If you think I don't—"

But staring into his face was no better than looking at his body. He was far too handsome, and looking at him always elicited a response in her. She'd known so few men, and none as handsome as this one. His hair, still too long, curled over his collar, and it was inky black against his tan skin. His skin was marred by a dim shadow of beard growth, the color on his chin and cheeks almost a stain on that chiseled face. And his eyes. She had the most trouble there. His eyes were far too soft when they focused on her. They seemed almost . . . kind.

She shook her head. "What was I saying?"

"Something about you unraveling my plan."

"Right. If you think I don't realize that a marquess needs children—heirs and legitimate heirs—then you must think me a fool, and you've treated me as one, too."

He pursed his lips, opened his mouth, and then closed it again. "I'm not sure I follow."

She sighed in exasperation. Of course he understood! "You told me it was my choice whether or not to share your bed. And you told me"—she pointed accusingly at the ring he'd given her—"this was a symbol of your promise. But what you neglected to mention was that if I chose not to share your bed, that would not solve your problem. Even if you have other women, you still need a legitimate heir."

"I see."

"Yes, I do, too." She crossed her arms. "So in truth, this ring means nothing, sir. You will either have to bed me against my will or throw me out to achieve your aims."

"Is that so?" He was still leaning against the desk, arms crossed, looking not at all concerned with what she was telling him. In fact—she peered more closely at his mouth—he almost looked as though he were amused by her.

"Sir!" she said forcefully, hoping her tone would make him see the seriousness of what she said. "I do not think you quite comprehend."

He began to work his way around the desk. "Oh, I comprehend, Catie. I think you are the one who does not understand."

She blinked, watching him take another step closer, though her cowardly feet desperately wanted to turn and flee. But she would stand her ground and see this settled between the two of them. "What do you mean, sir?" He was standing close now, and she had to tilt her head up so she could look into his face. "What do I not understand?"

He lifted a hand and brushed a loose strand of hair from her face. She shivered at the intimate touch. He was so close now that he was beginning to have an effect on her. She could smell his scent. It reminded her of their ride yesterday morning—a combination of leather saddles, pine trees, and new spring mornings. She leaned closer.

"Many things, my Catie," he said, and this time

when he lifted his hand to stroke her hair back, she anticipated his touch and bent into it.

Her heart was pounding now, and she was so terrified that she needed to count to at least a hundred before she would feel better. But the blood rushing in her ears and the warm zing of Valentine's touch on her cheek made it impossible to think. She could not even remember her numbers. She knew three was a number, but what came before?

Valentine tilted his head down so that his eyes were level with hers. "What you do not understand is that you will come to my bed willingly. You want me as much as I do you."

She shook her head, not managing to move away from him at all. Instead, she actually worked her cheek against the rough palm of his hand. She felt his calluses against the skin of her face and wondered how they would feel on other parts of her body. Lord, Valentine was right. She did want him.

"I don't want you," she lied. "Last night, I was tired. I was not myself."

He put a finger over her lips. "Last night your defenses were down, and you acted on your true impulses. You are afraid of men. How could you not be after living with a man such as your father?"

She felt as though a fist slammed into her belly, the shock and surprise so real she hunched over. "B-but that was just a dream. It wasn't real."

The finger pressed against her lips again. "You don't have to lie to me, Catie. You don't have to pretend with me."

Catherine took a deep breath and looked away.

Valentine's hand stroked her cheek. "He hurt you, didn't he?"

"No!"

"Locked you in a closet."

"I never said that."

"Not with words, no. But I need to know what to believe. Tell me the truth, did your father force you into this marriage?"

"I already told you—"

"I need to hear it again. The truth."

Catherine clenched her jaw. How many times did she need to prove herself? She was tired of defending her innocence. "I told you the truth, and I don't care if you believe me. Lord knows I'm used to being doubted."

Tears stung her eyes and spilled onto her cheeks. Valentine reached forward to wipe them away. "You're right. I should trust you. I'm sorry I doubted you before. You're not a liar." He lowered his head so that his forehead touched hers. "How can I make you see that there's more to the world than the way you grew up? How can I show you that there can be tenderness between a man and a woman? And there can be passion. It can be so exciting you forget to breathe. I can make you forget to breathe."

"No." She began to withdraw, and Valentine caught her hand.

"I know you're afraid of men. You protect your emotions because you had to survive with your father. But I'm not your father."

She shook her head, unable to put her fears into words. She'd never felt so close to anyone as she'd felt to him last night. She'd never needed anyone as she'd needed him. But she didn't deserve him or his promises of happiness and security. She'd never felt truly safe or happy. She didn't know what it was to have that.

"You're my wife," Valentine said. "I want you in my bed. I want you in every way a man wants a woman. Let me show you how it can be."

"No."

"Yes. Don't you think you deserve pleasure and happiness? Don't you think you're worthy enough?"

She stared at him, wondering how he'd managed to read her innermost thoughts.

But Valentine was looking into her eyes, and his own softened at what he saw. He released her hand and cupped her cheeks with both of his hands. She allowed it, though his touch unsettled her. "You are so beautiful and so strong. Look at the misfortunes the world has dealt you, and yet you approach every new challenge as though it were an adventure. Let me show you how you deserve to be treated."

"No." She tried to pull away again, and he allowed it. "No, I don't want you to touch me."

"Very well then." He held his hands out in a gesture of surrender. "You kiss me."

She'd been slowly backing away, but at his suggestion, she stopped.

"I won't touch you," he promised. "I won't even kiss you back, if you don't allow it. I'll be completely at your mercy, under your command."

Catherine bit her lip and considered. Inadvertently, her eyes went to his lips. They were well shaped, full, with a hint of color. Last night they'd been warm and firm.

"I give you my word, Catie," Valentine said, leaning that slim hip against his desk again. "I will not touch you."

She stood still, considering.

"Catie, if the prime minister trusts me, surely you can."

Oh, now he was all but daring her. As though she were afraid. As though she hadn't been the one to kiss him last night. "Very well. I shall kiss you." She held up a finger. "Once."

He wrapped both of his hands around the edge of his desk behind him, then slouched so that he would be at an accessible height. "I am at your disposal," he said, and closed his eyes.

And still she did not move. He stood waiting blindly, hands immobile, legs braced apart, a warrior at her mercy.

She took one step forward, then another. And then she stopped. She was only a few steps away, and the closer she got, the more daunting the whole task seemed. Was she just supposed to walk up and kiss the man? This had been so much easier when she was already in his arms last night.

She put her foot out to take another tentative step forward, and her shoe hovered.

He cracked one eyelid. "You're not going to leave me standing here, are you?"

"Ah—"

He'd closed his eyes again, and she thought how uncharitable it would be if she ran away, leaving him this way. After all, he was practically helpless.

She took another step and then another until she was directly before him. She was close enough to kiss him now, close enough so that he could have reached out and grasped her, but he did not. He kept his eyes closed and his hands locked on the desk, even as she leaned forward and pressed her lips to his.

She quickly withdrew, and he did not grab her and gobble her up. In fact, he still stood like a statue, eyes closed.

She frowned at him. That was all the reaction her kiss was to receive? He looked as though he were still waiting.

"Lord Valentine?"

"Quint," he said. Then, "Hmm?"

"I kissed you."

He cracked one eye again. "When?"

She put her hands on her hips. "Just now. A moment ago."

"Are you certain?" He frowned. "I didn't feel anything. You'd better do it again." And he closed his eyes.

She frowned back at him. She might be inexperienced, but she was no fool. Of course he had felt the kiss. He just wanted her to do it again. She almost turned and left, but again, it seemed unkind to leave him thus. And so she tilted her head and kissed him once more, this time harder and lingering a bit longer. Her pulse jumped as she remembered the feel of his hands on her last night.

When she pulled back, he was looking at her and smiling. "That was better," he said. "And you haven't turned into an ugly toad yet from putting your lips on mine."

"Best not to chance it further."

"You chanced it last night. Kiss me like you did last night."

Catherine shook her head. "No. Last night was—it was—" What was it? "I cannot, sir."

"Why? Don't you want me?"

"Of course I want you, it's just that—" She slammed her hand over her mouth and closed her eyes. Oh, Lord, how mortifying.

He put his hands around hers and pulled them down. "Catie, you are free to reject me and my bed, but wouldn't you like to know what you are rejecting first? Don't you deserve to know?"

She turned away. Why was she listening to him? And how could she not? She did deserve to know pleasure. Everyone would assume she'd shared his bed no matter what she did. Shouldn't she reap some reward? She wanted him. Perhaps it was a mistake. Perhaps she was a fool, but she needed him to touch her again like he had last night.

She turned back to him. "Would you"—she paused and took a deep breath—"would you kiss me?"

"Oh, God, yes." He bent toward her then pulled back again. "But this is purely by your request. I'll stop whenever you say." He leaned close again. "Remember what I said about the prime minister," he whispered. "You can trust me."

Slowly, he lifted one hand, and she could not help but pull back.

"I'm going to cup the back of your head." His voice was level, and his eyes never left hers. "You'll like it. In fact, it would be nice if you did the same." He moved slowly, sliding his fingers through her hair. "Touch me," he murmured.

She cupped the back of his neck. The action drew her closer to him so that her body was almost flush against his. It was an awkward and heady feeling, but not a wholly unpleasant one. And she decided that she actually liked having her hand on the back of his neck. It gave her some power and some control over what he did.

Or at least the appearance of it.

Then Valentine slid his other hand about her waist, and the blood began to thrum in her ears again. She looked up at him and found she was lost in his mahogany eyes.

Three, eight, seventeen . . .

And then he bent and put his mouth on hers. She tensed at first, expecting an assault, but his mouth was cool and dry, as she'd remembered it from last night.

He moved his lips against hers, lightly at first and then with more pressure. He almost seemed to be nibbling at her lips, and the thought made her smile. But she wanted so much more. She wanted to feel again what she'd felt last night.

To her pleasure, the light pressure of his lips increased, and she felt the flick of his tongue. It was a jolt, and she almost stepped back, but he held her close with the hand on her back. Still, she could not help but tense up, and that was when the hand on the back of her neck began to do its work. He kneaded and worked his fingers into her skin until she relaxed again.

By then, she knew what he wanted. He wanted her to open her mouth, and she was surprised to find that she wanted the same. She was not disappointed at what she felt. His lips slanted over hers, warm and moist and making her feel sensations even more mesmerizing than she had felt last night. Her whole body seemed to come alive against his, and she couldn't seem to get close enough to him. She pulled his head down farther with the hand on the back of his neck and ran her other hand along his back.

She thought she heard him groan quietly, but then he flicked his tongue into her mouth, and she was not sure of anything. Heat flooded through her. She knew her face was flaming, and she knew that if anyone ever saw her doing this, she would die of mortal shame. And yet she did not stop him. With each moment, the kiss grew more into a caress, his tongue probing and searching and spinning her to new heights of sensation.

His touch and his kiss sent heat flooding through her. Her hands tingled with it. Her breasts ached with it, and her stomach clenched. And then the heat reached that spot between her legs, and she felt her thighs become wet. She had the oddest sensation, and she wanted to rub herself. Even more, she wanted him to touch her there.

He'd withdrawn his tongue now, but their mouths were still fused. The sensation between her legs was growing, making her restless and excited, and when he withdrew his tongue she followed him. With a thrill of adventure, she entered his mouth. He met her there, kissing her harder, pulling her closer, showing her what to do and how.

And then, as though he knew what she was feeling, he parted her legs with his own and slid a leg between her thighs. He kept one hand on her back and the other on her neck, still kneading away her inhibitions, but she felt his thigh press against her. At first the touch was light and tentative, but she felt a jolt when his warm body caressed that inner part of her, even through her skirts and petticoats.

His touch grew more insistent. He rubbed against her again and again, the strokes of his tongue mimicking the thrusts of his thigh.

And Catherine could not take it anymore. She broke the kiss and gasped. But the gasp came out sounding much more like a moan, and not the kind of moan a lady like her would make. She sounded like a common whore.

It was all too much, and she released him and pushed her hand against his chest. Reluctantly, he allowed her to go. She stumbled back, her hand to her throat, and stared at him.

Unbelievably enough, he looked as flushed and affected as she. His hair was mussed, the dark waves falling over his forehead, his eyes were bright, and he breathed in rapid bursts that matched her own gulps.

"God, I want you," he said on a gasp. "Please."

She stared at this man, the only man she'd ever known who asked before taking. The only man she'd ever known who told her she was worth something, who told her she deserved more. More than anything, she wanted to yield to him. But again, if she submitted, if she let him sweep her away, allowed him to make her believe she meant more to him than she did, and then he took it all away . . . what then?

She took another step back. Her head was spinning, and she knew she needed time to think. She needed so much time to think these days.

"It's still your decision," he said, straightening. "I won't touch you unless you allow it. But now you know how it can be. God, Catie, please trust me."

She turned and fled to her room. She threw herself on their bed, quick to bury her head in the counterpane so that she could hide the blush from her face.

She took deep, soothing breaths until her heart slowed and she was able to count to a hundred. And then she opened her eyes and stared at the green-and-yellow-papered walls.

She could still feel the pulse beating between her legs, still feel the moist ache that begged to be quelled. Hand trembling, she put her fingers there and pressed against her flesh, hoping to staunch the feelings, but they only intensified, and the image of Valentine, his hair disheveled and his eyes hot and full of desire for her, made her want him more.

Quickly, she withdrew her hand and tried to think of banal topics: the weather, bread pudding, horses. But there again she thought of Valentine. He'd allowed her the pick of the best horse. He'd shown her his home, and she could still remember the way he'd beamed and the pride in his face when they'd ridden about the property. And then last night, when she'd been frightened, he'd held her and soothed her.

She shook her head, but she could not deny the inevitable. She had married a good man. He was nothing like her father. Quint Childers was a good man.

With a sigh, Catherine flipped onto her stomach. And so what?

That didn't mean she had to fall in love with him. That didn't mean she had to trust him.

He spoke of passion, of pleasure, but he didn't speak of love.

Because he didn't love her. He loved Elizabeth. Catherine knew she would only open herself to a lifetime of pain if she allowed Valentine into her heart. All her life, Catherine had fought with Elizabeth—for her parents' affection, for space in their shared room, for respect—but she would not fight Elizabeth for Valentine's heart.

That was a battle Catherine feared she would never win.

Chapter 15

Quint sat behind his desk and tried to concentrate on the documents in front of him. His recommendation to the prime minister was due soon, he had a speech to write for Parliament, and he still had to go through piles of correspondence. Here was a letter with information on a labor law he was researching, there a request from an MP for support of a new tax bill.

Quint stared at the work for the better part of the afternoon and made no progress whatsoever. It seemed no matter which issue he turned his attention to, the only issue he could really concentrate on was that of his marriage. He was not a violent man, but at that moment he could have cheerfully murdered Edmund Fullbright.

Quint had been wrong about Catie. He could see that now. Not that he hadn't had reason to distrust her, but no more. Now he felt nothing but righteous fury for her. Edmund Fullbright was the worst kind of scum—the kind of vermin who belittled those weaker than himself, the kind of man who made himself feel powerful by knocking down people like his wife and daughter.

Quint hadn't lied to Catie when he'd said that relationships didn't have to be like that. He had promised not to hurt her, and he meant it. He would protect her, cherish her. He'd give her confidence and power, all that her father had stolen from her.

Quint leaned back in his chair and scrubbed his fingers over his face. If only all his plans were as easily executed as devised. He needed to return to his political work, but Catherine, with her long black hair, large hazel eyes, and blatant mistrust of men—and him in particular—plagued him far more than the reports of American discontent on the seas. The Americans he could deal with. His wife was another matter.

Still leaning back, he linked his hands behind his head and tried to consider the issue of his marriage as he would that of a pesky foreign dispute. In many ways, his wife was similar to a rebel colony. She was submissive but willful, coarse but full of potential, beautiful but teeming with hidden dangers. Quint imagined the early settlers of the American colonies coming ashore and seeing their new home for the first time. It had probably not felt any more like home to them than his marriage to Catherine felt like the union he had hoped for with Elizabeth.

Still, the colonists had weathered the storm. They'd suffered through the cold winters and hot summers, they'd fought back the threats, and they'd carved out a niche for themselves. And look at them now. The bloody colonies were a proud, confident country in their own right. And he supposed that was what he needed from Catherine. If she were to share the political stage with him, she had to be proud and confident.

And here was Meeps, speaking of a Cabinet position. How few men were ever considered for such an honor at the tender age of thirty, and yet the opportunity was there for the taking—if Quint played his part well.

And if Catherine played hers.

But how did one take a raw, new land and mold it into a nation? Quint sat forward and made a note on a scrap of paper littering his desk. First, one staked one's claim. He could check that off. He felt a bit like Christopher Columbus must have when he mistook the Americas for India. Quint himself had been promised India, but he was in possession of America, and he would make the best of it. Not that that would be any hardship.

He closed his eyes and felt Catherine's warm, soft body against his. One hand had been on the long column of her neck and the other just above the sweet curve of her bottom. How he'd wanted to take her in both hands, grasp her hips, and pull them against his straining erection—his need for her the result of her innocent but oh-so-tantalizing kisses.

But that was not the way. He'd known it, and held himself back as best he could. Even when she'd met him thrust for thrust, their tongues mimicking the ancient rhythm both their bodies knew instinctively.

Quint let out a long breath and went back to his list. Yes, he had staked a claim, and he had not frightened the native away. He was wooing her and would continue to do so. But what next?

One worked to make the colony profitable. One built settlements and organized laws and—

Quint sat back again and smiled.

—and one cultivated the land. One plowed the virgin earth and planted one's seed and hoped the endeavor would come to fruition. It was only after a successful harvest—after the settlement reaped what it had sowed—that a great nation could be born.

And Quint saw it was this way with Catherine as well. He'd bed his wife, earn her trust and her affection, and then he would begin to build her confidence and her skills until he'd molded her into the wife that he wanted. Until she was the perfect political hostess.

There was only one small problem with his

colonization scheme: it took decades to forge a nation, and he needed a political hostess in a matter of weeks. The Cabinet position would not wait. If he did not take it, his rival Charles Fairfax surely would. Fairfax had the political clout and the perfect wife.

Quint ran a hand through his hair and peered out the window beside his desk. The midmorning rains had ceased, and the sky was once again blue and clear. It was a perfect day to go for a walk or . . . to ride into the small village nearby.

He looked back at his work. It was still waiting for him, and he really could not justify leaving so much undone for an afternoon of pleasure.

Except that when he looked outside again, he saw Catherine as she'd been yesterday morning. She'd been walking along the copse of trees, her long, dark hair blowing out behind her, her thin dress molded to her legs and her breasts, the color high and bright in her face. His groin tightened, and he looked back at the documents, then, with a resigned sigh, he rang for his curricle and sent a note to his wife. The government of England would have to wait. Quint Childers, Earl of Valentine, had colonizing to do.

An hour later, he sat beside his wife in his curricle and drove at a fast clip toward the village. She had acted reluctant to venture out with him and had barely been able to meet his eye when she'd come down from her room, but he had seen that beneath her embarrassment and mistrust of his intentions lay excitement.

She was a colonist as well—eager to explore a new world—or at least a new village. When he'd seen her still wearing the thin, too-tight muslin gown, he'd bundled her up in his cloak, and that gave him a brilliant excuse for going into the village.

She needed new clothes. There was a seamstress there who had sewn for the family for decades, and Quint told Catherine they would call on her and perhaps have dinner in one of the pubs.

She'd protested at first, but it was not hard to convince her. But when was it ever difficult to convince a woman she needed a new dress or a hat? The village was only five miles or so, and when they'd left Ravensland behind, Quint turned to her, and said, "I wish I could apologize for my behavior this morning."

She'd been staring at the view of rolling hills and blue skies in the distance, but she turned those hazel eyes on him quickly enough. "You *wish* you could apologize, sir? I wish that you would apologize. Your behavior was most . . . disconcerting."

He hid a grin. What she really meant was that her own response had been disconcerting. There was a passionate woman inside her somewhere, and he intended to free that woman. "Yes, well, as I said, I wish I could apologize, but as it stands, I cannot. In fact, I think that you ought to be the one to apologize."

"Me?" she screeched, and swung her body toward him. "What have I to apologize for?"

"Being irresistible for one."

"Oh, please."

"Being so beautiful and so tempting that I had to have you. You went to my head," he said, giving her a sideways glance, "and I lost control of our kiss."

She shook her head. "Men always blame women for their own lack of control. I see you are no different."

"But I had meant the kiss to be controlled and"—he swallowed and attempted to say the word without laughing—"chaste, but you have a power over me—"

She snorted.

"—that renders me quite helpless."

"Lord Valentine, if this is your idea of wooing, you will have to do better than falsehoods and exaggerations. I know I am not beautiful, and I know I am not irresistible. Men have been resisting me for twenty years, and I imagine a man like you has little problem doing the same."

The words were edged with emotion, and he knew she spoke from her heart. He could not stop himself from taking her hand, nor could he dam up the hole her statement made in his heart. "Is that what you really think?"

She nodded and tried to free her hand. "It's what I know."

He let her hand go. "Then you have been misinformed. I wanted you last night and this morning—before that even—and I still want you. I sit here beside you, and all I can think about is how good you felt in my arms, and how soft your mouth was, and how much I want to—" He cleared his throat.

She was staring at him, hazel eyes wide.

"You are a powerful woman, and a beautiful one, Catherine. I wish that for one day you would try to see yourself as I do."

She began to protest, but he took her hand again and kissed the gloved fingers. The village was coming into view. "Today, Catie. Just for today, when you are in the milliner's or the dressmaker's shop, try to see yourself as I do. Try to see how truly beautiful you are."

And then he steered the horses through the village, releasing her hand so that he could raise it in greeting to the locals he had known since he was a child. The first stop was the dressmaker. He escorted Catherine inside, spoke with Mrs. Punch, the proprietress—a woman who had dressed his mother and sisters when they were in the country—and promised to return in time to take Catherine to dine at the pub.

As he was leaving, he slid behind Catherine, meeting her eyes in the mirror. "See yourself as I do," he whispered.

* * *

"What a scamp," Mrs. Punch said, as Valentine disappeared out the shop's door. "I can only imagine what the boy said to make ye blush so. Pretty girl like you. I'm sure he doesn't deserve ye."

Catherine blinked. Now Valentine's silly words and phrases must really be going to her head because she thought the old woman had actually called her pretty.

Catherine looked about the shop. Mrs. Punch had led her to a back room filled with mirrors and half-finished sewing. But the space was neat and clean, and she'd been led to a spot before one of the mirrors in the center of the room. At the back of the room was a door to another area, and behind her was the door to the main shop. It was a pretty shop, with large windows and plenty of bright materials arranged neatly within.

The whole village appeared neat and simple. The buildings lined the street in pretty rows, each with a sign hanging out front, indicating its name. Most of the shops also had window boxes, and they were already bursting with flowers in pinks, yellows, reds, and purples. The people were friendly. Almost everyone they had passed had waved a hello to Valentine, and some were so cheery, Catherine had found herself smiling.

Now, in the dress shop, Mrs. Punch called for her assistant, and the girl swished in from the front room, holding an armful of lace. "Put that away," Mrs. Punch said. "I need you to fetch me all the best muslins and silks."

The girl blinked. She had a large rosy mouth, straw-colored hair, and enormous blue eyes. Catherine was glad Valentine had not been here to see her. Unlike her, this assistant was truly desirable. Catherine imagined that she had no lack of suitors.

The girl swished away, and Mrs. Punch shook her head after her. "Lazy girl, my Clare, but she's got a good eye and can sew better than anyone else in these parts. Well, better than anyone else but me." She hobbled behind Catherine and began unfastening her gown. "Let's get this ill-fitting thing off ye and get some measurements."

A sudden flush of modesty lit her cheeks in the mirror across from her, and Catherine said, "Oh, but can't I leave the dress on?" She did not want to stand about half-naked, especially when the beautiful, rounded assistant would return any moment.

"Nonsense. Ye have nothing to be ashamed of. You're a lovely girl, and I can't stand seeing ye in that ugly dress. It's all wrong."

And so with little other choice, Catherine submitted to having Maddie's gown and stays removed, and she stood in her shift with her arms up, then out, then down as Mrs. Punch took measurement after measurement.

"Have you known Lord Valentine long?" Catherine asked when Mrs. Punch stopped to scribble a number on the paper she kept in her apron pocket.

"Oh, yes. I've known the lad since he was so high." She held her hand off the floor to about the height of Catherine's knees. "And I'll tell ye, he was always a rascal."

"I can believe that," Catherine muttered.

"The boy could argue with a tree trunk if he felt so inclined." Mrs. Punch wrapped the measuring tape around Catherine's bust, and Catherine swallowed and tried not to blush. "Never got in trouble, no, not Master Quint. Whenever he was at fault, he managed to argue his way out of it. No surprise to any of us that he ended up in Parliament."

She was writing on the pad again, and Catherine peered more closely at the older woman. "You seem proud of his accomplishments."

"Oh, the whole village is proud that one of our own done so well. Put those on my chair," she told Clare, when the assistant returned laden with various shades of muslin and silk. "And finish these measurements."

The girl obliged, taking the measuring tape and stringing it along Catherine's back. Catherine closed her eyes and tried to pretend she was somewhere else. "But Lord Valentine told me he did not grow up here," Catherine said, when the assistant had paused in her efforts and was making a note of the measurement.

"Oh, well, him and his family were here often enough."

"What is his family like?" Catherine asked, then thought better of the question, but as it was too late to take it back, she added, "As we've only just married, I do not know them very well."

Or at all.

"The Lord and Lady Ravenscroft are proud but good," Clare said, though Catherine had not been speaking to her. Mrs. Punch nodded her agreement. "Why, I never seen a noble lady who cared so much about people like us." Clare paused and glanced at her. "Excepting yourself, of course, my lady."

Catherine raised her brows. Noble lady! Ha! If only this seamstress had seen her scrubbing floors last week, she wouldn't think her so noble.

"That family has always been good to me and mine," Clare went on, while Mrs. Punch held up various colors and materials against Catherine's skin to judge their effect. "My mother hasn't been well for years, since my papa died when I was just a babe, but Lord Valentine makes sure that we have something to eat. He even gave my brother John a position as a footman at his estate."

She would have expressed her surprise, but Mrs. Punch suddenly threw a mass of blue silk over Catherine's head and shoulders. She had never thought Valentine particularly chivalrous. In fact, he appeared more single-minded. After all, hadn't he plainly told her that he wanted a wife not for love or companionship but to advance his own interests?

And still, as the fitting continued, neither Mrs. Punch nor Clare had a bad word to say about Valentine. They sang his praises, so that by the time the styles and gowns had been decided on, Catherine felt that her husband was all but a stranger. If Mrs. Punch and her assistant had the right of it, Catherine was married to the most handsome, most intelligent, most successful, kindest, and best man in all of England.

Clare left to make a note of their selections and write up the bill, and then the shop bell rang and Mrs. Punch disappeared for a moment as well. Catherine was left alone in the dressing room in her shift and bare feet. She looked about for her shoes and stays, lifted chairs and bolts of material, but she could not find either. Finally, she stood and, turning, caught sight of herself in the mirror.

What had Valentine asked her to do today? See herself as he did? He'd said she was beautiful and irresistible. Now she stared at her reflection in the mirror and tried to see that girl. She supposed that her face was not bad. Her skin was too dark, but it was smooth and clear, and her eyes were pretty. She liked their honey hazel color and their almond shape. And she liked her nose. It was straight and not too big. And her mouth was wide and she had even teeth. She smiled and admired the way her eyes lit when she was happy.

Lifting her hands, she extracted the pins from her simple hairstyle and let the mass of dark hair fall about her shoulders and back. Her hair was straight and soft but thick. She liked the way it felt when it swished against the bare skin of her arms.

To her surprise, she liked the way she looked. She was by no means the temptress Valentine described, but she was pretty.

How had she never noticed that before? Was it because she was always comparing herself to Elizabeth's petite blond beauty that she had never admired her own assets?

Clare was another blond beauty, but she was not petite. She had large breasts and hips that were barely contained by her work-worn clothing. Perhaps men like Valentine preferred women who were not so small and slim but were robust with rounded bodies.

Catherine lifted her hand to her neck and brushed the hair back over her shoulders. Her skin tingled at the sensation, and she closed her eyes and ran her hand down to her collarbone and then the drawstring of her shift. She opened her eyes, and peered about her. She could still hear Mrs. Punch speaking in the other room, and Clare did not seem to be hurrying back. With a quick motion of her hands, Catherine loosened the strings and allowed the cotton to fall down about her elbows.

In the mirror she stared at her breasts. They were the olive color of the rest of her skin, but the nipples were dark and jutted upward. In fact, now that they were free and exposed to the cool air, they hardened in much the same way they had when Valentine had kissed her this morning. She remembered the ache she'd felt and lifted a hand to cup one breast. It was heavy in her hand but also soft and full. With one finger, she flicked the hard nipple and felt a surge of pleasure rush through her. Her thighs tingled, and the skin became damp.

She took the other breast in her hand, holding them both, molding them, and then she closed her eyes and thought of Valentine doing this to her. The heat between her legs flared and burned, and she had to catch her breath.

It was a good thing she had, too, because she heard the bell outside tinkle again and the sound of Mrs. Punch's footsteps. Quickly she righted her underclothing and was just securing her drawstring again, when the older woman entered. Catherine flushed, certain her face would betray what she had been doing and thinking, but the old woman seemed not to notice.

"Oh, my! Ye look as cold as an icicle! Where are your clothes?" And she hobbled after Clare, returning with Catherine's clothing and shoes, which had been mixed in with the new materials.

She helped Catherine dress, and when Catherine looked in the mirror again, she expected to feel like her old self. But the woman in the mirror was not the Catherine she was used to. Even as she pinned up her hair and righted her clothing, she now noticed her breasts pushing against the material. She noticed the curve of her jaw and the slant of her eyes. She noticed the high color in her cheeks, and for the first time, she did feel beautiful. For the first time, she saw what a man like Valentine might see in her.

That was, if he had not forgotten her. She checked the clock and saw that it was past the hour he'd promised to claim her. She tried not to look hurt as she watched as Clare and Mrs. Punch right the store and make ready to close. As casually as possible, Catherine inched her way toward the shop's front window, peering out in search of her errant husband.

"I bet I know where Master Quint is," Mrs. Punch said. Catherine frowned. Apparently, she'd not been as surreptitious as she'd thought. "Clare, take Lady Valentine to Myrna."

Clare smiled. "Do I have to come back?"

Mrs. Punch laughed and shook her head. "No, be off with ye. Take Lady Valentine, and then yer free to gallivant about with that man of yourn. But remember what I told you. Get the ring on yer finger before ye open yer legs."

She winked at Catherine, and Catherine, supposing that she was a married woman now

and supposed to find such humor amusing, tried
to smile.

A few minutes later, Catherine was following
Clare across the main street and down an alley to
where she supposed Myrna lived. Catherine was
not certain what her husband would be doing
there, but she was prepared for anything. Like
the rest of the village, the alley was clean and the
houses small and well kept, but there were fewer
shops now, and Catherine saw more children and
dogs in the street. They continued walking until
they finally reached the end of the alley, and this
section was dark and shadowed.

Catherine felt a shiver of fear as she watched
Clare point to an old wooden house with sagging
windows and roof. The face of the house seemed
sinister, the door a yawning cavern ready to swallow her. It reminded her of home. But she took a
deep breath and followed Clare inside.

Chapter 16

Catherine ducked under the low opening to the house and squinted in at the darkness. Her nose twitched at the greasy smells of old food and the musty smell of sickness. As her eyes adjusted to the dimness, she was able to take in the small room with its hearth, rough dining table, and several children seated splayed-legged on the hard floor. Clare greeted the children by name and explained that they were her siblings and cousins.

Catherine gave them each a smile and watched as they smiled back and then returned eagerly to the porridge in their bowls. How she wished she had brought something for them. They were obviously not starving, but she knew what it was to go hungry, even if just for a few days. She would not have anyone suffer the pang of emptiness she remembered often feeling in her belly as a child.

Then Clare motioned her toward another area of the house, where a curtain had been strung to give the occupant a bit of privacy. As Catherine watched, the curtain parted and a familiar face looked out at her.

"Lord Valentine," she said in surprise.

He looked just as surprised to see her. "Catie, what are you—?" He seemed to fumble for something, and she realized he was looking at his pocket watch. "Damn, I didn't realize the time."

And then Catherine heard another voice, a female voice, though weak and frail, say, "I've kept you too long again, Master Quint. I'm sorry."

Quint turned back to the woman, whom Catherine could barely make out in the darkness behind him. "Don't talk rubbish, Myrna. It's not every day I get to see you. Besides, now you can meet my new bride." He gestured to Catherine, and she stepped closer, brushing by the coarse curtain as she ducked into the alcove where the woman lay. She was Catherine's mother's age, but shrunken by illness and confinement.

The woman reached up and grasped Catherine's hand, and she knelt beside her. "She is just as pretty as you described," the woman said to Valentine. "And what a sweet face."

Catherine smiled. "Thank you. I hope I have not disturbed you."

"Ha! I am glad to meet you. Your new husband here can talk of nothing else. I see you brought my daughter with you."

Clare stepped forward, and the woman gestured to her. "Going out again, are you?"

"Not if you need me here, Mother."

"No, go out and have a good time. All of you. I'm tired now and will sleep."

Catherine nodded, rose, and backed out of the small alcove. It was then that she noticed a large basket filled with food in the corner of the room. The basket looked familiar.

Her husband said his good-byes, swinging the children into his arms and around in a dizzying dance, before escorting Catherine from the house. When they were in the alley again, she turned to him, "That basket of food in the corner. You brought that from Ravensland. I remember seeing it in the curricle."

He looked down at her. "I did. Myrna is an old friend. She'd been sick for many years, and I promised my mother I would care for her. I send food and pay her rent, and I visit whenever I am in the village."

He took Catherine's arm and led her back toward the main street.

"You are very kind," she murmured. "You buy me dresses, you visit sick women. What other secrets do you hold?"

"You'll have to wait and see," he said with a smile, as they reached the main street. Taking her elbow, he directed her along the buildings until they reached a cheery pub with men and women from the village streaming in and out. The owner's wife greeted them warmly, saying, "Milord, it is so good of you to come and sup with us. It's a bit busy today. Would you like me to sit you somewhere quiet?"

Valentine nodded. "Please. Then bring us two glasses of wine and some of the crusty bread you make so well."

The woman smiled with pleasure at the compliment, seated them at a table in the back, and, having delivered them two glasses of wine, scurried away to see to the bread and a bowl of her best stew. Valentine sipped his wine and sat back. Catherine marveled that he looked as comfortable here as he did on the back of a horse or in his well-appointed office.

She looked about the pub and noticed that while the locals were interested in them, they did not stare or ogle. They weren't about their business, only tipping their hats or nodding politely when she caught their eye.

The pub itself was large and cozy, with rows of tables and benches and several smaller tables and chairs in the back, where she was seated. The ceilings were high and the walls filled with paintings. Catherine looked at the walls beside her and saw that they were actually seated beside a curtain leading to another room. The curtain was parted slightly, and she could see a bed and a chair on the other side.

"They rent that room out for the night," Valentine told her. "I don't imagine the occupants get very much sleep, but it's better than nothing when you can't afford one of the rooms upstairs."

Catherine looked away from the curtain and went back to sipping her wine.

"Did you have a good afternoon?" he asked, after they sat in silence for some time. "Were the gowns Mrs. Punch selected to your liking?"

"Yes." She nodded to the woman as their bowls of stew and warm crusty bread arrived. "Mrs. Punch has a very good eye, as does her assistant. I believe she said the first gown will arrive in a matter of days."

Valentine scooped up stew onto his bread and took a large bite. "Of course, you'll have gowns made in London as well. But Mrs. Punch knows the latest styles. She will do a good enough job for the present."

Catherine watched as the pub door opened again, and Clare entered. She had changed out of her work clothes, and now wore a brightly colored dress with a low bodice that emphasized her assets. Most of the men gave her appreciative looks when she entered, and Catherine looked at Valentine to see if he had noticed; but he was tearing at another chunk of the bread.

Clare moved easily among the other locals,

speaking to some and passing among them, but she seemed to be looking for someone. And Catherine knew when she had found him by the way the girl's mouth erupted in a smile. It was a boy of seventeen or eighteen with long brown hair hanging in his face. He'd been in and out of the pub, alternately serving, cleaning the tables, and delivering tankards of ale.

And when the boy spotted her, his face went from pale and haggard to handsome and robust. Catherine smiled. The two were obviously in love.

"And what has you smiling?" Valentine said. He followed her gaze to Clare and her young man and then looked back at Catherine. "Young lovers. I should have known."

"They seem very happy," Catherine said, tasting her stew and then, taking a cue from Valentine, breaking off a piece of the bread and swabbing it through the thick chunks of meat and vegetables.

"Yes, they do. I'd like to see you that happy."

Catherine looked up. "Wooing me again, my lord?"

"I try my best. And what of you? Did you do as I suggested today? When you were bedecked in silks and laces, did you try and see yourself as I do?"

Catherine blushed, embarrassed to have her thoughts returned to her wanton behavior in Mrs. Punch's shop. "I tried," she said finally.

Behind them, the curtain swayed slightly and they heard the muted sound of voices. Catherine turned her head and saw that Clare and her young man had entered the room by a back door and were standing, talking at the far end. She could not hear their words, but the sound of their low, confidential voices was audible.

"And did you succeed?" Valentine was saying. "Did you see anything of the temptress that I see?" His voice was as low as those of the two lovers on the other side of the curtain, and it sent a shiver up her spine. Then, as she watched, the boy took Clare in his arms and bent his head to kiss her.

"I beg your pardon," she said when she saw Valentine watching her, waiting for a response.

He began to speak again, but as he did, Catherine caught sight of the couple through the crack in the curtain again. She really did mean to attend to Valentine, but she could see the lovers almost without any effort, and now the man had reached down and cupped Clare's bottom, sliding his hands over her rounded rump as the girl pressed her body against him.

Catherine's own body tingled in response, and she jumped when Valentine put a hand on her arm. "Are you well? You look a bit flushed."

"I-I'm fine," she said, and took a large gulp of her wine. Valentine frowned at her, but she gave him a weak smile, and he went back to his stew.

Catherine tried to do the same, but she found

her eyes drawn again to the lovers. She had only to move a fraction of an inch to see them. Now the boy was no longer kissing Clare's lips, but he'd moved to her neck, and his hands were loosening the low-bodiced gown she wore. As Catherine watched, he freed Clare's breasts and took each rosy nipple in his mouth. Clare threw her head back, giving him full access, and Catherine caught her breath at the quick rush of sensation she felt between her own thighs.

"She seems to be enjoying that." Valentine's voice was low, a murmur in her ear.

Catherine stiffened, and her eyes met his. He'd angled his chair so that he could see through the crack in the curtain as well, and he'd moved closer to her. Catherine had been so absorbed, she had not noticed.

"I-I was not watching," she said. Her cheeks flamed and she stared hard at the remnants of her stew.

Valentine chuckled. "You weren't watching? Is that why you didn't hear a word I said these past five minutes?"

"Perhaps we should ask for another table," Catherine said, still staring at her stew and acutely aware of Valentine beside her, his gaze on the entwined couple on the other side of the curtain. Catherine heard a low, female moan, and had to exercise great restraint to keep from lifting her head and looking.

"We probably should ask for another table," Valentine said, "but I rather like this one. Oh, now that looks like fun."

She snapped her head up and stared at him. "Sir, you should not be looking. It is obscene."

His eyes met hers. "Obscene? How?"

She shook her head, unable to explain, and not wanting to. But he kept his gaze on her face and waited. Finally, she was able to stammer, "Wh-what they are doing. It is not right."

"Not right? If it is not right, then you and I and all of these people in this room are wrong. How do you think you came to be, Catie?"

She shook her head and looked away from him, inadvertently catching sight of the couple again. Now Clare's breasts were completely exposed, and the boy had her seated on the bed. He was kneeling before her, ruching up her skirt, while she kneaded his hard member through his pants.

Catherine looked away. "I understand how children come about, sir. But that is not their intention. They are doing this solely for—"

"For what?" he said, his gaze flicking past her. Her heart sped up when she imagined what he saw. "For pleasure?"

She nodded. "Yes, and that is obscene."

He took her chin between two fingers and brought her gaze to his face. "Are you telling me that feeling pleasure is obscene? That the physical expression of love between two people is obscene?"

She had not thought of it that way, and she had no ready answer.

"Look again through that curtain, Catie," he said, releasing her chin. "Now you tell me if what you see is obscene."

The couple was close together again, she still sitting on the bed, he kneeling on the floor before her. His hands were under her skirts, but he'd risen up and was kissing her passionately. Clare returned the kiss with equal fervor.

Valentine whispered in Catherine's ear. "What is obscene about that? Was it obscene when I kissed you this morning? When I touched you?"

"No." She watched Clare move against the boy and remembered her own urge to move closer to Valentine. "No, but you did not touch me like that."

He chuckled softly, his breath tickling her ear. "Oh, but I want to. Look how the lad has lowered her gown, how her breasts spill forth. If that were you, I would bury my face in your flesh, kissing your nipples until they were hard pebbles against my tongue."

"Sir!" Catherine shifted uncomfortably in her chair as warm wetness dampened her thighs. Her own breasts tingled in response to his words, her nipples growing hard once again. "You should not say such things."

"Would you rather I do them?" And then she felt his hand, solid and light, on her knee.

"No, you mustn't," she hissed.

"Look through the curtain," he said. "Do you see where his hands are?"

Lord help her, but she could not stop herself from looking.

"Tell me what you see," Valentine prodded, even as she felt him lift her skirts under the table. She glanced about the room, praying no one could see what he was doing. But no one was looking at them, and Valentine's body blocked hers from view.

"Tell me what he is doing, Catie."

She glanced behind the curtain again and cleared her throat. "He is touching her."

"How?" Valentine murmured, his hand sliding under her skirts to touch the bare skin of her knee. "Where?"

Catherine could barely find her voice. She could not believe she was answering Valentine's questions, allowing him to touch her thus. But his warm hand felt so good on her, that she could not seem to stop her words from tumbling out. "He's sliding his hand up her thigh."

Valentine's own hand slid up her thigh. She shivered.

"And then he slides it back down again."

Valentine complied and then repeated the gesture. As Catherine watched, the boy did the same to Clare, but his hands were not on the top of Clare's thighs, as Valentine's were.

Catherine tried to speak and had to clear her throat again. "His hands slide up the inside of her thigh."

Valentine paused for just a moment, and Catherine almost turned to look at him, but she dared not meet his gaze. She would feel too much shame at what she was doing then. Valentine's hand slid up her inner thigh and back down again, and Catherine gasped.

"You like that," Valentine said, his hand stroking her flesh again, this time his fingers reaching even higher so that Catherine had to restrain herself from moving to meet him. "Now what is the lad doing?"

Lord, help her but she knew if she said it Valentine would do it. "He's spreading her legs."

"And what is she doing?"

Catherine glanced at Clare as Valentine's hand exerted gentle pressure, widening her own legs, just as she'd hoped and feared. "She's sitting on the bed, bare on top, her head thrown back." Indeed, Clare's chest was heaving, and she appeared to be mewing with pleasure, and then Catherine gasped.

"Now what?"

"He has—he has just—" But she could not finish, and Valentine looked past her, then leaned back and smiled.

"I would like to do that to you." As he spoke,

he spread her legs farther and worked his fingers in ever-widening circles. Catherine could not stop herself from scooting just a bit farther down the seat. She needed him to touch her there.

Valentine was saying, "I would like to take you home, lay you on the bed, and spread your legs, as I am now. And then I would delve between them and kiss you here." As he spoke, his fingers caressed her core, and she almost jumped from the pure pleasure in it.

She glanced through the curtain again and saw the boy's head between Clare's legs. She leaned back on her elbows, her breasts jutting out, her breaths coming in ragged moans. Catherine moaned herself as Valentine continued to caress her, his fingers moving assuredly over her sensitive skin. And then he entered her, softly at first, with just the tip of one finger, but she almost jumped off the chair.

"Easy," he said, as though he were calming a skittish horse. "I feel how wet you are," he whispered in her ear when she was still again. "My fingers are damp with your excitement."

He stroked her again, allowing another finger to enter her. Catherine tried to remain still, but she could not stop her body from writhing subtly against his hand. She prayed no one would see them, she prayed he would cease, and she prayed he would never cease.

Her gaze flicked to the couple again, and she saw that Clare's legs were shaking now, spread far, and taut with effort. Her gasps of pleasure were far too loud, and Catherine feared the whole pub might hear. And then she realized that what she heard were her own gasps in her ears as Valentine's fingers stroked her, bringing her higher and higher until she could not think, until she was so warm and the heat so intense that she was certain she would burn up.

And then she exploded. Her knee hit the underside of the table, but she did not feel any pain. All she felt were spirals of bone-numbing heat hurtling through her so that every muscle went limp and flaccid, and her entire body was heavy with pleasure.

And then she opened her eyes, and her gaze met Valentine's.

One, two, three . . .

Oh, Lord, she did not know what to say, what to do. How could she have allowed this to happen? She was obviously a very wanton woman.

"I-I—" she trailed off, unsure what to say. Finally, she managed, "I didn't know I could feel like that."

"I spoke to you of pleasure," Valentine said softly. "The marriage bed holds many pleasures."

She met his gaze again, and he reached out and stroked a lock of her hair back. Under the table, he righted her skirts and slowly brought his hand into view again. She stared at it. It was an ordinary hand, and yet it had given her so much pleasure.

"You're embarrassed," he said, his eyes full of concern. "I'm sorry. I should not have done that here. I just wanted to show you—" His gaze moved to the curtain again, and she followed. The boy was now standing, and Clare was unfastening his bulging trousers.

"I think it best we go now," Valentine said, taking her hand. He tossed the owner a pound as they exited and then led her quickly to where his curricle waited.

It was dark by the time they left the village. They rode back in silence, Catherine barely breathing for fear Valentine would hear and mistake the sound for an opening for conversation. She could not speak to him, not because she was angry or even embarrassed any further but because she wanted to keep what she felt close to her heart.

In the space of only a few days, everything she had thought she knew about men, and especially about Quint Childers, had been turned upside down. Men were not all violent brutes who sought to hurt women. They did not all drink to excess and then launch into tirades, terrifying their wives and children. Valentine had either spent his time quietly reading in his office or with her. He cared about reform and about the less fortunate.

He treated his servants and indeed all that he met well. He treated her well. He was understanding and authoritative but not a bully. He hadn't pounced on her, even when it was clear he wanted her. He treated her gently, with respect. When he took her riding, he had given her his best horse. He had made sure she would receive the best dresses.

And then when they had been in the pub and had seen Clare and her young man, he had not scolded her for looking or taunted, he had found it as arousing as she. He found her arousing, and had awakened a passion within her she did not know existed.

She had not known it could be this way between a man and a woman. She had not known men could give pleasure as well as pain. And now she was torn. She knew, even without the physical closeness developing between them, that she was beginning to have feelings for Valentine. He was a man above men, and she feared that he was too good to be true. What if she misjudged him? What if she gave herself to him, became his wife in all things, made this marriage true and real, and then it proved the wrong decision? What if Quint Childers was not the man she hoped?

She stared at the ring he'd given her.

And what if he was?

Chapter 17

The next few days were painful for Quint. He felt as though he were constantly on edge, constantly aware of his wife, and constantly aroused by her.

He had not intended it to happen. At the start of this seduction, he had planned to remain emotionally detached. But every day he spent with her weakened his resolve.

They had gone riding every morning and for walks in the afternoon. They supped together and sat in his study after dinner, reading and talking. Over all that time, how could he not notice that she had a quick mind and a kind heart? Even worse, she seemed to grow lovelier each day. When the first two gowns had come from

Mrs. Punch's, Quint had been amazed at the transformation that gowns designed for Catherine had made.

Catherine changed from a lovely young woman to a true beauty, her exotic complexion and those honey hazel eyes making her even more alluring. His desire for her reached heights he could not remember feeling for any other woman.

He watched her, even when she did not know he did, and he knew she watched him too. She was contemplating their marriage, considering— he hoped—coming to him, to his bed, becoming his wife in truth. He still slept on the chaise longue in their bedroom, and he had not pushed her to change this. He would not. He wanted her invitation, not her acquiescence.

That did not mean he did not take any liberties. She allowed him to hold her hand and to wrap an arm about her, and he kissed her as often as possible. She allowed the kisses and kissed him back, but she did not allow their embraces to go beyond a few fervent caresses. She did not allow what had happened in the village pub to happen again.

Despite his slow pace, Quint was not dissatisfied with his progress. He wanted her in his bed—rather, wanted to share his bed with her— but he wanted her as trusting, loving wife even more. She was becoming that woman every day, and he only wished he could speed the process along. The letters and documents he received from Meeps each evening increased Quint's hopes for attaining the Cabinet seat. But Meeps also reiterated the need for Valentine to be in London. Fairfax was beginning to mount his own campaign for the seat.

And Quint felt the pressure. Why had he married at such an inopportune time?

He knew why. Because he'd thought his wife would be an instant asset to his career, not force him into seclusion in the country. But if he returned to London now, what would happen to the burgeoning relationship between Catie and him? What would happen when she was thrust into his world and forced to stand on her own?

He would have liked to keep her here forever, sheltering her from the harshness of his life in London. He would have liked to keep her safe, but he knew that path would only lead to resentment. He needed a wife who could be his political counterpart. He needed a wife who made him happy at home and in the political arena. He could not love a woman who could not give him both—at least that's what he told himself because the truth was that she had made a muddle of all his calculated plans. He wanted to keep his emotions out of this relationship, and yet each day he felt his heart opening to her.

He wanted to change his wife into the political savvy hostess he needed, and yet the better he knew Catie, the more he admired her for who she was.

It wasn't supposed to be this way. It was supposed to be purely physical, and here he was beginning to care for the bloody woman. He didn't have time for emotions.

He had a career to think of.

That night, after dinner, they sat in his study as usual, and he pored over Meeps's latest correspondence, while she sipped tea and read from a book. While she turned her pages placidly, he read line after line and became more agitated.

"What are you reading?" Catherine asked, looking up from her book. "You are frowning as though another war has broken out."

He looked up at her, torn between telling her and putting all business aside and devoting the rest of the night to stealing kisses from her lovely mouth. She saw him looking at her, and her eyes darkened in a way he was coming to know well. She wanted him to steal kisses.

Instead, he exercised the small measure of restraint he still possessed, sat back, and said, "I think the country has been good for you. You seem happy and well."

She smiled. "I'm both. I don't know why I argued against coming."

"Because you feared you would miss your friends. Do you?"

She set her book down and uncurled her legs from underneath her. "Yes, I suppose now that you mention it, I do miss my cousins, though I have had letters from them, and that helps. But it is nice to be away from London, to have the quiet of the country and the solitude."

Quint frowned. He was thinking of taking her back into an even noisier, more populated world than she had ever lived before.

"What is wrong?" she said again. "You seem displeased."

In a short time, she'd become quite adept at reading his moods. Perhaps she was so intuitive because she'd had to live with a difficult and domineering father. Whatever the reason, she had read him well. "Displeased? No, not at all. I have been thinking." About taking you back to London. Even more about taking you to bed.

She didn't speak, merely waited with one arched brow for what he would say next. A week ago, she would have shrunk back, fearful of his conclusions, but now she knew him better, had learned to trust him.

"Would you like to return to London?" he asked. "Are you ready?"

She blinked, obviously not expecting his suggestion. "We have barely been at Ravensland a week. I thought we would stay longer."

He shrugged. "We might." The stack of correspondence on his desk mocked him at that. He could no more afford to stay in the country than he could afford to pay off the endless debts of the prince regent's residence Carlton House. "Honestly, I need to get back to work. But I don't want to rush you," he said, allowing his gaze to lift from the piles of paper on his desk and drift back to hers. "I want you to be happy."

She smiled then, but her eyes were sad. "You've sacrificed so much for me." She rose and came to him, walking with the graceful stride of a long-legged woman. At that moment, he didn't feel as though he'd sacrificed at all. Politics seemed to fade into the background, and all he could think was how he yearned to see those legs, caress them, have them wrapped around him, clamped tight.

"I am very happy here in the country." She came around his desk. "You make me happy."

She stood before him and he reached out and cupped her waist in his hands, drawing her between his knees. She went without protest, allowing his touch and seeming comfortable with it.

The color was rising in her face, and he knew she felt the thrill of being this close to him, much as his own blood began to thrum in his veins when she was within reach.

And then she said something completely unexpected. "What can I do to please you?"

Quint did not answer for a long, long time, fearing he'd misheard her.

Finally, she said, "You've given me everything that I want and need. I want to give you something."

"Allow me to come to your bed," he murmured, his voice husky as the words all but caught in his throat. "Invite me to your bed tonight."

She glanced away, looking at something he

could not see, and then she leaned down and gave him a kiss filled with promise. A moment later, she was gone. He could hear her steps on the stairs, and then all was silent.

Catherine stood in their room before the cheval mirror and tried to take deep, calming breaths. She had known this night would come. She had been anticipating it for days now, even wanting it to come. Since that day in the village, she had watched Valentine. No, not Valentine—Quint was his name, and she would use it. She had watched him partly out of self-protection. If he were not the man he seemed, he would do something to give himself away. But the more she watched, the more she grew to care for him. He was gentle with his horse. He was kind to the stable lads. He did not overtax his servants with labor. He was agreeable even when she knew something troubled his mind, as it did tonight.

He was more than the ambitious politician she had initially thought him to be. Certainly his career mattered to him, but perhaps it was not all. Perhaps he had learned to care for her enough that he could accept her limitations, and they could be happy as they had been this past week. She worried now that he wanted to return to London. Elizabeth would be there. Undoubtedly, her sister had used this time to formulate a plan to snatch Quint back. But Catherine wanted to trust him. She wanted to believe he would not be tempted by Elizabeth. Catherine wanted to believe the desire in his eyes was for her alone.

And she desired him. He'd awakened something in her that night in the village pub. Now it seemed all she had to do was look at his hands, and her whole body was aware and alive. How she yearned for those hands to touch her again, stroke her, bring her pleasure. But she had not allowed it. She had kissed him and been held by him and stroked him as boldly as she dared, but she had not allowed his hands to wander where she truly wished.

Tonight was the end of the restraint. She had known what he would say when she'd asked how to please him. She had known what he wanted because she wanted it, too, and now, nervous as she was, she must submit.

She glanced in her mirror again and straightened the long, flimsy nightrail she wore. It was white, and she could see the outline of her body beneath the material. She pulled the matching robe closed, but it too was flimsy and did little to preserve her modesty.

She glanced behind her at the door to the hallway beyond. She wondered how many other skittish brides stared at doors tonight, preparing for their husbands to walk through. She wondered if they felt half the fear and exhilaration that she did. She prayed he would not hurt her—her body or her heart—and she prayed she would please him.

A moment later, she heard his soft tapping on their door. It would have been easy then to jump in bed and feign sleep. He would not be angry. Instead, she said, "Come."

He'd obviously been anticipating this. He carried a bottle of wine and two glasses, which he set down on the bedside table. Then he blew out the lamps so that the room was lit only by candlelight. When he was finished, he poured the wine and held one of the glasses out to her.

"You look lovely," he said, and she knew he meant it. His gaze traveled over her white silk nightgown and robe appreciatively, and Catherine made a mental note when she was next in the village to thank Mrs. Punch for sending it.

As Valentine did not immediately leap on her when he came into their room, she took another cautious step forward. He remained where he was, holding the wineglass out to her. "I'm not going to attack you, Catie," he said finally, still holding both wineglasses. "You are in control."

She frowned, relieved and annoyed at the same time. How was she supposed to be in control? She did not know what to do. She wanted him to take her and kiss her senseless so that she did not have to think about what she was doing. She wanted to step back and allow this thing to happen to her, not take responsibility for it. But he was obviously not going to allow her that luxury.

He was still holding the wineglasses and, needing fortification, she put aside her fear and went to him, taking one of the glasses in her hand.

Hands free, he now set about removing some of his clothing. With quick efficiency, he stripped off tailcoat, waistcoat, and cravat and opened his shirt at the throat. Her gaze trailed down the snowy white of his shirt to where it ended in the waistband of his charcoal trousers. The trousers were tight, molding to his legs in a way that made her catch her breath.

She'd all but drained the liquid before she heard his low chuckle. She glanced up, gaze meeting his.

"Nervous?" he said.

"No," she answered immediately, and then swallowed the remaining contents of her glass. She looked at the empty vessel. "Perhaps a little. I-I don't know what I'm supposed to do." Her cheeks went hot, and she wished she had a hood so that he would not see her blushing yet again.

But he only placed a finger under her chin and notched her gaze back up to his. "What do you want to do? Whatever you want will be right."

She considered this, embarrassed that she had wants at all, really. Weren't men supposed to be the sex with wants and desires? But she was here now, and she had to do something if she ever wanted this ordeal to be over. She tried to remember the way she'd felt in the pub, and when her legs grew weak at the memory, she said, "I want you to kiss me."

Valentine—Quint, rather—smiled and lowered his head, obliging her. But the kiss was not what she wanted. It was quick and perfunctory. She wanted much more. He pulled back and then raised a brow. He made her insides melt when he did that.

"What's wrong, sweetling? Not what you'd had in mind?"

She shook her head.

"Then you must tell me what you need me to do." He took a sip of his wine, and then retrieved her glass and set both of them aside.

"I want you to kiss me," she said again, but when he made to kiss her in much the same way, she stopped him with a hand on his chest. Oh, dear. His skin felt very nice under her fingertips.

"No, not like that," she managed, though her voice was low and husky. "Kiss me"—she lowered her voice, mortified at the words that were about to escape her lips—"with your tongue."

She saw those dark mahogany eyes grow even darker at her words, and he bent to do her will.

His tongue entered her lips, mating with hers. She could not stop her entire body from shaking at the sensation of his lips claiming hers.

Her hand, still on his chest, seemed to smolder and catch fire from the heat of him, but as his gentle plundering of her mouth grew more insistent, as he opened her lips and delved inside, she found her hand closing on the material of his shirt and pulling him closer.

And then, just when she had begun to feel so warm and her body had begun to ache so that she needed to rub against him to decrease the building pressure, he stepped back and broke the kiss. She gasped from shock and indignation, but he only lifted his wineglass and drank again.

"What's wrong?" he said, watching her over the rim of the glass, the liquid red and fiery in his hands. "Was the kiss not to your liking?"

She wet her lips, wanting to speak but feeling the bands of propriety choking her voice. "May I have another?" She indicated her empty glass, and he nodded and went to refill it. She watched him walk across the room, stunned to find herself admiring the way the trousers fit his backside. She remembered how his bottom had looked without those trousers. She licked her lips again.

He turned back and, caught staring, she quickly averted her gaze. He handed her the refilled glass and then took a seat on the bed. She swallowed a good deal more of the red wine than she'd intended before she had the nerve to say, "Will you kiss me again?"

"Is that what you want?" he asked, and she felt like hitting him. Of course it was what she wanted—that and a great deal more. Why did the obstinate man insist on playing games?

"Yes. I want you to kiss me again. Like the last time. Only . . . more."

He grinned. "More?" Reaching toward her, his

hand looped in the sash of her robe, and he pulled her closer. "I want more as well. May I see more?"

She nodded, her throat so dry and parched, she could not speak. She watched as his hands worked the knot she'd made in front of the mirror. With patience and skill, he loosed the knot and parted her robe. Her body grew warm and liquid as his gaze devoured every inch of her. Slowly, he slipped the robe down her arms. The feel of the silk sliding off her shoulders was so delicious and the cool air such a contrast to his hot gaze that she closed her eyes to savor it.

When she opened them again, he patted the space on the bed beside him. "Come and sit here."

Her heart sped up as she stared at their bed. She had slept in it for a week. It was large, far too large for only her, and it was covered with a plush velvet blue counterpane. When she had slept in the bed alone, she had no trouble imagining that it would sleep three or four people easily. But now that he sat perched on it, the bed looked tiny. Anywhere she sat on it would be too close to him to calm the pounding of her heart. And yet she wanted to be this close to him.

He lifted a hand and caressed her cheek, then ran his fingers through her loosened hair until his fingers kneaded her tense neck muscles. She began to relax, to close her eyes and lean into his ministrations, when he pulled her to him.

With more slow, tantalizing skill, he kissed her

again. And again, the kiss was over far too quickly. This time when he pulled back to grasp his wineglass, she caught his hand in hers, stopping the glass's progress.

She guided his hand and the glass to her own mouth, took a small sip, but held the liquid inside her mouth. And then she kissed him, giving him the wine when he parted her lips. He groaned quietly, and she felt the low primal sound deep in her belly. She put her hand on his neck, then in his hair, wrapping her fingers in it and pulling his mouth to hers. She kissed him. Or more accurately, she devoured him, at least that was how she felt. But she needed him at that moment. She needed much more than the stingy kisses he'd given, and he seemed to sense this and abandon all games and kissed her fully back.

At some point her hands moved from his head to his open shirt. She fumbled with the fabric, parting it further, then bending to kiss the exposed skin of his neck. His pulse beat rapidly there, and his scent was heavy. The scents she always associated with him—spring, leather saddles, and pine were there—but she smelled something else as well. Something dark and musky and undeniably him. It made her heady and drew her mouth again and again to kiss and nip and take him there, and she began to think of the scent as the smell of arousal.

She was nipping along his throat, small quick bites with her teeth, when she heard him drop his glass. And then his hands were on her, and he lifted her into his lap. He cradled her bottom before setting her down, and then she felt the hard bulge of his manhood.

She pulled away, suddenly afraid, but he held her with one hand just above her waist. He was out of breath, and for some reason that pleased her. "What do you want now, Catie?" He gasped out. "Remember, I am in your control."

She certainly didn't feel in control. Her head was spinning, and she could hardly get her bearings. But when she looked in his eyes she felt everything lock into place. "Kiss me again," she said and leaned forward, ready to assist him from her new position, but he stopped her by leaning back slightly.

"Is that all you want? Just a kiss?"

"Yes, of course—" But then the image of Clare in the pub flitted across her brain, and she glanced down at her own nightrail. "Kiss me here," she said, lifting a hand and caressing her neck from her chin to the hollow at the base of her throat.

His hands were still about her waist, and he pulled her close so that her breasts brushed against him. And then she felt his firm, warm lips on her throat. They teased and traced and tantalized her until she let out a low moan and felt herself arch for him. His tongue darted out, and he ran it down the column of her neck, making her shiver with desire at the wet trail that cooled as his mouth moved.

Then he pulled away and looked up at her, awaiting further instructions. They were difficult for her to give. She had never given a man orders as long as she had lived. She had feared men and their directives and feared the possibility that she would ever be in the position for a man to order her into his bed.

But with Valentine it was different. Tonight he took orders, did not give them. He waited for her, his gaze patient and filled with desire for her. He wanted her, but she also knew with absolute certainty that if she were to stand and walk away from him, he would allow her to go.

"What are you thinking?" he said suddenly. "I can see something going on behind those beautiful honey eyes."

She glanced down. "I was thinking that if I wanted to stop now, if I wanted to go, you would allow it."

He tensed—her only indication her words displeased him—then he relaxed his hold on her waist so that he would catch her if she lost her balance, but he did not restrain her.

"If you want to stop," he said, tilting his head so that he met her gaze, "that is your choice. You are in control. I mean that."

She nodded, seeing the truth in his face. "What are you thinking?" she asked, her heart speeding up when the words left her mouth.

He raised a brow. "Provocative question, Lady Valentine. Are you sure you want to know?" His hands tightened on her waist again, caressing her through the nightgown until they molded to her hips and adjusted her so that she was pressing directly against his erection.

"Yes," she said on a breathless sigh. "I want to know."

"I am thinking"—he leaned into her and kissed her neck again—"that you are the most beautiful woman in the world."

She shivered as his lips trailed over her skin, warming it as he traced the curve of her jaw. "That's not true. There are many women—"

"To me, you are the most beautiful." His teeth nipped her earlobe and she let out a small moan. "Do you want to know what else I am thinking?"

"Tell me," she ordered, wiggling just a bit from the tickle of his breath in her ear.

"I am thinking how much I love your scent. You smell like peaches. And I wonder if you taste of them, too. If the skin of your breasts and your stomach"—he touched her lightly in the places he spoke of as he talked—"and your thighs taste as sweet and succulent."

She swayed as his hands grazed her thighs and then rested on her hips again, holding her up. "What else are you thinking?" she whispered, eager for more of his words, his seduction.

"I am thinking how much I want you. How I want to lay you down beneath me and drive into you until you are writhing from pleasure."

She had a brief flash of her father's angry face

and remembered her mother's screams. Fear sparked inside her, and she drew back, but Valentine caught her. "What is it?"

She shook her head. "Nothing. Something you said reminded me—" Tears pricked her eyes, and he put a finger over her lips.

"Shh. Don't think of that tonight. Let me change the look in your haunted eyes. Let me show you that my touch can pleasure you. Will you let me prove to you that I would not harm you for anything?"

"Show me," she said. "I'm so tired of being afraid." He kissed her again, a soothing kiss full of sweetness and care, and then he drew back and buried his face in her hair. With trembling fingers, she lifted her hands and let them find their own way to the knotted strings of her nightgown. As he pulled back, she loosened the strings and let the gown fall down her arms and about her waist.

He stared at her, then met her gaze.

"Kiss me here," she said, letting a finger trail over one erect nipple. "And kiss me here." Her hand went to the other breast, and then she cupped both and offered herself to him.

He did not pause, and she felt his hot breath on her flesh as he loved her with her mouth, sucking and licking and laving her until she was arched back and breathing heavily. The more he touched her, the more she wanted his touch. She needed him, the ache in her heart and between her legs growing to almost unbearable heights. She ground against him, ignoring her wanton behavior, only seeking to assuage the twinge between her thighs.

And then she was beneath him. His weight was more of a comfort than a prison, and he was stripping off her nightgown and kissing her everywhere, loving her flesh with his hands and his mouth and his eyes.

He sat back and looked at her, then lifted his own shirt over his head, revealing his muscled chest. He was a politician but no stranger to hard work and exercise, and when she ran her hands over his abdomen, she admired the hard ridges of his muscles. He had a light sprinkling of golden brown hair on his chest, which tapered to a line below his belly button and disappeared beneath his trousers. Catherine followed the line of that hair down with one fingertip, but Quint stopped her before she could touch the part of him that made her truly curious.

"Let's take this slow," he said, his voice almost a groan. "Let me love you first. If you're ready, there's less chance I'll give you any pain."

She nodded, and he began to slip off the bed. "Where are you going?" she asked, propping herself on her elbows. She was embarrassed by her nakedness at first, but the longer he looked at her, the less self-conscious she felt. There was only desire in his eyes, only pleasure at what he saw, and Catherine reveled in it. She wanted him to look at her, wanted him to desire her.

"I'm not going anywhere," he said. "But I need you to come closer." Then grasping her about the hips, he pulled her to the edge of the bed and parted her knees, standing between them.

She gasped, feeling vulnerable and excited at her new position. He leaned over her, planting his hands at her sides. "Do you remember that night in the village pub?"

She nodded. The memory was all too clear to her. She wanted Quint to make her feel that way again.

"Do you remember what that young man was doing to that girl?"

"Clare? Yes," she whispered.

"I want to do that to you. But I have to have your permission."

She nodded, her legs feeling numb and tingly at the thought of his mouth between them.

"So I have your permission to part your legs like this?" He nudged her knees apart until she was open to him. He kept his gaze on her face until she gave her consent, and then he looked down, wetting his lips at the sight of her.

Catherine's heart pounded so hard she feared it would burst, and the burst of heat between her legs at the intensity of his stare made her cry out. She emitted a low moan as he reached toward her. "Touch me," she pleaded, watching his hand move far too slowly. "Touch me there."

His fingers brushed against her lightly, and she threw back her head and moaned again. This was what she had wanted. This was the feeling that had given her dreams, that wakened her sweaty and full of need.

"Catie," he murmured, fingers still caressing her. "I want more. With your permission, I'm going to get on my knees."

She made a sound that was incomprehensible even to her, but she felt him lower himself.

"And now I'm going to kiss you. Here." His fingers pressed her sensitive flesh again, and then they withdrew. "May I kiss you here?" he asked.

"Yes," she said. "Please."

At first she felt nothing but the warmth of his body between her legs, the rasp of his stubble on her inner thigh, and the gentle pressure of his mouth against the juncture between her legs. And then she felt his tongue—at least she thought it was his tongue.

His touch was light and delicious, darting against her sensitive skin. The contrast between the whisper of his mouth and the intense, rapturous sensation overwhelmed her.

She couldn't think at all. There was nothing but sensation. Nothing but white heat and pulsing pleasure. Nothing but the zing of blood in her veins and the spiral of pleasure spinning through her body until she rose with it, lifting herself up and screaming her release.

Chapter 18

Quint stepped out of his boots, freed his erection from his trousers, and stripped off the last of his clothing. Naked, he stretched out beside Catie and allowed one hand to rest on the curve of her olive-skinned hip. Her back was to him, but he could hear her all but purring with the pleasure of her climax. The sound of her contentment gave him immense satisfaction. He didn't think he'd ever like anything better than giving Catie fulfillment.

Gradually, Catie turned toward him. Her eyes were heavy-lidded as she looked at him, and he couldn't stop what he knew must be a cocky smile. "Feeling better now?"

"Umm-hmm." She closed her eyes and

stretched. He took the opportunity to allow his gaze to travel the length of her naked body. Her legs were as long as he'd anticipated, her thighs slim and muscled like a good Thoroughbred's. He could picture those legs wrapped around him, her rounded hips rising to meet his every thrust.

When he looked back into her face, she was watching him. "Thank you," she said, her hand reaching out to trail a finger lazily over his mouth. He closed his eyes and soaked in the moment of tenderness. He had not had many such moments in the last ten years.

She ran her finger over his lips and then across his cheek and over his eyes. Her touch was light and exploratory, as though she wanted to memorize every inch of his face. Then her hand strayed to his neck and his shoulder. She pushed lightly, indicating she wanted him on his back, and he obliged her, knowing what she would see when he moved to allow her more access.

Her hand trailed down his chest and then stopped. He felt her tense beside him and opened his eyes to find her looking down. His erection hardened and throbbed the longer she stared. "I still want you," he said quietly, and her eyes jerked up to his. "But the decision is yours. We can stop now, if you like."

She blinked. "That hardly seems fair."

"Fairness is subjective, and the sole property of those who make the rules. Tonight you make the rules. What do you think is fair?"

She chewed her lip and looked down at him again. "I think it only fair you feel the same pleasure I did."

He nodded. "There are many ways to accomplish that, but only one that will truly make you my wife."

"Is that what you want?" she said.

"More than anything."

"Then I want that, too. What do I have to do?"

"I'm afraid I will hurt you this first time." He leaned over her, pushing her back against his bed gently and stroking a lock of her hair back from her face. "Will you tell me if it hurts too much?"

She nodded, and he could see the fear creep back into her eyes. He couldn't resist propping himself up on one elbow and kissing her. And then he could not resist touching her, running his hands over her body in much the same way she had touched him only a few moments before. He learned the texture of her skin, the dips and the rises of her body, the weight of her breasts and the swell of her hip.

It was not long before her fear subsided, and he heard her breathing catch and then come in shorter bursts once again. She was wonderfully responsive, this bride who was to be his wife. She was a confusing mixture of temerity and confidence, trust and wariness. She was a work in progress—an early draft that was awkward but so genuine that he could not help but feel tenderness for her. And she gave it in return.

How he needed something tender and genuine
in his life. The rhetoric, the political shouldering
and selling—he'd mastered and thrived on them.
He could be a bully when he need be. He could
wheedle and he could demand and he could
compromise.

But here, at home, he just wanted to be Quint.
He wanted tenderness and pleasure and his
wife's contented sighs. She moaned beneath him,
and he nudged her legs apart, this time settling
himself between them. He was gentle and careful not to crush her with his weight. Her eyes
fluttered open at this new feeling, but he kissed
her again, and after a few minutes she relaxed
and began to respond.

She was soft and pliant under him. She also
felt small and vulnerable, and he ached to protect
her and to bring her pleasure as well. He worried
that between her fear and his complete lack of
experience with virgins, this first time would not
bring her much pleasure. He tried to think of the
many nights to come.

It was not difficult to think of her on other
nights and in other positions. He imagined her
on top of him, her breasts jutting out as she
arched back and took him inside her. He imagined her looking over her shoulder at him as he
entered her from behind. And he thought of her
in his arms, both of them lying sated after a night
of lovemaking.

He could imagine her heavy with his child;

then smiling at him with a baby in her arms; then coming to greet him, leading their children by tiny, unsteady hands. He wanted all of this from her, and it began tonight.

He'd been stroking her breasts and her stomach, but now he reached between them and stroked the moist slit between her legs. She was warm and wet, and he knew she was ready for him—her body, if not her mind.

"Sweetling," he whispered, and her eyes fluttered. She moaned as his fingers found the hard nub between her folds. "I'm going to enter you now."

It was the closest he could come to asking her permission. It was already taking most of his willpower to keep from plunging into her.

"Yes," she moaned, pressing against him. "Yes, I want you inside me."

He rose up and inserted the tip of his manhood. She moaned again, and he paused, knowing that her pleasure might soon end. "I'll try to be gentle," he murmured, entering her more fully and feeling his own pleasure build just as he encountered her barrier.

She was still moving against him, moaning and asking him for more. Her pleas and the feel of her tightening around him were driving him to madness. He pulsed and throbbed inside her, wanting to thrust hard and deep, but holding himself back. And then he felt the prick of her fingernails dent the flesh of his back, and he could hold off no longer. As slowly and gently as he could, he broke her barrier, opening her up, and entering her fully.

He bit his lip to stop the cry of ecstasy. She was so hot and tight. God, she felt so good. He moved within her and almost came. The only thing that stopped him was the small prick of pain in his back.

He opened his eyes and looked into her frightened face.

"I'm hurting you," he said, seeing the pain now and the tears escaping onto her cheeks.

She nodded. "You-you're too big. You don't fit."

"It's only this first time," he murmured, lowering his mouth to kiss her gently. "I'm fitting you to me, sweetling. After this time, I promise our joining will bring you nothing but pleasure."

He moved within her again, and her nails dug deeper.

"Do you want me to stop?" he asked. God, he prayed she would not ask him to stop, but he mentally girded himself for the possibility. He could still cease, but if he did not pull out soon, he would not be able to control himself. Already, instinct began overriding reason. Unable to resist, he moved within her, sliding against her sleek folds. He bit back a groan.

"Sweetling," he said between clenched teeth, "if you want me to stop, you have to say so now. I can't"—he moved inside her again, thrusting deeper into her warmth—"hold on much longer."

And then he felt her legs wrap around him, and her body relax enough so that she seemed to accommodate him. "You are my husband now in truth," she said, and kissed him with passion. "Don't stop."

He didn't. He was gentle and cautious, holding back as much as he could until the urge to plunge into her a final time overtook him. He was aware that her fingernails dug into his bunched shoulders, that she smelled like peaches and him, and that he had never known he could feel so much pleasure. And then he could hold back no longer, and he didn't want to. He went over the edge and plunged into her with body and soul.

When they finally parted, he pulled her close and fit his body around her, cradling her in his arms. "Next time," he whispered into her hair, "I promise I'll give you only pleasure."

"Yes," she murmured, her breath tickling the skin of his shoulder.

He held her like that, staying awake and vigilant until she slept. And even then he did not doze. He lay beside her, listening to her quiet breathing, feeling the rise and fall of her chest, and losing himself in the heat her woman's body generated in slumber.

She was gone when he awoke the next morning. He was disappointed at not finding her beside him, but admittedly he'd overslept. He dressed quickly, hoping to catch her before her morning ride and perhaps join her, but as he strode down the steps of his house his butler announced that Meeps was waiting for him in the study.

Not the person Quint wanted to see just then, but business would have to win over pleasure today. Meeps was sitting in one of the armchairs, reading the *Times* and sipping tea when Quint strode in. The assistant stood, bowed, then gestured to a lone sheet of paper on Quint's desk. Quint went to it immediately. As he read, he had to sit down.

It took a moment for Quint to find his voice, and then he said, "Why didn't you tell me this earlier?"

"My lord, I told you others were in competition for the Cabinet seat."

"Others, yes. You said Fairfax had not been given a nod."

Meeps inclined his head. "It was a foregone conclusion, especially once your name was thrown into the ring."

Quint swore. Fairfax and he had been contemporaries at Oxford, always in competition with one another. They were not enemies, not even on opposite sides of the political fence. Their careers had been on a parallel course until last spring when Fairfax married Lady Honoria, daughter of the Duke of Astly.

Quint had watched as Fairfax's popularity

soared. Lady Honoria was polished and beautiful. She was schooled in the social graces by those
who made the rules of etiquette, and the political
salons and soirees she hosted for Fairfax were
immensely popular among the secretaries and
Cabinet ministers.

Lady Honoria had been one reason Quint decided it was time he seek a wife. He could not
hope to keep up with men like Fairfax without
some ammunition.

And now he had his ammunition—the niece of
an earl—nothing to scoff at. Except he had not
married the charming Elizabeth Fullbright, but
her shy, socially awkward sister.

"Fairfax. Goddamn it," Quint grumbled now.

"I advised you to stay in London."

Quint glared at Meeps, and his assistant shrank
back in his chair a bit. "Since you seem so adept
at advising me," Quint said in his most scathing
tone, "why don't you advise me what to do now?
Fairfax is the undisputed favorite for the Cabinet
seat. How do I change that?"

"You must return to London. Posthaste."

"Damn it, but I *knew* you were going to say
that."

"And then you must launch a three-pronged
attack."

Quint sat forward, leaning his elbows on the
desk. He liked organized strategies. "Go on."

"Your first line of attack will be Parliament.
You must quickly attach yourself to the new act

sponsored by Lord Graves. It's bound to be controversial."

Quint shuffled through the stack of papers Meeps had moved aside until he found the documents he sought. "Ha! Graves wants to lower taxes on"—he flipped several pages—"hell, on a whole host of items."

"Fairfax opposes the bill."

"What a surprise. It's not going to be popular."

"Except with the people. Pass that bill, gain the people's support, and the prime minister cannot afford to overlook you."

Quint nodded. "The second prong of attack?"

"You have to attend every rally, every plebeian meeting, every reform society gathering. You'll give rousing speeches, and your name will be all over the *Times*."

Quint began taking notes. "I've already received several invitations to speak. I'll have you accept for me. Hire Black and Clarion to write my speeches."

"Black is working for Fairfax now."

Quint looked up. "Get him back. Pay him whatever he asks. No one turns a phrase like Black." He went back to his notes, his hand writing furiously but not as quickly as the rapid-fire ideas in his mind. He loved this feeling at the beginning of a political campaign. He felt like a general, eager to rally his troops and yell, "Charge!"

"I'll need you to return to London today," Quint told Meeps in between shuffling through papers and scratching notes. "I want you to talk to Graves, prepare the way for me—"

"My lord, you know I will be happy to, but we still have one more avenue of attack to discuss. Perhaps the most important one."

Quint stopped writing, but he did not look up. "I know. My wife."

"She must host the party to end all parties. Fairfax has proven himself. Invitations to his affairs are some of the most highly sought. There is not an MP in Parliament who doesn't seek his favor the week before one of his wife's soirees. You must do the same."

Quint sat back slowly and his attention drifted to the window overlooking Ravensland's lawns. Catherine, in one of her new pale muslin gowns, was a cloud of yellow and white among the green landscape as she meandered closer. Her dress was simple and pretty, her dark hair caught up in a knot on top of her head. Her face was peaceful, with a slight smile that hinted she knew a secret. He knew some of her secrets, too. He'd shared them with her last night.

She was beautiful and innocent, and no match for Lady Honoria and Fairfax. He'd seen her all but wilt when she was surrounded by people and noise. How would she ever host an affair?

"Is that your wife?" Meeps said, peering out the window closest to his chair.

"Yes. I'll speak to her about the party. She can begin to plan it as soon as we return to London."

But Meeps was still staring out the window. "She's lovely. I don't remember her seeming so lovely before."

Quint steepled his hands. "When we return to London, we'll make sure she is the admiration of the *ton*. No one will forget how lovely she is."

Meeps looked at him. "And you think that's possible?"

Quint sincerely hoped so.

As soon as she entered the house, Catherine noticed that the door to Quint's study was closed, but she did not think anything of it. He was awake, and he was only a few feet away. She could not wait to see him.

She hurried through the foyer and with a quick tap on the door, opened it, and said, "Are you finally out of bed? Thor and Hazard are waiting for their morning ride."

Quint was indeed behind his mammoth desk, as she'd expected, but he rose awkwardly when she entered and glanced to his right. There another vaguely familiar man was also rising from one of the armchairs, and the heat bloomed in her cheeks. "Oh, I see you are busy. I am sorry." She turned to close the door, but her husband's voice stopped her.

"Lady Valentine, please, join us."

Catherine did not want to join the men. The man with Quint looked harmless, but new people made her uncomfortable. She could never think of anything to say. But, dutifully, she turned around and, closing the door behind her, stepped into the room.

"Please." Quint gestured to one of the couches near the hearth. She was accustomed to sitting in the armchairs, but Quint's guest was in her usual spot. She went to the couch and arranged her skirts carefully so that she did not have to look at the men right away. Quint came to sit beside her.

"Lady Valentine, you remember Mr. Meeps. He is one of my advisors."

Catherine glanced up at the pale, red-haired man. He was thin, wore small glasses, and dressed completely in black. He looked like a clerk. "Sir, it is a pleasure." But it was not. If a political advisor had come all this way to speak with Quint, it meant something important was happening in Town. It meant the end to this short-lived idyllic time alone with Quint.

Apparently, she was to be involved as well. She did not want to be involved.

Meeps nodded at her and retook his seat in her chair. She looked at Quint. It was strange to see him like this. After all they had shared last night, here she was sitting beside him, acting as though they were complete strangers. Why, she knew what he looked like without his trousers on. He knew what happened to her when he . . .

Her face began to heat, and she decided not to think of that at present. But it was difficult when every time she looked at her husband, images from last night came rushing at her. She wondered if he had a similar feeling, but he seemed completely at ease.

No, that was not exactly true. He was saying something to Mr. Meeps, but his gaze kept darting back to her. He had the look of the jailer whose duty it is to escort prisoners to their executions.

The jailer looked at her, a sympathetic and yet determined look on his face.

"What is it?" Catherine said immediately. "What's wrong?"

He smiled at her, but the happiness didn't reach his eyes. "Nothing is wrong. We're returning to London, as we discussed last night."

"And Mr. Meeps?" She knew that was not all. The ax had yet to fall.

"Mr. Meeps and I were discussing political strategy. And I thought that while we are in Town, we might host a ball or a soiree."

Catherine blinked. Her head felt light, almost as though it had come unattached and was tumbling fast and furious toward the Aubusson rug beneath her feet. "A ball?"

"Yes. I'll help you, of course." He said something else, but his voice was murky and she could not comprehend.

A ball. A party with dancing, loud music, and a crush of people. An opportunity for her to make a hundred mortifying mistakes, especially if she were the hostess. Everyone would be looking at

her, watching her. She clutched her fingers together tightly.

One, two, three . . .

Meeps began to speak. It was a moment before
she understood him. "—for Lord Valentine's career. Of course, you must invite the prime minister, the prince regent, the Cabinet ministers—I
will send you a complete list. As your town house
is rather small, you might think of having the
ball in one of the assembly—"

The prime minister? The prince regent? No, no,
no. She could not possibly host these men. What
would she say? What would she do? The preparations for an event like this were unimaginable.

The cozy study began to feel hot and cramped.
The walls inched closer until they crouched over
her like angry beasts.

Four, five, six . . .

Catherine stumbled to her feet, and Valentine
caught her arm. Both he and Meeps jumped to
their feet. "Are you well?" Quint asked.

"I think I shall go upstairs and lie down," she
said. She tried not to look at the walls hunkering
closer, not to hunch as she strode through the
shrinking door, but she could not force her feet to
slow as much as she should have. She darted
through the door, and when she heard it click
shut behind her, she broke into a run for the stairs
and managed to make it to their room before she
lost her breath entirely.

Catherine was gulping for air when she closed

the door to her chamber. She leaned against the door and shut her eyes, thankful this room was still its original size. She counted to ten and climbed onto the bed she'd shared with Quint just a few hours before. Curling into a ball, she pressed her fingers to her eyes to hold back the sting of tears and tried to breathe deeply.

How could he? How could Valentine do this to her? He knew hosting a ball like this was her greatest fear. And yet he'd thrown the suggestion at her as if it were nothing—a choice between a lemon or apple scone at tea. And not only did he want her to eat this enormous, fearsome scone, he wanted her to do so in front of the whole of London Society.

London Society. The upper ten thousand. The *haute ton*. The most scheming, most unforgiving, most vengeful collection of people since the Romans. And here she was, a defenseless gladiator, thrown in the pit with the lions.

And for what? His career. His ridiculous career.

"Catie?" There was a tap on the door, and the knob turned. Belatedly, she wished she'd thought to block it. Not that that would have stopped him. She sat and tried to smooth her hair.

"I don't want to talk right now. I'm not feeling well," she managed. Lord, he looked handsome this morning. He must have finally accepted that his hair had grown too long, and he'd pulled it back into a queue, secured by a black string. His shirt and cravat were white as snow, and he was dressed to ride, boots, riding coat, and all.

She watched him stride across the room toward her, ignoring her wish to be alone. If she were a gladiator, he was the lion. She knew his body now, could imagine the bunch and pull of his muscles as he moved. She looked at his hands and remembered how they'd felt on her flesh, how they'd stroked and caressed until she was breathless with needing him.

She looked into his eyes, trying to distract herself and hold on to her anger. But looking into his face didn't help. That too brought back memories— the rough scrub of his beard against the inside of her thigh, the way his long lashes framed those mahogany eyes, the feel of that full mouth on her nipple.

She turned away from him but felt the bed dip as he sat beside her. It was strange to have him so near her again. Here they were on the bed, where they'd shared so much last night, but now all she felt was betrayal. She'd thought he had finally accepted her, was coming to care for her. But he hadn't changed at all. He still cared more about his career than anything else.

She wanted to turn her back on him, to walk away and never look around, but she could not because she had changed. His wooing, his gentle nature, the way he'd loved her last night—those things had changed her. She needed him. She had fallen in love with him.

And he loved his career.

He sighed. "Catie, I know this is not what you had in mind when we discussed returning to London. You get nervous when you attend balls—"

"Not what I had in mind?" she whispered, but her words were loud enough to silence him. "No, it wasn't what I expected, but perhaps that's because you deceived me into believing you cared how I felt. What was it you said? You wanted me to be happy?"

"I do want you to be happy."

"Then don't force me to host this ball." She turned to him and met his gaze head-on. "In fact, don't force me to return to London at all. Let's stay here for the rest of the Season." She prayed he would accept her suggestion, prayed he would be the man she wanted him to be, but he was shaking his head.

"I cannot. I'm needed in Parliament."

"Then you go back. I'll stay here, and you can join me when the session is over."

"I'm not leaving you," he said, taking her hand. It would have been a sweet statement had not his eyes been hard and determined.

"Why?" she said, withdrawing her hand. His touch still evoked too many memories. "Surely, I have not become indispensable to you in so short a time. Surely, you can live without me for a few weeks."

He stood and ran a hand through his hair, disordering his neat queue. "Why do you have to make this so difficult, Catherine? I understand your fears, but I need you. Can you not do one thing for me?"

"For you or for your political ambitions? That's what this is really about."

He shook his head, then suddenly turned and knelt before her. "I have a chance at a seat in the Cabinet. Do you know how long I have wanted this and worked for it?"

She looked away. Already her heart was melting. How could she resist his pleas? After last night, after the gentle way he had been with her, how could she deny him anything? Even when the one thing he wanted terrified her.

"I have worked my whole life for this opportunity, and I am so close," he was saying. "I deserve this, but I need you. Charles Fairfax is my competition, and he's been gathering his supporters this past week you and I have been away."

"And he's married to the Duke of Astly's daughter." She glanced at him. "I must seem a poor choice in comparison. Especially considering whom you really wanted." And Elizabeth would be waiting for him back in London.

"Damn it!" Valentine rose and paced away from her. "I don't have time for this right now, Catherine. I want you, you know I do, and I need you right now. I need your support." He turned on his heel. "Do I have it?"

She gave him a long look, took a deep breath, and said, "Yes, you have it, but let's be clear, Lord

Valentine. You need a wife. You don't need me. You've considered me a liability from the start."

"That's not true."

"Isn't it? And why should I believe you, when you lied to me last night?

"I did not lie—"

She stood and crossed to him. "Then look me in the eye and tell me that you did not have your career in mind last night even as you spoke of our returning to London only to make me happy."

To his credit, he did not look away. "Catherine, I care for you. What happened between us last night—"

"Don't speak of it to me," she said, forcibly restraining her tears. "Do not ruin that for me as well." A rogue tear escaped her defenses. He reached out to stroke it away, but she realized his intention too late and flinched back.

"Goddamn it, Catie. I'm not going to hurt you," he said.

"It's too late for that. Just go." She turned away from him, staring at the white walls of her room. "I'll begin packing. We can leave as soon as you are ready."

Chapter 19

Quint didn't understand women. He didn't understand why they had to mix everything up in their minds until everything a man said or did produced offense in one way or another.

He'd traveled back to London with Catherine a week before, and since that time, he'd exchanged barely half a dozen words with her. Not that he'd seen her very often. He'd been so busy that he could not even remember the last time he slept.

Forget sleeping with her. He supposed he could add that to his list of transgressions—deserting the marriage bed. She probably assumed he'd neglected her on purpose. Nothing could be further from the truth. He wanted her, thought of her constantly, but he did not have time to smooth her ruffled feathers.

She'd been angry, and he could understand that. The anger came from fear. He'd asked her to do something that terrified her. Naturally, she was frightened and lashed out. But he did not understand how she managed to connect one small favor with everything else he felt for her. He still cared for her. He still wanted her. Why would her hosting a ball for his political allies change anything between them?

But it had.

Now when he looked into her eyes, he no longer saw fear and wariness. He saw pain, and somehow he was the source of that pain. He supposed she saw his request for her to host the ball as a betrayal of some sort, but that was ridiculous. Why couldn't she see that hosting the ball would actually be a good thing for her? It would help boost her confidence. The ball was as much for her as for him.

Well, that supposition might be stretching things a bit, but the ball was at least not solely for him.

As he strode into his London town house, he tried to remember the last conversation he'd had with his wife. Barring that, he tried to remember when he'd last seen her. It had been at least a day. Surely not more than that. Not two days.

The clock in the foyer struck one. She was

probably asleep by now, but Quint could not afford to wait any longer to see her.

He'd mentioned the ball to the prime minister, and Quint had to be sure the plans were going according to schedule. And, of course, there was another transgression. Quint had promised to help her plan the thing, and he hadn't lifted a finger to do so. He'd been too busy, overwhelmed by bills, speeches, and correspondence.

But he would rectify everything now. He would apologize and renew his offer of assistance—or at least the best efforts of his own assistant—and she would forgive him.

He hoped.

And after she forgave him, he would kiss her, make love to her, and all would be right between them again.

He hoped.

He took the steps two at a time and clomped down the hallway. Her door was open, and he slowed as he neared it.

"Oh, good, Lord Valentine. You have returned."

Quint peered into Catherine's dimly lit room and saw her seated on the low plush bench used at her dressing table. A valise crouched at her feet.

He frowned. "It's after one in the morning. Why are you awake and dressed?"

"I was waiting for you. I wanted to tell you good-bye." She stood and bent to lift the valise.

"What are you talking about?" His eyes swept

the room. Her armoire was open, and except for a few scattered linens, it was empty. The dressing table was bare of combs and brushes. Nothing personal remained in the room.

Quint felt the old prickle of unease at the back of his neck. He lifted a hand, rubbed it away, but it returned with a vengeance. Nothing good came from that prickle.

Catherine stepped before him. "I'm leaving you."

"Oh, no you're not," he said, reaching for her valise, but she drew it away.

"Catie, do you want me to pack this robe?" Her cousin, Lady Madeleine, walked into the room through the open dressing-room door. As soon as she spotted him, she halted and began to frown. "Oh, it's him."

"What the hell does that mean?" he barked. Of course it was him. He lived here. "What are you doing here?"

She glanced at Catie. "Didn't you tell him?"

"Of course," Catie answered, still keeping her gaze on him. "But he's not taking it well."

"I'm standing right here," Quint said. "You don't have to speak as though I'm not home."

"But that's exactly the problem," Lady Madeleine said, narrowing her eyes at him. "You never are home. That's why Catie's leaving you."

"The hell she is. She's my wife. She can't leave."

Catherine raised her brows at him. "Watch me."

She turned to her cousin. "We can send a servant for the rest of it. Let's just take this and go."

Lady Madeleine nodded, and the women stepped forward, but Quint blocked their exit. "You're not leaving." His heart was racing now, panic galloping through his blood. "You're my wife."

"You'd hardly know it the way you treat her," Lady Madeleine spat.

"The way I treat her? What have I done?"

"Nothing at all except practically desert the poor girl. She's lonely here by herself all the time."

Quint opened his mouth to defend himself, but Lady Madeleine waved him silent.

"Not to mention, you're making her host that ball. You know how social events frighten her. How could you?"

Quint felt his panic being quickly replaced by anger. "I do not have to defend myself to you, but be assured, Lady Madeleine," he directed his words to her cousin, but looked at Catherine, "I would not ask her to host this ball if I did not think she would rise to the challenge. The experience will be good for her."

"Of course, it will be good for her," Lady Madeleine said, "but that is not the point."

"Now you are speaking as though I am not here," Catie said with a scowl at both of them. "I have heard quite enough. I am leaving."

"Don't even think of it." Quint stepped closer,

but Madeleine jumped between them. He spoke over her head. "Your place is here with me."

Catie gave a bitter laugh. "There's nothing for me here."

Quint wanted to reach out, grab her, and shake her until she saw sense. "What are you blathering about? *I'm* here."

"No you're not." She thrust her hands on her hips. "You're never home. Why, it's taken you two days to realize that I'm leaving you!"

Quint opened his mouth to protest, but he was speechless. She'd been planning this for two days? As he watched, she pushed past her cousin to stand nose to nose with him. She was proud and strong and brave, no trace of the fearful Catherine he had first known.

"And now you've come home." She poked his chest. "And you expect me to jump to do your bidding. Well, I won't. I'm leaving."

Quint narrowed his eyes and restrained himself from gripping the finger she poked at him and hauling her away with it. "Are you saying you want a divorce?"

"I don't care. I'm leaving. I'm going to—" She glanced at her cousin.

"The Americas," Lady Madeleine provided.

"That's right. I'll leave for the Americas and start over."

Quint leaned close to her, not touching her, but his face only inches away. "You are not going to the Americas. You're staying here with me."

She glared at him. "Make me."

He growled, prepared to do just that.

"If I go, you can have your divorce and then marry Elizabeth. It's what you've wanted all along anyway."

Quint's brain felt twisted and hazy. "What the devil are you talking about?" Why didn't women ever argue logically?

Suddenly Lady Madeleine was pushing them apart. "Now, just a moment." She put her hands up. "Let's not say or do anything we'll regret later."

"It's a bit late for that," Quint said, and Lady Madeleine rounded on him. Quint took a surprised step back.

"That's right, sir. Keep stepping back."

"I think it's time for you to go home, Lady Madeleine."

"Not until Catie is happy. No one does anything until everyone is happy. We have to fix this mess."

"But I don't want anything fixed," Catherine protested. "I have a long trip ahead of me. I want to get some sleep."

"Then you'll go to sleep in my bed," Quint said. "You're my wife."

"Not for long," she shot back.

"Goddamn it!" Quint started for her, but Madeleine was between them again.

"Why don't we all sit down and talk this

through," Madeleine suggested. "Catie, you sit there at the dressing table. Lord Valentine, you take that blue armchair."

Quint watched as Catherine took a seat at her dressing table, and he grudgingly moved toward the armchair. He sat slowly, and then Madeleine said, "Good. Now, the most important thing is finding a way to bring the two of you back together."

Catherine glared at her. "Why would we want to do that?"

Maddie glared back. "Because it's obvious you're miserable without one another."

Quint straightened. "I am not miserable."

"Oh, hush," Madeleine said. "You are miserable, and Catie is too. She hasn't slept for crying so much."

"Traitor," Catie said.

Quint glanced at his wife. She did look tired, and her eyes were swollen.

"What we have to do is to find a way to make both parties happy."

Quint raised his eyes to the ceiling. His wife's cousin was obviously a politician in training, but if Lady Madeleine's efforts would make Catherine stay, then he'd play along.

"Very well," Quint said, trying to sound magnanimous, "what do you suggest?"

"A compromise," Madeleine said. "Catie will agree to host your ball."

Quint glanced at his wife. She nodded. "But that's only provided *you* agree to a few conditions."

"That's right," Lady Madeleine said. "Catie would like—"

"There are conditions?" Quint spat out. "This is a marriage, not a treaty negotiation."

"It won't be either if you keep interrupting," his wife said. "I *will* leave."

He refrained from rolling his eyes, and finally ground out, "Go on."

"First of all, you have to be home for dinner every night."

"Don't be ridiculous—"

"Good night, Lord Valentine." She rose and motioned for her cousin to follow.

Quint clenched his fists. Goddamn it! What the hell kind of negotiation was this?

"Catie," he said, though his jaw was locked. She paused and looked over her shoulder. "Every night is a bit steep. Perhaps—"

She turned back and started for the door again. Quint closed his eyes. "Fine. I'll be home for dinner every night. What else?"

She turned back to him, smiling. The smile almost made his concession worth it.

"You must help with the preparations for the ball. Your job is to deal with the invitations."

"Fine. No problem."

"Not one of your assistants. You. Personally," Catherine said.

Quint frowned. "What difference does it make if I do it or Meeps?"

She shook her head. "If you're going to argue, I'm going to call for the carriage."

"I'm not going to argue," Quint said, clutching the arms of his chair. "I agree. Put your things away. You're staying."

She smiled again. "Right away."

To Quint's relief, his wife picked up her valise and headed into the dressing room to unpack. He smiled. Finally.

"Obviously, you think you received the better end of the bargain." Lady Madeleine was standing before him, hands on her hips. Quint's smile faded.

"Two things," she said. She gave him a look Quint supposed was meant to strike fear in his heart. "You had better fulfill your end of this bargain. Catie wants you home, and you can stop giving speeches and fawning over the prime minister long enough to be there for her."

Quint did not so much as blink. "I do not fawn."

Lady Madeleine shook her head. "One of these days, you are going to realize that there's more to life than bills and debates. Cabinet posts and undersecretary positions are all well and good, but they won't ease the loneliness. They won't warm your bed, and they won't comfort you when you're old and sick. You will lose Catie if you take her for granted."

Quint rose. "I know what I'm doing, Lady Madeleine. I don't need your advice."

She rolled her eyes. "That's what men always say. You do realize that you almost lost her tonight?"

He inclined his head civilly, but inside, his stomach pitched and roiled. "I won't lose her," he said. "You can be certain of that."

Later that night Quint rose from where he lay beside Catie's warm, naked body. He paced the room and eventually went to sit at his desk. He had more work to do tonight, and the new rules his wife had forced him to agree to would not lighten his load.

He looked at his sleeping wife. Her goddamn cousin was right; he'd almost lost her. She'd almost slipped right through his fingers while his mind was on political matters. The thought terrified him, even now. He would have probably said or done anything she'd asked to get her back.

He didn't know what terrified him more—that he was completely at his wife's mercy or that he no longer seemed to mind that he'd lost control of their relationship.

She had all the power now. She all but had him in the palm of her hand. If he were not careful, he would soon find himself in love with her.

Quint swallowed and glanced back at his wife.

Did she feel anything for him? Did she love him?

Damn! He rose and paced the room. He didn't need her to love him. Her needed her to trust him, to obey him, to host his friends.

He didn't need her to love him.

And yet he wanted her to, he wanted to hear her say those words.

He'd made love to her tonight with a possessiveness he did not know was in him. He would never let her go. Never. But he would not abandon his dream of the Cabinet position either.

Quint looked at the papers on his desk. The two desires—his wife and his career—should not be mutually exclusive, but increasingly Quint feared that's exactly what they were.

Chapter 20

"No, that one is too white," Madeleine told Josie. She held up another sheet of vellum from the sheets spread over Valentine's dining-room table and admired it. "What about this one?"

Josie huffed. "There's absolutely no difference. Those two papers are exactly the same shade."

"Ridiculous," Maddie scoffed, holding the first up again. "This one is bright white. This is ivory. What do you think, Mr. Meeps?"

Catie looked up from the menu she was trying to perfect and watched the poor, overworked Mr. Meeps look from one of her cousins to the other. The small man pushed his glasses back on his nose. "I think—"

"This one, right?" Josie said, holding her choice out.

"Don't influence him!" Maddie broke in. She waved her choice at him. "This is better, is it not?"

Catherine shook her head. "Leave poor Mr. Meeps alone, girls. The invitations are Valentine's responsibility, and I told him he had to do it himself."

"But, Lady Valentine, his lordship has given me leave to make decisions in his stead," Meeps told her.

"I don't care. He is going to keep to his end of our bargain. Either he does the invitations or there are none."

"Good for you, Catie!" Josie said, applauding.

Catherine smiled, but it was short-lived. Valentine's housekeeper bustled in and said breathlessly, "The table covers you ordered are here, milady. Where should I put them?"

Catie pressed her lips together and thought for a moment. "The drawing room, I suppose."

"But milady, we can hardly open the door for all the items crammed inside. You told Webster to store the extra tables in there yesterday."

"Oh, that's right." Catherine glanced at Josie and Maddie for help. They blinked back at her. "Um, I suppose we have no choice but to put them in Lord Valentine's study."

Mr. Meeps shook her head. "Oh, no, Lady Valentine. I do not suggest—"

"You absolutely must taste this cake!" Ashley

said, rushing into the dining room, a slice of white cake balanced on a fork before her. "It's divine. We should order at least three for the ball."

She shoved the treat at Catherine, so that Catherine had little choice but to take a small bite. Ashley then scampered over to Josie and Maddie and offered the cake. Josie leaned forward to taste, and shook her head. "It's good, but it's lemon. I liked the vanilla we tasted yesterday. It works better with our theme."

"Theme? What theme?" Maddie said. "Ah-ha! That's why you want that awful bright white vellum."

"It goes with the white theme," Josie protested.

"If you are going to start with the white theme again, then I will have to hit you."

"Madam," the housekeeper said.

Catherine tore her gaze from her arguing cousins and tried to swallow the dry cake.

"What about the table linens?"

"In his lordship's study," Catherine mumbled around the food.

"Madam," Webster, Quint's butler, strolled regally into the room. "The extra china has arrived."

"Oh, Lord," Catherine said, dropping her head in her hands. She'd been working nonstop to organize Valentine's ball and had been fortunate to catch three or four hours' sleep a night. Her cousins had been immensely helpful, and she didn't know what she would have done without them. Hosting an unplanned ball in the midst of the Season was no small feat, especially when one considered that Valentine's house and staff were not prepared for such an undertaking.

Not only was Valentine's town house too small for the event, he did not own enough of the accoutrements one needed. His solution had been to have the ball at an assembly hall and rent everything. He wanted only the best. The problem was that the best china and linens had already been spoken for by hostesses who had planned far earlier than she. But with help from her cousins, Catherine had managed to secure items she hoped would be acceptable.

Now she just had to figure out what to do with them, and that was not easy. She was too tired to think clearly at this point. The ball was in less than a week, and she still had so much to do.

She looked up at Webster. "The china is here? Are you certain? I thought that was not to arrive for two more days."

"It is here, madam," he said.

"Catherine, where are you?"

She turned at the sound of Quint's voice and the tap of his boots on the marble in the foyer. A moment later, he poked his head into the dining-room door. He was wearing evening attire, very rumpled, as though he had not changed from the night before. Catherine vaguely remembered that he had mentioned dining at his club after the parliamentary session, but she had not seen him since. Thinking back, Catherine realized that she should have made him promise not only to be home for dinner but also to stay home.

"Webster," Quint said, swiping his hair back from his face. He had obviously lost the thong he had been using to hold it back, and now it hung free about his neck and forehead. "Who are all those people outside?"

Webster looked at Catherine. "Ask your wife, my lord." And Webster turned and walked away.

Quint glanced at her, eyebrow raised. Lord, every time she saw him it was like the first. Her heart still sped up, her stomach did quick somersaults, and her hands trembled. How could someone like her have married such a kind, handsome man?

She wondered if he still thought of Elizabeth, and if he regretted the exchange of one sister for the other. As for herself, Catherine would never have told her cousins, but she rather liked being married to this man. Especially at night. Try as she might during the days, she could not forget the nights they spent together. She could not forget the possessive, urgent way that he came to her, taking her into his arms and making love to her.

She was still trying to accustom herself to sleeping with a man. She liked the pleasurable sensations he made her feel, especially when he used his tongue—

She felt her face heat and looked away. She caught Josie staring at her, a knowing look on her face. Obviously, Madeleine had not kept quiet about the events of the night she'd almost left Valentine. Maddie was certain that Valentine's actions, his easy capitulation and insistence he would never give her up, was a sign that he was in love with Catherine. Catherine begged to differ. As usual, Valentine had his career in mind. If Catherine left him, his career would be ruined.

And yet there had been something about him that night that spoke to her. She would never have defended him, have agreed to host this ball, if something in Valentine's face had not touched her. It had almost looked as though he needed her.

Catherine shook her head. How silly of her.

Valentine welcomed Catherine's cousins and then looked at her. "How are the preparations coming?"

Catherine frowned, all good feeling for him fading. Did he care about anything but this ball? He did not even take a moment to ask how she was.

She cleared her throat. "For my part, the preparations are fine. How are yours, my lord? Mr. Meeps says you have not yet chosen the paper for the invitations."

Valentine turned to his assistant and gave him a dark look. Meeps looked away. Obviously, Meeps was not to have spoken.

"I am finalizing the wording and the paper choice," Quint said.

"Oh, good. Have you spoken with the stationer yet?"

Her husband ran a hand through his hair, and she knew the answer.

"I am only asking," she said, glancing down at her menu, trying to appear absorbed, "because I took the liberty of approaching several stationers myself. None of the gentlemen I spoke to can accommodate us until next week."

Catherine glanced up at Valentine. Her father would have berated her for impertinence and interfering, but Catherine felt only mildly worried that Quint would react the same. She knew in the logical part of her mind that he would not. But the primal, instinctual part of her brain—that part that had cowered in fear and fought for survival since birth—still kept its wary vigil.

As expected, Quint only frowned at her pronouncement. "That won't do." He paced away and then turned back. "I have an idea."

Now it was Catherine's turn to frown.

"Perhaps we can write them by hand. You ladies are always perfecting your handwriting, are you not? Perhaps handwritten invitations would be more . . . personal."

Catherine blinked. "Handwritten invitations? How many guests are you inviting?"

"Ah, good question." He tapped his tailcoat, first the right pocket and then the left. Finally, he extracted several papers from his waistcoat. "Here is the guest list. I believe the total number of guests is about"—he flipped through one, two, three, four—she lost count—"four hundred."

He handed the list to Catherine and tapped his fingers on the table in front of her.

Josie gasped and Maddie looked as though she would choke. Ashley spoke for all of them. "If you think we are going to handwrite four hundred invitations and then hand address them, you are mad." She popped the last piece of cake in her mouth and crossed her arms.

"Very well, then I shall find a stationer," Valentine said.

Ashley snorted. "Best of luck to you."

Catherine watched Valentine clench his jaw. She moved back slightly, but he put a hand on her shoulder, reassuring her. She was not even certain he realized he did it.

"Thank you for your support."

With Quint's warm hand on her shoulder, Catherine glanced down at the list, running her eyes over the endless columns of names. Valentine's guest list included the most powerful, most prestigious men and women in the country. The air at the ball would indeed be rarefied.

She began to feel ill. Her head swam, and she had to remind herself to take a shaky breath. It was not only that the most powerful, most awe-inspiring members of the English government would be attending a ball that she planned that made her nervous. The sheer number of people who would be in attendance gave her greater pause. As hostess, she would never be able to escape if she began to feel overwhelmed. And just looking at the list overwhelmed her.

She clasped her hands on the table and forced her mind to focus on one detail at a time. She would not think of that night until it was upon her. Gradually, her heartbeat slowed.

Perusing the list one last time, Catherine tried to focus on the names of people she knew. Her cousins and aunts and uncles would be there. They would support her.

She flipped another page then, and one entry jumped out at her. She leaned closer and read it again.

Miss Elizabeth Fullbright

Her head shot up. "What is this?" she said, jabbing the paper.

Valentine looked down at her and frowned. "The guest list. I told you."

"No." She slapped the list down. "What is this?" She sliced at the offending name with her finger.

Valentine took the pages and peered at them. "That is your sister." He handed the pages to her, and she handed them right back. Valentine's face darkened, but Catherine did not inch back. She was not scared of him. And today, she was too tired to feel much of anything but exhaustion.

"Why is Lizzy on the list?" Maddie said, rising, and moving protectively toward Catherine. Catherine doubted Maddie was actually worried Valentine would strike her, but she appreciated the support nonetheless. Still she kept her gaze locked with Valentine.

"She is on the list because she should be," Valentine replied, not turning away from Catherine. "In fact, I should have invited your father and mother. It will seem strange that they are not in attendance." He looked at Catherine, his hand cupping her chin briefly. "But I know that would be too hard for you."

Maddie had reached her side. "And it won't be hard on her to have Lizzy there? You were betrothed, after all."

Valentine shrugged. "All of that is in the past now."

Catherine's jaw dropped. All of it was in the past? Had he forgotten how he'd felt when he discovered that her father had drugged him and then tricked him into marriage? She had certainly not forgotten how she had felt when she'd awakened in the middle of the night to find her father selling her to a brute she had never even seen before.

"You seem an unusually forgiving man," Maddie was saying. "But do you not think it will be even slightly awkward to bring your wife and your betrothed together in such a public forum?"

"Elizabeth is no longer my betrothed."

"Fortunate man," Josie grumbled.

Valentine looked as though he would protest and then glanced at Catherine and seemed to think better of it. Catherine's heart sank. No matter what he said now, she had seen the truth in his eyes just then. He obviously did not think himself fortunate. She felt her heart swell into her throat. Even after all they had shared, he was still in love with Elizabeth. And now she would be at the ball, and Catherine knew she would lose him. Lizzy always got what she wanted.

Valentine adjusted his cravat. "Elizabeth is a sweet and lovely girl. There's no need to impugn her character or punish her for the sins of her father."

"A sweet and lovely girl?" Josie gasped. She glanced at her cousins. "Does he know Lizzy?"

Catherine rolled her eyes. "He knows her. Just not very well. But, in truth, the real issue is not mended family relations, is it, Lord Valentine?"

"Don't start this again," he said.

And then, as Catherine watched, he turned his back on her and marched out of the dining room. Catherine stared after him, then looked at her cousins incredulously.

Ashley shook her head. "Just like a man. He said his piece and walked away."

"I wouldn't put up with that," Josie agreed. "Who does he think he is?"

"He is Lord Valentine," Mr. Meeps interjected. "Soon to be a Cabinet minister."

"Well, he's also my husband," Catherine said, turning on her heel to follow. "And I'm the one who has to live with him."

"Be gentle," Maddie called after her. Catherine raised her hand and marched after her husband. He was striding determinedly toward his study.

Catherine swerved to avoid a servant carrying a stack of table covers. "Valentine!" She increased her pace to catch up with him, but he did not look around. His back stiffened, and he marched on.

"Valentine!" she said, practically stepping on his heels. "I want to talk to you. Now."

She grabbed his arm and was pulled along with him. He opened the door to his study and froze. Inside, piled on every available surface was china. The pattern was quite pretty—Catherine had chosen it herself—white with pink roses along the edges, but it did nothing to complement the décor of the masculine study.

Valentine went very still, and his arm flexed under Catherine's fingers. "What is all this?" He gestured to the plates stacked in twelve piles, three or four feet high on his desk. There were bowls on his chair and more on the leather couch. Beside the bowls the servants had placed cups and saucers. The larger platters and serving bowls littered the floor, stacked carefully, their dainty designs daring any man to try and walk among them.

"I had nowhere to put the china we rented," Catherine said. "The drawing room is full of the extra furniture. Oops." She pulled him aside to make way for the servant carrying the table linens. "Here are the tablecloths and napkins."

The servants moved around them and set the linen on the edge of the rug just inside the door to the study. Quint stared after him, narrow-eyed. Then he turned on Catherine.

"How am I supposed to get inside and work? My desk is covered, and I can't concentrate in this chaos."

Catherine pulled him aside as another man loaded with table linens approached. "You will manage. I want to talk about the guest list."

He sighed and pulled her farther back, away from another troop of men and women carrying an endless supply of china and tablecloths. "Catie," he said softly, and Catherine's heart leaped in her chest. Why did he have to call her that? And why use that tone? Did he know the effect it had on her? Every time she heard it she thought of their nights together, his arms around her, his mouth on her, his whispered endearments as he'd plunged inside her.

She closed her eyes and tried to close her heart.

"Catie," he said again, "I know there's no love lost between you and your sister, but perhaps this night is a chance to let bygones be bygones."

"Quint." She put her hand on his arm, and he looked down, seeming surprised at her gesture and her words. It was probably the first time she had ever voiced his given name. "You have a good heart. You see the best in people. I admire that."

And she did. From the beginning, he had seen the best in her, and he saw the best in her sister. It was a good trait for a man to possess. She loved him for it, though he would probably never feel the same for her. He did care for her. How was she to convince him that his faith in her sister was misplaced without ruining the small faith he had in her?

Finally, she continued, "But my sister and my father, they are not like you. I don't trust them to come to this ball with honorable intentions."

"I have not invited your father—"

"Do you think that will matter?" she asked. "He will come."

"He'll never get past the door. I will be sure the footmen know to refuse him entrance. I won't let him near you again, Catie." He caressed her jaw with one finger, and Catherine sighed. How was she to fight against such tenderness?

Catherine bit her lip and tried to concentrate. "Quint, you don't know my father and sister as I do. They will—"

He reached out, taking her by the waist and drawing her to him. Catherine stiffened, intent on continuing her argument, but finally she went.

"Sweetling, you are good to worry, but there's no need. I was short with you earlier. I'm sorry."

He brushed a loose tendril of hair away from

her face and then pulled her into a small alcove in the wall, away from the eyes of the servants.

"You are doing a wonderful job with the preparations. I should have told you so before. I should have been here to help you. But you know that everything I do is for both of us. This Cabinet position is not just for me, it's for you as well."

Catherine raised a brow. "It's for me as well?"

"Yes, it will mean more prestige for you, more money for us, you'll be admired and copied, and your invitations will be sought after."

Catherine shook her head and took Valentine's face in her hands. It was rough with stubble that he had not had time to shave in a day or so. She ran the pads of her fingers over it. "But I don't want any of that, Quint. I don't want to be copied or admired. I just want to be with you."

His eyes widened in surprise, and a slow smile spread over his features. "So you do care for me?" he whispered. "I wondered. I-I hoped."

She frowned. Had she said too much? Shown too much of her heart? He hadn't said he cared for her, but she, too, had hoped.

She cleared her throat and went on, trusting that she said the right words. "Of course, I care for you." She tried to keep her tone light. "But all this Cabinet position has done so far has taken you away from me. Can't we forget all this and go back to the country? We were happy there."

He took her by the shoulders. "We'll be happy here. I'll make you happy. In a few days, I'll have the position, and I won't have so many functions to attend. And after the session, we'll have all the time in the world to spend together. Believe me, one day you will thank me for this."

Catherine did not believe him, not at all, so she let her hands drop. He caught them, leaned forward, and kissed her gently on the mouth. She realized that she missed his kisses. Those gentle ministrations she had been so afraid of at first had come to mean more to her than she would have ever believed. Why couldn't he forget all the politics and balls and just love her?

He stepped away as another servant barreled toward them, arms piled to his chin with linens.

"I'm going to my room to get some work done," he said. "I'll come down later to check on you."

She nodded, dejected at yet another of his escapes. "What about the stationers?" she asked.

"Right."

She tried not to frown. He'd already forgotten.

"I'll have Meeps take care of it," he said as he walked away. "He can be quite helpful."

She sighed. Perhaps she should have married Meeps. Quint gave his assistant so many of his personal duties that Catherine figured eventually she'd go to bed and find the little man there, too.

She trudged back to the dining room to find her three cousins still fighting over vellum. Now even Ashley had an opinion. Catherine, fed up with the whole thing, strode to that end of the table, picked up a random sheet—ivory with a gold border—and handed it to a Meeps. "This is the one. Take it to the stationer."

Meeps took the paper and looked at it, then her. "But, madam, I do not know—"

Catherine narrowed her eyes.

"Yes, madam." Meeps hurried to do her bidding.

Catherine turned back to her cousins and saw Maddie and Ashley gaping at her.

"But we'd decided that one was all wrong," Maddie said.

"Actually I rather liked it," Josie chimed in. She was the only one of the girls smiling.

"Did you even look at it?" Ashley crossed her arms, full of indignation.

"What does it matter?" Catherine said. "No one will remember the invitation. After the ball, everyone will be talking about what a fool I am."

Maddie, always her supporter, put an arm around her waist. "We've already talked about this. You'll be fine. One of us will be beside you at all times. You'll take deep breaths and get lots of air, and if it gets too overwhelming, we'll say you have an important matter to attend to and sweep you away for a few moments."

"You have to have confidence in yourself," Josie said, taking her other side. "There's nothing to be afraid of. The assembly rooms are huge. You won't feel trapped."

"I suppose Valentine won the battle of the guest list," Ashley said, as usual seeing right through to Catherine's real dilemma.

"He's such a good man that he can't imagine anyone else isn't," Catherine told them. "He has the best intentions."

"Misguided intentions," Josie spat.

"And now you have to deal with *her*," Maddie said.

"But not alone." Josie waved her arms expansively. "We'll be right beside you. Lizzy's no match for any of us. We'll keep her from doing anything horrible."

"I know you will," Catherine said with a weak smile.

"If you know that, then why do you still look so sad?" Maddie asked.

"You're hurt that he still can't see who your sister really is," Ashley said suddenly.

Catherine shook her head, but Ashley put a hand on Catherine's arm. Ashley always saw too much.

"You think, given the chance, that he'd trade you for her. He won't, Catie. You said yourself that he is a good man."

"I'm tired." Catherine drew away. "I need to get some rest."

Josie grabbed her arm before she could turn away. "Wait a moment. We are your cousins. Don't try to avoid us." She looked closely at Catherine's face. "Are you in love with him?" This last was whispered as though it were a mortal sin.

Catherine refuted it without thinking. "Of course I'm not in love with him."

"You're lying," Josie said. "You love him."

"Is that true?" Ashley demanded.

"She said it wasn't." Maddie at least defended her. "She didn't even want to marry the man, she would never fall in love with him. She's a founding member of the Spinsters' Club."

"That was a child's game," Josie said, still staring at Catherine. "She's in love with him. I know the signs."

"Don't be ridiculous," Maddie said.

"I'm not! I know the signs of love and pining, and she's got all of them."

"No, I don't," Catherine said.

"Oh, yes, you do," Josie countered. "Look at you, you're moping around all day, but when Valentine walks in the room your face lights up. And you're even hosting this ball for him, and you hate balls. If that isn't love, then what is?"

"How do you know so much about it?" Catherine asked. "Are we about to lose another member of our club?"

"Don't be ridiculous." Josie turned away.

Ashley grabbed her shoulder. "You had better not be in love, Josephine Linet Hale."

"I'm not!"

"But there's a man, isn't there? You're not telling us everything."

"Stop harassing me. We're trying to help Catherine."

Catherine was perfectly happy with the attention off her for once, but when the three girls' eyes swung back to her, she quickly changed course. "I think we're all tired and ready for bed. Let's start again with all this in the morning."

"You're avoiding us," Ashley accused.

"Of course she's avoiding us," Maddie said, "but she has a point. Let's give it a rest for tonight. We'll be back in the morning for more preparations. I think your dress will be here by then, and I can't wait to see it!"

Chapter 21

Edmund Fullbright fingered the white vellum with the gold border between fingers
grubby with sweat and tobacco. He'd taken the
invitation from his younger daughter's hands,
though the chit had been loath to allow him to
see it.

He'd slapped her and told her not to show her
worthless face to him for the rest of the night. He
could still see the surprise in her bright blue eyes.
She wasn't used to being slapped, but since Catherine had left, the little bitch had developed an
attitude he didn't care for.

Perhaps she'd always had it, but it galled him
now more than ever. She was going to end up
worthless. Her sister had been married over a

month and was hosting a grand ball with her husband, who would soon be a hoity-toity government official.

What had Elizabeth done except preen and simper and waste his money? Had she secured the hand of a duke or one of those foreign princes? No.

In fact, last week he'd taken her to a ball and found her in an empty room, locked in an embrace with a lowly baronet. The man had had his hands all over his daughter. Little whore.

Edmund sipped his gin and leaned back in his desk chair. And now this. Now she'd been invited to her sister's fancy ball, and she hadn't wanted him to know. Of course he hadn't been invited. No, Lady Goddamn Valentine hadn't seen fit to invite him or her own mother. That was gratitude for you.

After all he'd done for her. She wouldn't even be Lady Goddamn Valentine if not for him. But did she appreciate all he'd done for her? And it was exactly like her to turn into an ungrateful little wretch just when his money problems had come to a boil. He needed money, and Catherine owed him.

Fullbright picked up the pretty little invitation once again. Perhaps it was time his daughter was reminded to whom she was indebted.

Chapter 22

Quint decided that he hadn't given his wife quite enough credit. She had not wanted to have this ball. She had protested every step of the way, and there were recent days when he was inclined to see the whole thing her way. He liked organization and consistency, and she'd turned his entire life, not to mention his study, upside down.

The house had been a mess. Their lives had been a mess, and yet he had enjoyed seeing her work. He loved watching her rise to this challenge, watching her put aside uncertainty and hesitation and become the confident, self-assured woman he knew she could be.

He took his gloves from his valet and pulled

them on. The ball was going to be superb. He had supervised the final preparations only this afternoon, and the assembly rooms where the event was to be held had looked absolutely stunning. Standing there, watching as the last touches were put in place, Quint knew that no duke's daughter could have done better.

Now, he could not wait to see Fairfax's face when he finally had to acknowledge that Quint was a formidable foe in the Cabinet race. Even more, Quint hoped to be on the receiving end of Fairfax's congratulatory handshake when the prime minister offered Quint, and not his rival, the position.

Quint knew he deserved the situation. He had sweated and worked harder for this than ever before. If all went well tonight—and he knew it would—then there was no reason the Cabinet post would not be his.

Quint took one last look in his cheval mirror, trying to imagine himself as a Cabinet minister. He could imagine it very easily. And once that happened, he would make up all the lost hours and all the sacrifices to Catherine. He would win back her affections and do everything in his power to make her happy. In the last few days, he had wanted many times to tell her how much he cared for her, but there just never seemed a right time. He knew she thought he still harbored feelings for her sister, but Quint never thought of the girl. He only had eyes for

Catherine. If his wife only realized how often he thought of her.

After tonight, there would be no doubt. He thought he already knew how she felt. Her words that day he had come home to find all of the china stacked in his study had reassured him. She'd said she missed him, that she cared about being with him. Those words had gripped his heart and held it.

She loved him. He was sure of it.

He wanted all those things, too. And he wanted to make her happy. He would make her happy as soon as he secured the Cabinet post. Once he was a minister, he would make all of this up to her.

He smiled at his reflection and turned to his valet. "Very good, Dorsey. That will be all."

Dorsey inclined his head, and Quint crossed through the dressing room to knock on his wife's door. She opened it herself and he, expecting her lady's maid, stepped back in surprise.

Or maybe the surprise was from seeing the goddess before him. He had never thought of her as a striking woman. That was not the word that came to mind when his thoughts turned to her.

Kind, proud, courageous, determined: Those were the words that described his Catherine. Now he had to add breathtaking. Simply put, her beauty was not even a matter of debate but a given fact. As he gazed at her now, all thought, all reason was sucked out of him.

She wore a gown with a low, square neck in

black velvet trimmed with silver cord. The velvet was heavy and gleamed, but not as richly as her hair. That was the next treasure he discovered. Her hair was pulled back from her face in an elaborate coil that twisted and turned and wound about itself until he was lost trying to follow the style. But he noted how heavy it was and that his fingers itched to feel that weight and to stroke the expanse of her neck just beneath.

He let out a breath, and murmured, "You look lovely, Catie. Truly. You take my breath away."

Modest as always, she ducked her head. Then he noticed that part of the shimmer in her ebony crown was from black pearls dotted throughout the shining mass. They were also wrapped about her neck in both short and long, lustrous strands. He reached out and touched one strand at her throat.

"They are only borrowed," she said. "My aunt Ellen lent them to me."

"They suit you," Quint said, moving his finger to trace the olive skin over her collarbone. "I will have to buy you a set myself." He touched the small pearl drop earrings and then brushed the skin of her cheek. Rather than tensing, as he was used to her doing, she leaned into him and closed her eyes.

Quint's blood fired hot. He had a quick and ardent vision of her naked with only the pearls clustered in her ample cleavage. And now that he was thinking of it, he noted that the low neckline gave him more than enough opportunity to observe that perfect cleavage. Quint frowned.

"Are you wearing a shawl with that?"

"No, why?" She looked down at her gown. "I thought you said I looked lovely."

"You do, but there is perhaps a bit too much of you showing."

Her face turned pink, then red, then burgundy. "I see-I-Maddie said the neckline was appropriate. She said it is higher than what most of the ladies wear, but if it looks ill—"

Quint realized his error and made a hasty retreat. "No, it looks well. Very well. *Too* well." He gave her his best rakish grin, which was rusty from disuse. "I am sure your cousin is right. I had just not expected to see you looking quite so alluring. After tonight I fear I will rarely have you all to myself."

"Nonsense," she said. "You may have me anytime you like. I worry that you no longer want me." She glanced down at the floor, and Quint saw her shuffle her feet, clad in elegant Roman sandals that matched her gown.

He took her chin between two fingers and nudged her face up. "Now who speaks nonsense? I'm standing right here, thinking what a fortunate man I am to have such a beautiful, accomplished wife." And he meant it. How the hell had he not seen this all along? Why had he ever wasted time doubting her? He should have been cherishing her, loving her all along.

"All eyes will be on you at the ball," he whispered. "I will be the envy of every man tonight."

Her eyes, which had been shining as they looked into his, dropped again, her long black lashes screening her honey hazel eyes from view. Once again, Quint knew he had said the wrong thing, but this time he was not sure why. "I know you are still apprehensive about tonight," he said, venturing a guess, "but I assure you all will go well. It will be an evening no one will forget."

Catherine met his eyes again. "I'm sure you are right."

When they entered the ballroom, still an hour or so before most guests would begin arriving, Catherine understood what Quint had meant when he said his breath had been taken away. As she looked at the assembly room in awe, she felt the same. It was the loveliest room she could ever have imagined. Actually, it was lovelier than she had imagined. Everything from the tablecloths and overlays, the flowers, the potted plants, and the white Greek columns draped with white silk were directly out of her own imagination. She had dreamed them all, put them on paper, and then—with the help of her cousins—made her dream a reality.

Lord, she had no idea it would look as good as it did. A footman finished lighting the last of the chandeliers, and as the other servants raised it to the ceiling, even more of her creation glittered into view.

She crossed the marble floor, pausing beneath one of the draped columns. Beside it, she felt so insignificant, as though all of her problems were nothing compared with the heavy problems of the world—problems her husband dealt with daily. Perhaps she was selfish to expect him to put aside those weighty concerns for someone as insignificant as she and her little needs.

Then she reached out and touched the column, pushing it so that it tipped slightly. It was light, made from some insubstantial material that the decorator—a man who worked as a set designer for theater productions—had convinced her to use.

The column reminded her that concerns that might seem weighty to some were often nothing more than illusions. Power. Position. Taxes and treaties. How could any of those possibly be as important as love?

She was afraid her husband had forgotten that. He had obviously known the rule at one time. She remembered the way the country villagers had looked at him with admiration and esteem. She remembered him taking care of the lady in her bare hovel. Quint was a man who cared deeply for others. She had thought he cared for her.

Or perhaps she was wrong, and he had never cared for her at all. Perhaps she had imagined the tenderness and the care he had shown when they'd made love. Perhaps that was one of his politician's tricks.

The guests would be arriving soon, and Catherine crossed the room to make a last check on the dinner preparations. Per her instructions, tables and chairs had been placed in a small room adjacent to the ballroom. At the back of the room were three large tables swathed in white silk with gold overlays. The china was already out, as were several platters of fruit. The rest of the sumptuous fare would not be set out until later, but perhaps she should check to make sure everything was as it should be.

She glanced at her small watch and saw that the first guests would arrive in less than twenty minutes. If she checked on the food now, she would be late in receiving them. It was a tempting escape. If she were overseeing preparations, she would not have to face the crowds and the crush of guests.

She closed her eyes, and once again the suffocating fear piled down on her. She remembered what it had been like to crouch in that closet as a little girl. She remembered the fear and the horror and the loathing she'd felt. Not for her father, but for herself because she was so afraid. She was pitiful.

She jerked her head up and opened her eyes. No more. She was not pitiful. She was breathtaking and capable and hostess of what would surely be *the* ball of the Season. And Quint had faith in her.

Her father no longer had power over her. He was a weak man; she saw that now. He made himself feel big by hurting her and her mother. But he could not hurt her anymore. She wouldn't allow it.

Catherine straightened her shoulders and marched back into the ballroom. She needed to do this, finally to put childhood fears and ghosts behind her. With a smile, she quickened her step. Maddie, Josie, and Ashley were coming up the stairs—Catherine could not see them yet, but she could hear their voices.

One by one, they came into view, each more exquisite than the last. First was Josephine. Her auburn hair was twisted and secured with small combs so that it curled about her head like a crown of fire. She wore a dark green satin gown that complemented her green eyes and made them appear huge in her pixie face.

Behind Josephine was Madeleine. She wore white. The gown had a low neck that showed the ample curve of her bosom and made her waist appear tiny. Her hair had been pulled away from her face, but the heavy mass of it flowed in chestnut curls down her back.

And then there was Ashley. She had always been the acknowledged beauty of the group, and tonight she lived up to her title. Like Josephine, she wore green, but her gown was the green of the sea before a storm. It matched her sea-green eyes and set off her pale porcelain skin. Her blond hair was secured in the most elegant of styles, and like Catherine, jewels dripped from her curls. But no simple pearls for Ashley. She was never so understated. Her hair glimmered and sparkled with small diamonds.

Catherine had come to a complete stop as her cousins ascended the stairs, and now she said, "I don't remember inviting any royalty. You three look like princesses."

Ashley smiled and dropped a curtsey, and Maddie looked embarrassed.

Josie scowled. "If this is what it feels like to be a princess, I pity their majesties. I've been pushed and pulled in every direction today. These stays are so tight I can barely breathe, and a hairpin is digging into my scalp." She reached for her coiffure, but Maddie swatted her hand away.

"Don't touch. You'll ruin it before the ball even begins."

"Look at you," Ashley said, making a wide circle around Catherine. "Catherine Anne Fullbright, I had no idea this was underneath all those drab gowns you always wore. The black velvet suits you."

"And so do Mama's pearls." Maddie clasped her hands together. "She's going to weep with joy when she sees you."

Josie pulled a handkerchief from her bosom. "Don't you dare start." She handed it to Maddie, who used it to dab her eyes.

Ashley finally ceased her perusal and stopped

before Catherine. "What happened when Valentine saw you? Did he ravish you?"

"What kind of question is that?" Catherine felt her cheeks color and wished that, for once, she could be as brazen as Ashley.

"The kind of question we virgins ask. We may be maidens, but that doesn't mean we're not curious."

"Nothing happened."

"Nothing?" Josie cried. "He just grunted and held out his arm?"

"No, he said"—Catherine thought back, her skin warming with pleasure as she remembered—"he said I looked lovely."

"That's all?" Even proper Maddie seemed disappointed.

Catherine glanced about her, made sure Quint was not in sight, and continued, "He said that I took his breath away."

Her three cousins beamed. "That's so romantic," Maddie said.

"It would have been more romantic if he'd ravished her."

"Ashley, shh. You can't say things like that," Catherine chided. "You're going to get a reputation."

Ashley shrugged. "What do I care? But I promise to be on my best behavior tonight. Look, there's the man of the hour."

Catherine turned to see Quint coming up the stairs. His smile was pinched and tight, and she could tell immediately by the way he held his shoulders that he was apprehensive. Her first impulse was to rush to him and reassure him that all was ready, but the sight of him in his evening attire always undid her, especially when he looked as he did tonight.

He wore the requisite dark blue tailcoat and breeches, the snowy white cravat, waistcoat, and white gloves. But his hair had been cut so that it no longer brushed his collar. It was short and neat in the back, the only untamed section the wave that fell over his forehead. He pushed it back, and then his mahogany brown eyes found her.

She knew the moment they did because his entire expression changed. He relaxed, and his smile became more genuine. Her own body reacted instantly. Her pulse fired, and she had the urge to go to him. He needed her, and she wanted to be there to help him.

Now and always.

"Catie, there you are. Are you ready to receive our guests? The footmen tell me the first couples have arrived."

"Oh, yes, of course." She lifted her skirts and went to him quickly. As she passed her cousins, Josie caught her arm.

"Take a deep breath and remember to keep breathing. Everything is going to be perfect."

"I know." Catherine smiled. She felt absolutely no fear, only the warmth of love and acceptance.

She took Quint's outstretched hand. "Ready?" he asked.

"I couldn't be more so."

Quint and Catherine descended the stairs together, a little family. She had never before been part of a family so much as the scapegoat. She had never felt as though she belonged in the drawing rooms of the *ton*. The only time she felt at ease was with her cousins, but since marrying Quint even their childhood club was closed to her.

She couldn't explain why, but being at Quint's side made her feel more a part of anything than she ever had. She felt right with him. She felt that she belonged, that she was where she was supposed to be.

And then he led her to the entryway, the door opened, and the footman admitted the first guests.

Chapter 23

Quint had been a bulwark beside her in the receiving line, and he'd stayed beside her for much of the night. When he was not beside her, one of her cousins was. Finally, Catherine had shooed Maddie and Josie away, insisting they dance and enjoy themselves. She was doing fine and wanted a moment to check on everything.

With a smile on her face, she glided into the dining room to make sure the servants had replenished the fare. It made her nervous to walk among so many people. There were reporters from all the papers, politicians, and what seemed like the entire *ton* in attendance. And all were staring at her.

The dining room was blissfully empty, and she

leaned against a chair, took a deep breath, and tried to calm herself. No one was looking at her. No one cared one whit for her. It was only that there were so many people in the rooms, jostling against her, closing her in. She was being foolish, especially considering that she had been doing so well all evening.

There was nothing to fear. And yet, she couldn't seem to take a deep breath. She closed her eyes.

"Out of breath, dear sister?"

Catherine opened her eyes and stared into cornflower blue ones. Lizzy.

No, not Lizzy. Not now. Catherine just needed a moment to collect herself, and then she'd be able to take anything Lizzy threw at her.

Catie straightened and shook her head, praying for courage. "Elizabeth, how good to see you."

"Liar. You're no more glad to see me than I am you." Elizabeth crossed her arms and cocked her blond head so that her curls bounced. "You stole my husband."

Catherine shook her head. "No, that's not true. Father—"

"You stole him, and you'll pay for making a fool of me."

"Lizzy, you know I would never do that. Besides, you've always said nothing less than a prince would do for you."

Elizabeth reached out and snatched Catherine's arm, digging her nails in deep. "He was *mine*, and I will have him back."

Fear stabbed Catherine's lungs. She knew Lizzy would do what she said. Lizzy always got what she wanted. Had she ever thought she could hold Quint when her sister wanted him? But she wouldn't give him up without a fight.

"Let go." The words were low, but Catherine knew she was losing the battle to keep this exchange between the two of them. Soon Lizzy would say or do something to draw the crowd's attention, and the ball would be ruined. Catherine's mind raced. She couldn't allow Lizzy to ruin this for Quint. She had to find a way to remove her sister before it was too late.

"Do you know what everyone is saying about you? They think you're a whore. They know Quint should have been mine."

Catherine shook her arm, and said firmly, "Let me go, Elizabeth. This is not the time or place."

"You would say that." She dug her nails deeper, and Catie hissed with pain. "You shall go home with Valentine tonight. I have nothing to return to but that hovel. Since you married, I haven't had a single offer. I'm going to be an old maid."

"Do not be ridiculous," Catherine said, finally managing to free her arm. Spots of blood welled up where Elizabeth's nails had taken hold. "You're only seventeen. You will have many suitors."

"I want Valentine." She swung her arm, sending a stack of china cups onto the floor. Catherine jumped back to avoid the shrapnel, but Elizabeth caught a strand of her hair and held on.

Catherine could hear gasps and whispers as people began to realize what was happening. She closed her eyes, knowing that whatever happened now it was too late. It would look to everyone as though Elizabeth were the wronged one. Quint would hate her. "Elizabeth, let go."

Elizabeth had her hair tight, and the tears were beginning to sting Catherine's eyes.

"You ugly whore. I hate you."

Catherine's blood boiled. "Not as much"—she wrenched her hair free of Lizzy's grasp—"as I hate you!" And then she pushed with all her strength.

Lizzy stumbled over a chair, knocking it over, and then was thrown off-balance. She threw an arm out in an attempt to stop from falling into one of the tables, but Catherine hooked a foot under her, and Lizzy went down, landing with a thud on the floor.

"Now, you'll pay," Elizabeth hissed, rising to her knees. Catherine knew she had to stop her sister before an even bigger fiasco ensued. She glanced around for something useful, but saw nothing other than the punch bowl.

The punch bowl.

Elizabeth was rising to her feet, spewing threats and curses, and Catherine grabbed the bowl and lifted it.

Elizabeth's eyes widened. "No!"

But it was too late. Catherine dumped the cold punch over her sister's head so that the red liquid cascaded over Elizabeth's head and shoulders, dripping onto the floor. Several guests dashed to get out of the way. Elizabeth looked up, her hair matted to her face. She looked small, like a wet cat.

"I think that's all the time I have to speak with you tonight, Lizzy," Catherine said. She signaled to two footmen standing speechless in the corner of the room. "Please escort my sister out. She is no longer welcome here."

"You bitch!" Elizabeth screamed as the footmen came up on both sides and took her arms. "Valentine was mine!"

Catherine saw the reporter from the *Times* standing in the doorway. He had his notebook out and was jotting something in it. Oh, Lord. Why did he have to see?

And then she looked past him and saw the prime minister and Quint. Both men looked shocked and slack-jawed. Catherine closed her eyes. As she'd feared, she'd ruined everything.

She turned away from her husband's disappointment. Tears wanted to well in her eyes, but she would not allow them to fall here, where anyone could see. Undoubtedly, her marriage was over. They'd come so far together, but none of it would matter after this. She'd ruined his chances at a Cabinet position.

Behind her, she heard the footmen returning, and then she heard Valentine's voice. "Is she gone? Good. Make sure she doesn't return. I don't ever want to see her face again."

Catherine turned to stare at her husband. He was glad Elizabeth was gone? He was throwing her out? In front of the prime minister?

Where was her true husband?

He stared at her across the room, and then he was walking toward her, his pace increasing the closer he came. And he didn't stop when he reached her. In spite of the fact that she was splattered with punch, he pulled her into his arms. Catherine was rigid from shock.

"Are you well?" he asked. "I'm sorry, Catherine," he whispered in her ear. "I'm so sorry."

"But why are you sorry?" she asked. "You have done nothing."

"I should have listened to you. I should never have invited her," he said.

Catherine blinked at him. "Then you don't blame me?"

"Blame you? Sweetling, you tried to warn me. I'm the one who's a stubborn fool. You were right about your sister. You'll never have to see her again."

Catherine opened her mouth, but no words would come. She swallowed. "Then you don't want her? You don't wish you'd married her instead of me?"

Quint shook his head. "Your sister pales in

comparison with you. How many times do I have to tell you that *I only want you?*"

"Oh, Quint." She wanted to say more, but the words lodged in her throat.

He took her hand. "Everyone is looking at us, expecting us to do something. Would you favor me with the next dance?"

"I-I—" She glanced about them. It was true. Everyone was looking at them. For once, it didn't matter. She was with Quint. "Of course."

Quint led her to the center of the ballroom, where they joined the line of couples in a country dance.

He stood across from his wife and smiled at her. The night was a disaster, and still he could not stop smiling at her.

He wasn't sure exactly what had happened. The evening had started out well enough. His wife was lovely, easily the most beautiful woman in the room. She had been a poised and gracious hostess, and the ball had begun without incident. The prince regent had arrived just as the dancing had begun, and he was in an agreeable mood and began the ball by partnering Catherine's cousin Lady Madeleine in the minuet. And then Quint had danced with Catherine, and he was pleased to note that she was an excellent dancer.

He had been more than pleased to relinquish her hand to the prime minister, and though she trembled when he released her, he thought that her time with the prime minister had been a success. Mr. Perceval had come away laughing and had shaken Quint's hand and told him that Catherine was a refreshing change from the usual Society hostesses.

Quint had deemed the ball a success—at least in his own mind. And when he'd seen Fairfax, he'd shaken the man's hand with equanimity. Why not? It had been a good fight, but one of them would have to go away the loser. Quint knew it would not be he.

Now, he was not so certain. The incident between Catherine and her sister would be in all the papers in the morning. He'd be the butt of jokes and speculation. He hated gossip, but after an incident like the one tonight, there was no avoiding it.

He had probably lost the Cabinet seat.

And still he could not stop smiling at his wife. She was so beautiful, so brave, so . . . Catherine. Looking at her, the Cabinet position just didn't seem to matter anymore. Nothing mattered except her.

"Thank you," she said, as they moved with the other couples in the dance.

Quint had to move away from her as his turn came, but when they crossed paths again, he said, "Why are you thanking me? I haven't apologized near enough."

She blinked at him but had no time to make a response before she linked arms with the man diagonal to her and executed the next movement of the dance. When they came back together, she said, "You stood by my side. That's all that matters to me."

Quint squeezed her fingers. "I'll always stand by you. I should have listened to you before. I was wrong about your sister, and I admit when I'm wrong."

They parted again, and it was ages before he finally had her in his arms again. He turned her, pulling her closer than necessary, and she whispered, "It takes a strong man to own up to his own mistakes."

Quint grinned at her, turned her about, and took her hand, leading her off the dance floor. "And it takes a weak one to succumb to his wife's charms in the midst of a ball, but I hope you can forgive this weakness as well."

"I can forgive anything of you."

Her voice was breathless behind him as he pulled her along. He nodded at guests and eyed a servants' door nearby. They had almost reached it when Mr. Hudson, the reporter for the *Times,* stepped in front of him.

"Lord Valentine," Hudson said, and Quint noted that the man was holding his notebook like armor. "Might we have a word?"

Quint gave Catie a quick glance, then pulled her to his side. "What is it, Mr. Hudson? As you can see, my wife and I have a ball to host."

"Yes, you've been busy all evening. That was

an interesting scene with your sister, Lady Valentine. Care to elaborate?"

Catie paled, and Quint stepped in for her. "No, she does not."

"Then what do you have to say, Lord Valentine? There have been charges of impropriety, even illegality, connected with your wedding. Were you not engaged to Miss Elizabeth Fullbright?"

Quint narrowed his eyes. He'd successfully deflected most of the questions and controversy by leaving Town and exercising his power as a peer. Why was Hudson bringing it up now?

Behind the reporter, Quint saw Fairfax standing a few feet away. His handsome rival was smiling smugly.

Quint turned back to Hudson. "How much did Fairfax pay you to ruin me, Hudson?"

He heard Catie gasp beside him and took her hand.

"I don't know what you mean, Lord Valentine," Hudson said smoothly. "I have quotes from Lady Valentine's own father and sister. Fairfax has nothing—"

"Fairfax has everything to do with it," Quint said, closing in on the reporter. Hudson stepped back. "You've always supported him over me. Perhaps I should mention something about the value of impartial journalism to your editor, Mr. Hudson."

"Perhaps I should mention the role opium

played in your wedding, Lord Valentine. An opium-eater in the Cabinet. What will the public say?"

Quint released Catie and grasped Hudson by the neck, thrusting him against a pillar.

"Quint, no!" Catie called. "Think of your position."

But he didn't care about his position anymore. He didn't care what anyone said or thought about him. He only cared about Catie. He would protect her.

"Listen to me, Hudson," he growled. "You print whatever lies about me you choose, but you leave my wife and my marriage out of this."

Hudson put his hand over Quint's and loosened his grip. "I would like to, my lord, but with the public so divided, and the prime minister so uncertain, I fear I must tell our readers the truth."

Quint breathed in and out, felt his head spin, and saw his dreams and his future slipping away.

And then he turned to his wife. She was there, beside him, looking at him with so much trust, so much faith. In her hazel eyes, he had all he needed—and more.

"Quint?" she said uncertainly.

"One moment, sweetling," he murmured. Slowly, he turned back to Hudson. "I have a new story for you, Mr. Hudson. Something I think your readers will find even more fascinating than my wedding."

Hudson raised his eyebrows and the pad. "I'm listening."

"I am no longer seeking the Cabinet position. In fact, I wholeheartedly endorse Mr. Fairfax's appointment."

Hudson's eyes widened. "You are serious, my lord?"

"Print it, Mr. Hudson. If you don't, I will." He turned to take Catie's hand again, then swung back to Hudson. "And leave my wife out of it, or I promise you, Hudson, you will have more than your story to worry about."

With that, Quint pulled Catie after him and headed directly for the servants' door. The corridor was dark and littered with forgotten serving trays and glasses. Quint hoped the servants had abandoned it temporarily as well.

Quint knew he'd just ended his career. He knew he'd just tossed away all his dreams, all he'd worked for. But as Quint pulled Catherine inside the servants' hall and leaned against the door, closing it, enveloping them in the dim glow of a distant candle, he didn't care. His career was nothing. Nothing mattered except Catherine.

"Quint," she said, her voice worried, "did you just tell that reporter you were ending your bid for the Cabinet?"

He ran a hand through his hair. "That doesn't matter to me anymore. All that matters is that I'm here with you." He leaned in to kiss her.

"But Quint," she said, holding him off with one hand, "your career means everything to you. You have to go back out there and tell that reporter—"

"No, Catie," he said, his finger brushing over her lips, "I meant what I said. As for going back out there, I'm perfectly happy exactly where I am right now."

Quint wrapped a hand around his wife's waist and tugged her against him. She was warm and supple in his arms, and he could not resist bending to taste the exposed skin of her neck.

"So sweet," he murmured against her ear and felt her shudder. "I wonder if you know what I'm thinking at this moment."

"Perhaps I am thinking the same thing," she said, pressing herself against him.

"Oh, God, I hope so."

He took her mouth with his, delving between her warm wet lips, tasting her hungrily. He tried to be gentle, but his need was too great. And she was having none of his tenderness tonight. Her hands tore at his coat, and then, when she could not remove it, her fingers tugged at his hair, bringing his mouth down on hers.

He removed his coat for her, and then her hands were inside his shirt, her touch heating his skin even further. His hands inched up her waist, cupping her breasts, and then fumbling with her gown and her stays to free her flesh for further exploration.

"My, but you did that rather easily," she gasped, as his thumbs brushed over her erect nipples.

"I have a confession." He dipped and laved a tongue over one pebbled nub. "I am rather eager to be inside you." He closed his mouth over one breast and kneaded the other with his hand.

"I think . . . I feel . . . the same." Her voice was breathless with need, and she arched against him, pulling his hair to keep his mouth where she desired.

When sampling her flesh with his lips was no longer enough, he reached under her skirts and stroked her thigh. Her skin was silky smooth under his fingertips. As he inched higher, she moaned in his ear. Her moans turned to gasps as his fingers penetrated the juncture of her thighs. She was already wet for him.

He plied her flesh with expert strokes until her breathing rasped against his temple, and then she tugged on his hair and he looked up at her.

The corridor was dark, but she had a mischievous smile on her face. "Let me show you what I am thinking," she whispered, and with one hand she reached out and stroked his hard length through his trousers.

He threw back his head and closed his eyes, reveling in the pleasure of her touch. Her fingers were uncertain at first, slow and cautious, but then, with encouragement, her strokes grew bolder and longer. And then with a flick of her fingers, she freed him from his trousers, and her hand touched his bare flesh. He stifled a growl in her neck, and pulled her hard against him.

Lifting her off the ground, he swung her toward the door, and pinned her against it. Her skirts were an encumbrance for only a moment, and then he felt her warmth against him.

"Wrap your legs around me, sweetling," he murmured in the peach-scented curls at her ear. "I'll hold you up."

She did as he commanded, and with slow, cautious movements, he entered her. But once again, she thwarted his best attempts at gentleness. She moved against him so that he filled her far more quickly than he'd intended. And God help him, but he loved the feel of her around him.

He withdrew and thrust again, trying once again to keep his movements gentle, but she tugged at his hair. "Harder, Quint. Faster."

He could not argue with that dictate, and he plunged into her, hearing the thunk as her body pushed against the door. And still she urged him on, her words frantic in his ear, her hands tugging at him, her body taking and demanding as eagerly as his own.

Her cries became louder, drowning out the thunk of the door and the orchestra music above that. She was riding the tide with him. He could feel it in the way her legs tensed, the way she threw her head back, the tiny ripples as she clenched and released around him.

"Quint. Quint," she gasped. "Yes, yes."

And then he was flying with her. He was part of her, and they fell down the waterfall together, tumbling over and over and over until he could barely catch his breath.

When he finally landed, her moans were a ragged echo in his ears. He held her as long as he could, his arms cupping her bottom, holding her close to him. She held him as well. Her hands clutched his back, her fingers digging into his shirt. Finally, he pulled back and began to set her down. But even when he released her, his arms did not stop shaking. He was trembling from the experience of being with her. He'd never given so much to a woman, never been with a woman who seemed to want him as much as he wanted her.

He glanced at her, and even in the dark he knew she looked debauched and disordered. And how was he to walk out of this door with her? They'd emerge in full view of all their guests, and what they'd been doing would be patently obvious.

"I suppose we must return to the ball," he said, brushing a stray lock of hair from her face.

She nodded. "I suppose we must, but I'd rather stay here with you. That was"—she paused, obviously looking for the right word—"amazing. I did not know that could happen when you were inside me."

Quint frowned in puzzlement. "What could happen?" Then he remembered her contractions. "Oh, *that*. Yes. You might have known before if I was not always so eager with you."

"But you were eager tonight."

He pulled her close and hugged her. "I'm always eager with you. But I promise that from now on I will take more time. I want you to feel pleasure every time I'm inside you." He whispered the last and felt her shudder.

He bent and kissed her nose. "I'd like nothing more than to stay here with you all night, but even if we've made a muddle of the event, we can't desert our own ball. I'll leave first. Then you follow in a few moments."

He bent to retrieve his tailcoat, and she straightened her skirts. Then she helped him arrange his clothes and hair, and he righted hers as best he could.

"There." She patted his chest. "You look quite presentable. How do I look?"

Her skirts were wrinkled, one shoulder of her gown kept falling off, and her hair had come loose and was trailing down her back in large sections. But Quint only saw her rosy cheeks and her bright eyes. "You look beautiful," and he bent and kissed her swollen lips, taking the time to taste them. She was so sweet. Every time he kissed her, it was a different experience.

And every time he kissed her, she kissed him back, matching his mood—fervent, tender, exploratory. With more willpower than he thought he possessed, he drew away from her. "We take a risk if we continue that much longer. I cannot wait to get you home. Soon." He kissed her again, then quickly opened the door and reemerged in the ballroom.

The orchestra was playing a slow, stately piece, and the dancing went on as before. Catherine's cousin Ashley was holding court with a bevy of admirers under one of the Corinthian columns and Catherine's other cousin, Josephine, was dancing with Lord Westman. He didn't see her cousin Lady Madeleine or her aunts and uncles, and he didn't see Hudson.

Good. Quint hoped the man was in his dingy office writing his wretched story. And then Quint saw Catie emerge from their rendezvous place. She looked sweet and pretty, though still a bit disheveled, and he forgot about the reporter and the story and just enjoyed watching her.

Catherine felt as though everyone in the room had ceased what they were doing and were watching her walk through the servants' door. It seemed the whole room was silent, and there was only the sound of her heartbeat, pounding incessantly in her ears. The beat echoed her thoughts: *they know, they know, they know.*

With a deep breath, she settled against the wall. There was nothing and no one to fear here. Elizabeth was gone. Quint had stood by her side. He had all but told her he loved her just now in the servant's corridor. What was she afraid of?

She spotted Maddie coming toward her and

plastered a smile on her face. "Are you well? I heard what happened with Lizzy. I wish I'd been there."

Catherine smiled at her cousin's clenched fists and determined expression. "Lord Valentine was there. He stood by me."

Maddie raised a brow. "Of course, he did."

Catherine glanced across the room and met Quint's gaze. He was always looking at her now, always watching her, his eyes full of promise. As she watched, he winked at her.

"Oh, Lord," Maddie said, and Catherine drew her gaze away from her husband.

"What's wrong?"

"Josie and Ashley were right. You do love him."

Catherine took her cousin's hand. "Yes, I do. I'm sorry, but I don't think I can be a member of the Spinsters' Club any longer."

Maddie laughed. "Oh, that old promise. I'm happy for you. And now I suppose you'd better be off. Here he comes."

Catherine looked toward Quint and saw that indeed he was coming for her. She went willingly into his arms.

"Let's go home," he murmured into her ear.

"Are you certain?" she asked. "We should not leave the ball so early."

"I don't care. I want to be alone with you. You're all that matters."

And then he swept her into his arms. She laughed at the surprise—her own as well as that of the people standing near them. There was a round of applause, and then she was being carried through the ballroom, down the steps, and into the night. He ordered their carriage and set her down, pulling her into his arms and holding her tightly. She closed her eyes, hearing his heart beat against cheek. She felt safe and wanted.

"You're a wonderful man, Quint," she whispered. "I've never thought anything less of you. I want you to know how happy I am that you married me."

He tilted her head up so that she looked into his clear brown eyes. "And I want you to know—"

"Isn't this sweet?" The low, malice-filled voice filled the quiet night.

Catherine pulled back and let out a yelp when she saw her father standing in the shadows. Of course he was there. Catherine shook her head. Had she really thought she would escape without seeing him tonight? It just seemed so unfair. She'd survived the ball and her sister, only to be faced with her father. And Edmund Fullbright was drunk. She knew that right away. Drunk and mean.

"Mr. Fullbright," Quint said, pushing Catherine behind him. "I don't remember inviting you."

"You didn't," her father said, swaying into the light. "And you made sure I couldn't get in." He lurched to the side, and Catherine noted that while he was dressed in evening clothes, his appearance was slovenly. His cravat was loose, and his breeches were stained. "Now, is that any way to treat your family?" Her father slurred the words at her.

Quint clutched her hand, holding it tightly to reassure her. "I hardly think you are the man to speak on that subject."

Catherine expected her father to boil over with rage, but he only gave Quint a thin, malevolent smile. "Perhaps not, but I am able to speak on any great number of other topics, including this dupe of a marriage." He tapped a thoughtful finger on his chin. "I wonder what the prime minister would think if he read the true story of how you two lovebirds were married? I wonder if the citizens of our fine city"—he gestured clumsily at the buildings surrounding them—"would want a Cabinet officer who couldn't even marry the right woman at his own wedding? What kind of official would that man be?"

Catherine felt Quint tense. "Your concern for the welfare of our fine government is touching, Mr. Fullbright," Quint gritted out. "But I have already dealt with your friend, Mr. Hudson. Blackmail won't work."

"Blackmail always works, my dear son. May I call you 'son' now? I hope so, as I believe you and I will have a long and profitable relationship."

Catherine lowered her head in defeat. It seemed that she would never emerge from the shadow of her father. But, to her surprise, Quint laughed. Her head shot up, and she blinked at her foolhardy husband.

"Go home, Mr. Fullbright. You won't get a shilling from me. Do you think that I would ever give a worthless bastard like you even a momentary glance? You're no better than the horse manure I wipe off my boot."

Her father's eyes widened in shock and anger, and Catherine shrank back. She knew that look and what it meant. "Quint, be care—"

"Who the hell do you think you are?"

"Catherine's husband, and I'll be damned if you hurt so much as her feelings ever again. Say good night, Catie." He put an arm on her waist and made to usher her away, but her father stepped in their path.

"You worthless—" His fist came up fast and hard, and Catherine bit back a yelp of fear for Quint. But her husband easily sidestepped.

And then, before she could react, Quint's own fist came up, and she heard the crack when it connected with her father's face. Edmund Fullbright went down in a heap.

Quint stared at him, nudged him with a foot, and then, turning, held a hand out to Catherine. She took it, stepping over her father's unconscious body. "Good-bye, Father," she said.

"Your carriage, madam." Quint gestured to the first carriage in line.

"But, sir," the coachman, who had been staying out of the way, stepped forward. "This is the prime minister's carriage."

"I'll apologize tomorrow." Quint placed her inside and climbed in after her. "Well, that was fun," he said, when the carriage was under way.

Catherine stared at him. "I dumped punch over my sister's head, you gave up the Cabinet position, had a public brawl with my father, and now we've stolen the prime minister's carriage. We're doomed."

"We're having fun," he corrected her.

"Fun? But your career—"

Quint pulled her onto his lap. "I don't care. I wasn't only wrong about your sister. I was wrong about my work. It's important to me, but not as important as you."

She stared at him. "It's not?"

He pulled her against him, and she burrowed her head in his neck, loving the way he smelled.

"I almost lost you to my obsession with work. I won't ever do that again. I forgot what was truly important. I forgot the reason I got into politics. I wanted to help people. I wanted to do good, and I let my ambition get the better of me." He stroked her hair, his breath warm on her cheek. "I don't want the Cabinet position, not if it means losing you. I've missed precious minutes and seconds with you, Catie. I spent hours at a desk when I could have been with you. I don't want to lose any more time together. I don't want to lose you."

Her heart swelled, and she murmured, "You won't. And you never will. I love you, Quint."

He answered her with a kiss that didn't end until morning.

Chapter 24

Catie thought she dreamed the sound. She tried to turn over, to ignore the ping, ping, ping, but finally she opened her eyes and listened.

Beside her, Quint breathed in and out deeply. He was asleep and his body was warm and heavy. She wanted to turn into his heat, feel his arms come around her, but she heard the ping again and forced herself to slip out of bed.

A quick survey of the room revealed clothes scattered over the floor, a tub with water that had long ago cooled, and a half-empty bottle of wine and two glasses. No shoes or a robe.

She heard the ping again, this one coming from her room, next door, and she pulled on Quint's tailcoat in an effort to cover herself. She hurried through the dressing room and looked out the window. Below, three women had their heads together. One was blond, one brunette, and the other auburn-haired.

Catherine pushed the window up and peered out. "What are you doing here?" she hissed.

The girls jumped and looked up at her. "We've come to help you," Maddie said. "Come down."

"I don't need help," Catherine whisper-shouted back. "Go home and go to bed."

Maddie nodded and began to pull her cousins away, but Ashley looked up and hissed, "What about Valentine? Did he really give up the Cabinet position? That's what people were saying when you left."

Catherine shrugged and shook her head sadly. "He did."

"Then come down. We want to help," Josie called.

Catherine did not see how her cousins could help. They had not made a scene at the ball; they were not going to be the subject of a resignation article in the *Times*. They had not absconded with the prime minister's coach.

She should close the window and go back to bed. Quint needed her now. He didn't need her three cousins' misguided attempts at patching up a hopeless situation. She dressed quickly, choosing the men's clothing Maddie had sent weeks ago because she did not need assistance to put it on. Then she tiptoed down the steps, past the sleeping footman in the foyer, and opened the door.

Her cousins were waiting for her on the front stoop.

Ashley took her hand. "Quick, let's go."

"Go where? I'm not going anywhere dressed like this."

"We have a plan to help your husband," Josie said. "We're going to see that he gets the nod for the Cabinet post."

Catherine looked at Josie and then Ashley and finally Maddie. All three girls were wearing trousers and men's shirts. Their hair was tucked under their collars or, in Ashley's case, she'd stuffed it under a farmer's cap.

"But I don't even know if he wants the position."

"Of course he wants the position," Ashley said. "He doesn't want you to get hurt."

Catie bit her lip. "You're right. I can't let him give this up."

"That's the spirit," Josie said.

"What did you have in mind?" Catie asked. "Are we going to scale the walls of Parliament? Break into Mr. Perceval's office?"

"Don't be silly," Josie said. "We won't have to break in. I have the key." And she held up a shiny gold key.

"I don't even want to know how you came into possession of that," Catherine said, "but I fail to see how breaking—"

"I told you that I have the key."

"Very well, I fail to see how entering the prime minister's office without permission in the middle of the night will secure Valentine the Cabinet post."

"That's because you have no imagination," Ashley said. "And it's not the middle of the night. It's almost dawn. By the time we reach Perceval's office and let ourselves in, he will be on his way. When he arrives, he'll have no choice but to see us. Then we can convince him that he'll do the country a grievous wrong if he does not appoint Lord Valentine."

Catherine looked at Maddie, usually her most sensible cousin. "And you agree with this plan?"

Maddie shrugged. "What other choice is there? If Valentine does not receive the post, then it's as though Elizabeth and your father and everyone who wishes you ill has won."

"It's time we reversed fortunes," Ashley said.

Catherine had no illusions that this plan would work. Why, they looked like a bunch of vagabonds. The night watchmen would probably arrest them before they made it two blocks. But she looked back at Valentine's dark town house, thought of him sleeping inside, and knew she had to try. Besides, her cousins were right. It was time for a reversal of fortune.

"After we see the prime minister, we have to find the reporter from the *Times* who was at the ball," she said, moving forward to take the lead. Her cousins followed as she started down the walk. "We may have to persuade him to change his story."

"He'll change it," Josie said, patting her hip. "You leave that to me."

Lord, Catherine hoped that was not a cutlass at Josie's hip, though for once, she could use the help of a pirate.

Quint was dreaming about his wife. He was dreaming about pulling her warm body to his and sinking into her. Groggily, he reached for her. And felt empty space.

He opened his eyes. "Catie?"

No answer.

He rose and padded across the room, through the dressing room, and into her room. No sign of her, except—

He lifted his tailcoat from the top of her bed, then looked at the window. It was open. The sun was just rising above London, and somehow Quint knew his wife was out there. He swore. He didn't have time to search for her this morning. She was probably at the assembly rooms, supervising the cleanup, but he could not stop by to check. He had an appointment with Perceval at eight, and he did not want to be late. After last night, he intended formally to withdraw his application for the position and concede to Fairfax.

Quint fully expected a dressing-down from the prime minister for the events of the ball. He'd made the government look foolish, particularly the article that would surely make the day's papers. Hell, he'd stolen Perceval's coach. Quint deserved a stern lecture, and he was prepared to take his lumps.

He'd take them and ask for more. He didn't care. He had Catherine, and that was all that mattered. One look from her, and everything became clear. He'd been such a fool. How had he not seen immediately that Catherine was the only thing that mattered? He dressed quickly, thoughts of Catherine never far from his mind. Why would she go to the assembly rooms so early? Would the servants have even arrived yet?

As he waited for his carriage to be brought around, he paced his foyer. What if she had not gone to the assembly rooms? He remembered the open window in her bedroom and swore again. Suddenly, he needed that carriage urgently. He had a very bad feeling that his Catie was trying to help.

"I really think this is a bad idea," Catie whispered from the prime minister's darkened office.

"Why?" Ashley said. She was sitting in the chair behind his desk, feet propped up before her. "Isn't it Mr. Perceval's job to make decisions for our country? We're helping him do that."

"Maybe we should split up," Catie said. "All four of us here might be too much. Perhaps Maddie and I could stay and you and Josie could go to the office of the *Times*."

"Not a chance," Josie said, letting the curtain she was holding aside fall back into place. "Once we leave, you'll convince Maddie this was a bad idea, and you'll be gone."

"This *is* a bad idea," Maddie muttered. She was sitting on the edge of a chair beside the desk. Her hands were clamped in her lap. "I don't need to be convinced of that."

"Shh. I hear something!" Josie ran to the door and pressed her ear against it.

Catherine pushed a hand against her stomach. It bubbled and churned with panic. One, two, three . . .

"He's coming," Josie said, and all four girls quickly arranged themselves in the chairs before his desk. Then the door opened, and Spencer Perceval strode inside. He was followed by two aides and Mr. Hudson, the reporter from the *Times*. At least that would be one less stop on this ill-advised expedition.

Perceval halted in midstride halfway across his office. Catherine figured it took him that long to spot them because the room was dim.

"What the hell is this?" he demanded. He

stopped abruptly, and one of the aides bumped into him.

"Ah—" Catherine tried to speak, but nothing more would come out.

Ashley jumped in. "We're here on a diplomatic mission, Mr. Perceval."

"A what?"

"Well, maybe that's not exactly what it is," Josie said, "but we need to talk to you."

"Then make an appointment with my secretary." He strode to the chair behind his desk and began straightening papers. "Now, get out."

"Sir, if you could just give us one moment of your time. We've gone to a great deal of trouble to be here." That was Maddie.

"I'll say. How the hell did you get inside?"

"Sir, would you like me to fetch someone?" one of the aides asked.

"I—" Perceval was staring at Maddie. He narrowed his eyes. "Wait a moment. You're Lord Castleigh's daughter." He looked at Ashley. "You're Sir Gareth's girl. And Miss Hale and"— he nodded at Catherine—"Lady Valentine. What are you ladies doing here? I thought you were a troop of gypsies."

Catherine finally found her voice. "I know how we must look, but if you'll just hear us out, we won't ever bother you again. It's a matter of great importance."

"Let me guess. It has to do with your husband."

* * *

Quint ran through the halls, sliding around the corner and into the prime minister's office. Immediately, he noticed there was no secretary to stop him, no aide working at his desk. The door to the prime minister's office was open, and he could hear a woman's voice.

Catherine's voice.

Quint rushed forward, then paused just inside the door. No one saw him. Hudson from the *Times,* the prime minister, Perceval's aides, and Catherine's three troublesome cousins were all looking at her.

"So you see," she was saying, "Lord Valentine really does want the position. More than anything."

Quint opened his mouth to protest, but no words came. There was something in Catherine's voice that pierced him through to his soul. God, her actions here were rash and ill-advised, but she wanted to help. She cared enough about him to come here, dressed like a vagabond, and plead for him. He'd never known anyone to do something like this for him.

"He only pulled out because he was afraid this man"—she pointed at Hudson—"would write something bad about me. But I don't care. I'd rather Quint took the post. He's the best man for the job."

Quint's gut twisted. She really had faith in him, and she was wiling to sacrifice her own reputation to ensure he had his career. His bloody career that meant so little to him compared to her. He didn't deserve her.

The prime minister glanced at the reporter. "Is that true, Mr. Hudson? Did you threaten to print a negative article about Lady Valentine?"

"No! Well, not exactly, sir."

Perceval held up an imperious hand. "We will talk later, Mr. Hudson." He looked back at Catherine and sat back in his chair. "This doesn't change the fact that Valentine stole my carriage."

"It was a rash decision," Catherine answered quickly. "And a rare one. Please don't hold that against him. He has worked so hard for this position. He wants it more than anything else in the world."

"That's not true," Quint said. He couldn't allow her to continue. This was not her battle, and he wouldn't let her fight it for him. All heads swiveled to stare at him.

"Quint," Catherine gasped. "What are you doing here?"

"He has an appointment," one of the aides remarked, consulting a paper.

Quint strode forward and took his wife's hands. They were as warm as her honey hazel eyes. He wanted to take her in his arms and keep her there forever. "The true question, Catie, is why are you here? I came this morning to tell Mr. Perceval that I don't want the position. It doesn't matter to me anymore."

"But you've worked so hard for it."

He cupped her face. God, was anything as precious to him as she? He loved her so much now it almost hurt. "Meaningless work when it took me away from you. I belong with you, Catie. I love you."

He heard a sob and saw Madeleine dabbing at her eyes with her sleeve. She waved his attention back to Catherine. His wife's eyes were filled with tears as well. "Do you mean that?" Catherine whispered. "Do you really love me?"

"With all my heart. I've never loved any woman until I met you."

Catherine launched herself into his arms, holding him so tightly he lost his breath. "I love you, too. You know I love you."

"Well," the prime minister said, banging on his desk, "now that we have that established, can I get back to work?"

"Absolutely," Quint said. "Just one more thing." And then he bent to kiss the woman he loved.

Epilogue

Article from the *Times*
by Mr. Hudson
PERCEVAL CHOOSES
NEW CABINET MINISTER

In these days of foreign and domestic unrest, the choice of a Cabinet minister is not a simple commission. Our illustrious prime minister was recently faced with exactly that difficult decision. As our faithful readers know, both Mr. Charles Fairfax and Quint Childers, Lord Valentine, were under consideration for the post. Early this morning, Mr. Perceval selected Lord Valentine to fill the position.

The choice may come as a surprise to those in attendance at Lord Valentine's ball last night. Rumors flew that Lord Valentine was no longer seeking the post, and guests reported that a fistfight broke out between Lady Valentine and her younger sister, Miss Elizabeth Fullbright. Indeed, some sources testify that Lord Valentine absconded from the ball in Mr. Perceval's own coach.

Despite the uproar, it appears Mr. Perceval would not be swayed in his decision. He said in his statement, "Lord Valentine will make a competent, reliable Cabinet minister."

When asked about the earl's erratic behavior of the night before, Perceval answered, "Let those among you who have not been in love, cast the first stone." This reporter will hold on to his pebbles.

"That's a lovely article," Catherine said. "I have it memorized now, but there is still one question I need answered."

Quint tossed the paper aside and leaned back in bed, beside his warm, naked wife. "And what is that, sweetling?"

"Will you take the position? You know I want you to."

"I am thinking about it," he answered, pulling her close and reaching under the covers, "but I think I may need one more dose of your excellent persuading."

"Then you shall have it, Mr. Cabinet Minister."